HEARTS OF STONE

A Selection of Recent Titles by Brad Smith

The Carl Burns Series

ROUGH JUSTICE *
HEARTS OF STONE *

The Virgil Cain Series

RED MEANS RUN
CROW'S LANDING
SHOOT THE DOG

* *available from Severn House*

HEARTS OF STONE

A Carl Burns thriller

Brad Smith

This first world edition published 2016
in Great Britain and 2017 in the USA by
SEVERN HOUSE PUBLISHERS LTD of
19 Cedar Road, Sutton, Surrey, England, SM2 5DA.
Trade paperback edition first published
in Great Britain and the USA 2017 by
SEVERN HOUSE PUBLISHERS LTD

British Library Cataloguing in Publication Data
A CIP catalogue record for this title is available from the British Library.

ISBN-13: 978-0-7278-8579-1 (cased)
ISBN-13: 978-1-84751-786-9 (trade paper)
ISBN-13: 978-1-78010-855-1 (e-book)

This is a work of fiction. Names, characters, places and incidents
are either the product of the author's imagination or are used fictitiously.
Except where actual historical events and characters are being described
for the storyline of this novel, all situations in this publication are
fictitious and any resemblance to actual persons, living or dead,
business establishments, events or locales is purely coincidental.

All Severn House titles are printed on acid-free paper.

Severn House Publishers support the Forest Stewardship Council™ [FSC™],
the leading international forest certification organisation.
All our titles that are printed on FSC certified paper carry the FSC logo.

MIX
Paper from
responsible sources
FSC® C013056

Typeset by Palimpsest Book Production Ltd.,
Falkirk, Stirlingshire, Scotland.
Printed and bound in Great Britain by
TJ International, Padstow, Cornwall.

ONE

C arl saw the flying dog from inside the workshop. He was standing at the vise, sharpening the aged Remington chainsaw, when something caught his eye and he looked out the window to see the young Border Collie soaring, twelve feet in the air, its front paws extended, ears laid back, teeth bared. The animal seemed suspended perfectly parallel to the ground for a second or two and then, having missed its prey, it hit the hard turf in an uncoordinated tangle of legs before leaping back to its feet, ready for another try.

Stacy Fulton, the young woman who ran the farm's online sales, was the dog's accomplice in this. As Carl watched, she walked over to retrieve the Frisbee from the grass while the pup raced back to the flatbed trailer that was the animal's launching pad. Stacy had taught the dog the routine, to stand stock still on the trailer until she shouted 'Go!' at the same instant she flung the Frisbee high in the air out over the lawn. The soaring dog would catch the disk two or three times out of ten and would play the game all day long if Stacy would accommodate it. As it was, she usually obliged the pup during her work breaks. With Carl in the fields a good deal of the time and Frances busy with the television show, Stacy had become the one closest to the animal. She had started in the warehouse a few weeks after the pup had arrived at the farm. She and the animal were both green and eager to learn and whip smart. Stacy was twenty-one; she'd gone to university for a couple of years and then decided to take a year off. Carl suspected that her leaving school was a financial decision but he didn't know for sure. Her family was out west, somewhere in British Columbia. She and Frances had become close. Stacy didn't know it but Frances had already decided to lend her the money for school if she decided to go back. For the time being, Stacy was helping run the warehouse and teaching the Border Collie aerial maneuvers.

Today the pup caught the Frisbee just as Carl came out of the workshop, carrying the Remington in one hand and a newer model Stihl in the other. He set both down by the door of the machine shed and went inside, where he fired up the Ferguson tractor and drove it around behind the building, to where the wood wagon was parked. A functional relic, it had been built by Frances's father fifty or so years earlier; it was a large rectangular hardwood box, crudely constructed, resting on two axles and supported by leaf springs salvaged from a 1936 Reo truck. Carl hooked the wagon tongue to the draw bar of the tractor and then drove back around to the front of the shed.

Stacy walked over, the tooth-marked Frisbee in her hand and the panting pup at her heels, as Carl put the saws into the wagon. It was a cool and cloudy autumn day and she was wearing jeans and a down vest over a cream-colored sweater, her hair back in a ponytail. As she walked, the dog kept nipping at her hand, begging for one more turn.

'What are you cutting?' she asked.

Carl indicated the forest lot, a quarter mile away, at the rear of the farm. 'Dead oak in the bush. I've been meaning to drop it all summer and never got around to it. Better do it now, it could snow any day.'

'Don't say that,' Stacy joked.

'Saying it or not saying it won't make a difference.'

'I guess not.' Stacy glanced toward the warehouse. 'I'd better get back to it. People are still ordering Thanksgiving stuff. They need to realize we don't offer drone delivery.' She smiled. 'Not yet anyway.'

'Christ,' Carl said.

'Frances is right, you're an old-fashioned guy.'

'Nothing wrong with being old-fashioned. I almost forgot – do you need a ride to the airport tomorrow?'

'I decided not to go home,' she replied. 'Flights were crazy expensive. And – I don't know – I wasn't real pumped about spending time with my dad's new girlfriend. Frances invited me to stay with you guys.'

'Good,' Carl said. 'My daughter's just started her new job in Edinburgh so it's a trade-off. You can do the dishes in her place.'

'That's a little sexist.'

Carl smiled. 'Hey, I'm an old-fashioned guy.'

'Bugger,' she said. 'Are you taking Boomer to the bush with you?'

Carl thought about it. 'I'd better not. That's a big tree to come down and I can't cut and watch him at the same time. The way he tear-asses around, he could get hurt.'

'I'll keep him in the warehouse until you're gone.'

After she took the animal inside, Carl pulled the Ferguson around to the gas pump and filled the tank. Heading for the lane he stopped at the house and went inside for a thermos and bagged lunch he'd prepared. He put them in the wagon and started out. As he drove along the dirt lane leading to the bush the sun came out, for the first time that day and for a few days before. The poplars along the lane had already lost their leaves, scattered in the mud of the fields. The maple trees in the bush were out in full color, brilliant red under the emerging sun. The oaks showed yellow. Their leaves would be the last to fall.

The tree to be cut was a massive white oak, the trunk forty inches or so across. It had died slowly over the course of the past couple of years, with more bared branches each season. Frances, ever vigilant of white ash bore and Dutch elm disease, had tried to find out what was killing the oak.

'Old age, I'm guessing,' Carl had told her. 'Trees get old, same as people.'

Frances had been unconvinced. She suspected that the chemicals sprayed by farmers using genetically modified seeds could be at fault. In fact, she took those farmers to task for everything from the disappearance of honey bees to ground water pollution to sickness in some kids. Carl didn't disagree with any of it. But he was pretty sure that the tree had just gotten old. He told Frances he would count the rings on the stump after cutting it.

Using the old Remington, that cutting took over an hour. The Stihl was nearly new – and more efficient – but it had just an eighteen inch bar. The Remington was a brute, weighing nearly fifty pounds, and had a cutting bar of twenty-four inches.

The tree hit the forest floor with a crash that shook the ground. Carl set the Remington aside and, taking up the Stihl, began to cut the top branches into stove wood lengths, stopping periodically to toss the pieces into the wagon. The tree, now that he saw it lying on the ground, was even bigger than he had previously thought. It would fill the wagon three or four times with firewood.

By the time he stopped for lunch, the wagon was overflowing and he had at least another face cord cut on the ground. He sat on the massive log and ate the sandwich and drank coffee from the thermos. The day was warm enough that he was down to his shirtsleeves. After eating he went to the stump to try to determine the tree's age. White oaks were slow growers and some years – depending on temperature, rainfall, amount of sun – would be slower than others, so some of the growth lines on the stump were tiny and inconsistent. Counting them, Carl was forced to make a guess. But that guess came in at about a hundred and forty years.

Old age, like he said.

Not that Frances would necessarily agree with him on that. She was a pragmatist who required concrete evidence before she believed anything. Not only that, but Carl suspected that she liked to argue with him. She didn't seem all that interested in arguing with other people, and by that he was flattered. It created within him a certain feeling which for a long time he couldn't identify. Eventually it came to him: it made him feel at home, not just with Frances but with simply being there on the farm. More than that, it made him feel at home with himself.

He realized that he had never in his fifty plus years on the planet felt that way. It wasn't something he thought about missing until he was no longer missing it. If he had given it any consideration he probably would have concluded that it was something available to certain people and not to others. It wasn't something a man could achieve simply by striving for it. It either showed up or it didn't.

He certainly had never felt at home with Frances's sister Suzy, whom he had married when they were both still teenagers. They had been a poor match, both reckless and wild, both destined for trouble. Suzy had died of an overdose and a few years later Carl had gone to jail for arson. The only good thing that came from the relationship was their daughter Kate, and it had been Kate who had indirectly led Carl back to the farm – and to Frances. Kate was involved at that time in a criminal trial, as a victim testifying in a twenty-year-old sexual assault case. Carl had returned to the area to support her, even though she wanted nothing to do with him. In trying to get closer to his daughter, Carl became very close to Frances. What happened between them surprised the hell out of Carl, and he suspected it had done the same to Frances. He was reluctant by nature to analyze the situation. He was perfectly content in the knowledge that he felt at home for the first time ever.

Not that he and Frances had a perfect relationship. Such a thing did not exist and they were both well aware of it. For instance, he hadn't told her that he was cutting the tree today and she was not going to be happy when she heard about it. She liked cutting firewood, she liked being in the bush, as did Carl. There was something mindless and yet gratifying about it. There was no politics to it, no agenda other than the obvious.

He would have waited but, as he'd said to Stacy, he wanted to drop the tree and haul the wood out of the bush before the snow came. Frances was in the city, shooting the Christmas special that would air two and a half months later. The Thanksgiving show – which they'd filmed in August – would be on this weekend.

The TV show had started out with her doing spots on a local morning program in Rose City – cooking segments using River Valley Farm products. After a dozen or so of those, the station had pitched the show to her and she had agreed, based on the logic that the program would boost the farm's profile and consequently increase sales. Which it had. But Carl had suspected from the start that Frances was not at all comfortable being a TV personality, that she had no desire to be famous, even if that fame only existed in a limited market in a few cities. He was pretty sure she'd rather be in the bush, cutting firewood and arguing with Carl. He wouldn't pressure her to quit the show because he wasn't certain that it was what she wanted. Still, he held out hope that she would. In a world where dogs could fly, anything was possible.

Carl went back to work now and spent the afternoon cutting, resorting back to the Remington for the larger pieces of the trunk. Even cut into stove lengths they were too heavy to lift. Eventually he'd bring back the larger John Deere tractor, with the front end loader, to lift them on to a hay wagon.

It was late in the day, the sun falling into the river, when he drove the Ferguson tractor, with the wagon behind, up to the wood shed. Dusk was coming on and he decided to unload the firewood in the morning. The warehouse was dark and there were lights on in the kitchen at the house. In the half-light Carl could see Boomer lying on the front lawn, fast asleep. Stacy must have tired him out; he didn't so much as raise his head when Carl drove the tractor around the corner of the shed. Frances wasn't home from the city yet but would be soon. They shot until five o'clock and rarely went overtime.

Carl stowed the saws in the shed and started for the house. He whistled sharply as he approached the dog, but oddly enough the animal still didn't move. In the gloaming, Carl didn't see the splash of red on the grass until he was twenty feet away. His heart in his mouth, he hurried to the dog.

The afternoon hadn't gone smoothly, although Frances hadn't expected that it would. One of the station managers – an enthusiastic type named Shawn, fresh out of community college – had come up with the idea of having several local sports figures join Frances in the make-believe kitchen in the studio to prepare their favorite Christmas recipes. The concept seemed sound enough but, as with most of Shawn's ideas, it fell apart in the execution. As always, the devil was in the details.

It turned out that the hockey player, who arrived unshaven and irritable, intended to make grilled cheese sandwiches as his special dish. He preferred processed cheese between slices of white Wonder Bread, the finished product smothered in ketchup. A second guest, a young woman who had competed in the most recent Olympics as a marathoner, wanted to make tofu stuffing. The college football star arrived with six different recipes, each with a bacon base.

Frances ended up assigning each a recipe of her own and after that things went smoothly enough, although the hockey player insisted on dousing his coq au vin with his signature ketchup. When everyone was gone and the cooking area cleaned, Frances sat at the fake counter with Christina, drinking real wine from a bottle that had earlier served as background.

'One of these days Shawn is going to come up with an idea that's a cropper,' Christina said.

'And the apocalypse will be upon us,' Frances remarked. She had removed the heavy pancake makeup and changed from her Christmas frock into jeans and a sweater. 'What's this about a remote?'

'You said you wanted to get out of the studio more,' Christina said. 'I have this friend who lives out near Butterfield who has a Christmas tree farm. You know – one of those places where you go and cut your own tree. Pretty standard stuff, but the hook is that they have these huge Belgian workhorses that pull a vintage sleigh into the woods. They have a couple of teams actually – it's a going concern. So you take the kids, bundle them up, go for a sleigh ride and cut your tree. Great visuals.'

Frances had another drink.

'What?' Christina asked.

'Let me think about it,' Frances said. 'What else are they suggesting?'

'You don't want to know.'

'Why?'

Christina poured more wine for both of them. 'They thought we could bring in Jimmy Trimble, the polka guy, and the two of you could sing some carols.'

'I'm not singing.'

'There's the Christmas spirit.'

'I am *not* fucking singing.'

Christina laughed. 'I kinda told them that already.'

Frances sighed and looked around the kitchen they had built for her. The cupboards with doors that didn't open and the sink that didn't run water. The refrigerator which had never been plugged in.

'I didn't think it would be like this,' she said.

'What?'

Frances gestured around her. 'Everything. I guess I was naive, coming in.' She laughed. 'I mean, this is show business! I wasn't looking for that. There's a difference between being a farmer and being a lifestyle maven. Even a small market lifestyle maven. I'm a farmer. Carl bought me rubber boots for my birthday and I got all excited.'

'Really?'

'Really,' Frances said. She took a drink of wine. 'And you know the sad part about all of this? Other than the fact that I just used the word maven twice?'

'Tell me the sad part,' Christina urged.

'There's a thousand of us sitting around in a thousand TV studios right now, desperately trying to come up with fresh Christmas ideas. What can we do that's never been done before? Can we shoot a turkey out of a cannon? Can we make a Santa Claus out of cranberries? Can we deep fry an elf?'

'I like the elf idea,' Christina said. 'Let me run it past Shawn.'

Frances smiled, then glanced at her watch. 'I have to run. I have a turkey to pick up.'

'You don't raise your own?'

Frances shook her head. 'Long story. We did raise a couple this year, one for Thanksgiving and one for Christmas. Ridley Bronze, heritage birds. We made the mistake of letting Stacy name them. Trust me – once you name an animal, you're not going to chop its head off and eat it for dinner. So we are now going to have two Ridley Bronze turkeys living with us for – well, for however long Ridley Bronze turkeys live.'

'Remind me who Stacy is?'

'She works for us,' Frances said. 'Good kid, still trying to figure out what to do. She's become a surrogate daughter. Plays with the pup and saves poultry from imminent doom. Carl's daughter is working an environmental study in Scotland, so the three of us are having Thanksgiving together. What about you?'

'Dinner with the in-laws,' Christina said. 'They eat around five o'clock. We'll be home by eight, settle in for some HBO.'

Frances put her coat on and started for the door.

'Have a good one,' Christina said. It was a phrase that Frances hated but she excused it. She liked Christina. She had the door open when she stopped and turned back.

'What if we made it about the horses?'

'What?' Christina asked.

'Your tree farm idea,' Frances said. 'It's not about a family going out to cut a tree. It's about a horse. Maybe the old mare, providing there is an old mare. We follow her for the day, from the moment she wakes up in the barn to when she's rubbed down at night. The kids reacting to her as she does her job, trudging back and forth. She represents the great proletariat of a time gone by.'

'I like it,' Christina said.

On the drive home, Frances stopped in Talbotville to pick up the turkey. They were holding it for her at Fred's Custom Meats, a local butcher shop that bought the free range birds from a farm somewhere up north. The animal was fifteen pounds, plump and pink, and it did not – so far as Frances would ever know – have a name.

It was dark when she got home. She drove past the house to park in front of the garage. Getting out, she retrieved the turkey from the passenger seat and headed for the back door. Had she glanced to her right she would have seen the pup Boomer on the grass.

Inside, the three men were waiting, scattered throughout the open kitchen and living room. All wore balaclavas. The man inside the door was barrel-chested and stank of tobacco and bourbon; he grabbed Frances roughly by the hair as she entered and flung her across the room with such force that she fell to the floor, pitching forward to crack her head against the wainscoting. She dropped the turkey and it bounced crazily along the hardwood and came to a rest by the stone hearth of the fireplace.

Glancing up she saw Carl lying on his side on the living room floor, his wrists bound behind him with plastic ties, his mouth wrapped with duct tape. Past him and trussed in a similar fashion, Stacy was on the couch. A tall thin man, wearing greasy coveralls, lounged on the arm of the couch, as if chatting with her at a party. The third man stood by the

bay window, hands thrust in his pockets. Frances turned to
Carl, who was staring at her across the floor. He nodded his
head, as if to reassure her.

Then the big man had her by the hair again, jerking her to
her feet. She saw now that he had a revolver in his hand. He
forced her to take in the scene, turning her this way and that
like she was a puppet he controlled. He put his face close to
hers, his foul breath in her nostrils.

'You see how things are?' he asked. 'Right now everybody's
still alive. You're the one can keep it that way.'

TWO

Two months earlier

Carl and Frances had been up before dawn. They had
coffee only before heading out to the ten acre field
on the river flats that was planted with sweet corn.
They picked thirty dozen ears, loaded them on to the wagon
and then into the GMC stake truck by the warehouse.
Finishing, they were both soaking wet from the dew-heavy
corn stalks. They went back to the house to change clothes.
Stripping down, Frances looked over at Carl.

'We have time for a quick shower?' Her smile was wicked.

'I have never had a shower with you that would qualify as
quick,' Carl said. 'Hold that thought until I get back.'

He drove the truck to a whole foods co-op in Rose City.
By eight o'clock he was unloaded and back on the road. In
Talbotville he stopped for breakfast at a Main Street diner
where a number of locals with time on their hands were
discussing ways to save the country from the certain ruination
that was apparently the goal of the current federal administration. Carl, with nothing of any real value to add to the
discourse, ate his sausage and eggs in silence and left.

He stopped at Country Grain & Feed outside of town and
picked up the order of chicken feed waiting for him. After

discussing the weather – which, like the political situation, Carl could do nothing about – with the store manager for a time, he headed for home. When he arrived the television trucks were already there – parked in the driveway, in the yard and along the road out in front of the farm. He'd driven past them and pulled into the warehouse drive before circling around to the chicken house. He parked and got out, then walked along the rear of the property to the patio behind the house. It was hot in the sun and he stepped into the shade to watch.

Frances was on the lawn a few yards away, wearing a hooded winter coat and work gloves, holding a rake in both hands. She was looking away from him, speaking.

'Before the big meal, there is always plenty to do to work up an appetite. It's autumn and that means raking leaves, stacking firewood, cleaning the rain gutters. Thanksgiving means that winter is on its way and we had better be ready—'

'Cut!'

Frances stopped, turning to the director, who was standing by the wall of the garage, surrounded by the production team. He was looking at a monitor on a stand.

'What?' she asked.

'We got a guy in the background. Walked out of the warehouse and went into the barn.'

'He works for me,' Frances said. 'What's the problem? I thought we were trying for – what did you call it – verisimilitude?'

'Guy was wearing shorts and a tank top,' the director said.

'Oh.'

'Let's try it again,' the director said now.

Frances said her lines again and began to rake the leaves into a pile. They did it twice more and then the director asked that the cameras be set for a different angle.

'Let's get one with the house in the background.'

The leaves were now in a pile where Frances had gathered them; two helpers went to work scattering them about the lawn again.

'We need more leaves!' one of them shouted after a moment.

Carl turned to where a pudgy kid – no more than eighteen

or nineteen – was on his knees behind the garage, spray painting green maple leaves that were spread across a plastic tarp. The kid had several spray cans on the go, various shades of red and yellow and brown. The painter was sweating profusely under the heat and the obligation of his task.

'They're not dry yet!' he shouted after a moment.

'Bring 'em anyway.'

While they set up for the shot, Frances walked over to where Carl was standing. She removed the coat and cap and tossed them on the scarred pine table where they ate grilled chicken and steaks from time to time. Under the coat she wore a T-shirt and khaki pants. She ran her fingers through her hair, mussed from the wool cap.

'I didn't see you come home,' she said.

'I snuck past the cameras,' Carl said.

'Wish I could. You get the feed?'

'For the hens,' Carl said. 'The pullet mix is back ordered. We're OK for a week or so there.'

Frances pulled the T-shirt away from her body to show him how she was sweating.

'How many shots of me raking leaves do we need?' she asked.

'That's rhetorical, right?'

'You're a lot of help.' Frances looked around. The leaf painter was now carefully dragging the tarp with the freshly colored leaves around to the front yard. The kid's hands were covered in paint and there were even splashes of red in his dark hair.

'Why did I agree to shooting here?' she asked.

'You wanted out of the studio, if I recall.'

'Yeah, and now the farm is the studio. Be careful what you ask for.'

'What's next after the leaves?'

'Me pretending to chop wood, and then me pretending to gather eggs that have already been gathered, cleaned of dirt and chicken shit and placed artfully back in the coop.'

'You'd better hope the hens don't unionize,' Carl said.

'I control the axe,' Frances reminded him. She sighed. 'After that, we move inside for the cooking.'

'Ah, the cooking,' Carl said. 'You're actually planning to cook a turkey?'

'It's already in the oven. Takes a while to cook a turkey, you know.'

Carl glanced toward the house. 'You have the oven on? It's eighty-five in the shade out here.'

'I know how hot it is. I'm the one who's been bundled up like an Inuit hunter all morning. I probably could have cooked the damn bird out here on the flagstones.' She glared at the director, who was sitting in the shade reading a magazine and looking cool in his shorts and shades. 'And it gets worse.'

'How?'

'I mentioned the firewood.' Frances said. 'The plan is we'll have a fire going in the hearth inside. A nice little Thanksgiving backdrop.' She turned to Carl. 'Sure you don't want to be on TV?'

'Surer than ever,' Carl said. 'I'm going to unload that truck. It's probably only ninety or so in the brooder. Come on down if you want to get cooled off.'

'No turkey for you, bub.'

'You're breaking my heart,' he called over his shoulder.

When Carl reached the pickup truck, parked by the side door to the chicken house, he looked back to the activity around the farmhouse. The newly painted leaves were properly scattered, the camera was set. Frances was back in autumn attire, standing once more in the yard, rake in hand. When she looked his way, he waved. She gave him the finger and he laughed as he began to unload the truck.

THREE

Chino sat spread-legged on the stool beside the work bench, smoking a cigarette while he went over the spreads for the coming week's games. He'd had a bad Sunday, losing five out of six bets. He'd had a hundred each on four of the five and dropped two hundred on the Rams,

who had won the game but failed to cover the spread when the chickenshit head coach had ordered his quarterback to take a knee on the Saints' five yard line, instead of kicking the field goal that would have put Chino over. Those lost three points meant that Chino was out five hundred on the day and overall three grand on the season. All on credit. Johnny K wanted his money. He had called last night to say as much and then, when Chino said he needed time, Johnny had called back an hour later to suggest that Chino have a conversation with Tommy Jakes about a job.

Chino had gone to see Tommy that morning. The job involved the border. If it worked out, Chino could pay Johnny off and maybe get him to extend his line of credit for this Sunday's games. He was due to win. Overdue, in fact. Chino flipped the paper over and looked at the night's NHL games. He didn't like betting on hockey because he didn't know anything about it. He might as well throw the names in a hat and let a monkey pick one out.

Tossing the paper on the bench he heard the blat of a blown muffler coming from the intersection a quarter mile away, the noise rising and falling as the driver shifted upward through the gears, approaching the yard. As the truck pulled into the driveway Chino stepped out of the shed, taking a last haul on the cigarette before flicking it into the dirt. He exhaled as the driver got out of the truck.

It was Digger Bagley, sliding his bulky frame from behind the wheel. His curly blond hair grew over his ears and even his eyes, giving him the look of an unkempt sheepdog. Digger had recently done eighteen months in jail for blowing up a guy's Camaro with a pipe bomb and was now getting back into the scrap iron trade. The Camaro's owner had been seeing a woman whom Digger considered to be his girlfriend, even though she had taken out a restraining order against him. Digger had broken into a shed at a local quarry and stolen enough blasting powder to take down a small town. There hadn't been much left of the Camaro. It had taken the cops less than twenty-four hours to arrest Digger.

Chino walked out into the heat to have a look at the load. The box of the GMC pickup was full of rusted rims and brake drums and ragged pieces of steel siding. On the trailer behind the truck was an ancient McCormick threshing machine, steel-wheeled, listing to the side as if it might topple over from age. It was tied in place by an assortment of ropes and straps. The thresher was eighty or ninety years old, maybe more. Chino took a walk around the truck and trailer. There was a lot of cast iron on the old harvester. It would weigh up.

'Where'd you find this relic?' he asked.

Digger was hanging back, all three hundred pounds of him. 'My grandpa's old farm.'

Chino shook his head. 'Hidden away in a cubbyhole, was it?'

'What's that?'

'You been finding goodies at that farm for years. Must be a big place, you never noticed something this size.'

Digger had a fat bottom lip that made a permanent pout. 'What's it worth?'

Chino nodded his head up and down while making a show of calculating. Really he was thinking about his problems with the football bets. He couldn't afford to pay Digger too much. 'Fifty bucks for the lot.'

'Fucksakes.'

Chino glanced over, still nodding to the music. 'What's your problem?'

'That damn machine weighs a ton,' Digger said. 'I ought to know, took me all morning to haul it from the weeds and load it. Shit's worth more than fifty.'

'Not to me.'

'I'll take it over to Peter's Salvage and have him put it on the scale,' Digger said. 'By the pound, be a sight more than fifty bucks.'

'Then take it there, fat boy,' Chino told him. 'See how you make out. Old Pete's above board, he just might ask you where you found this junk. He might make you produce old grandpa.'

'Thing's a million years old. Who cares where I got it?'

'I don't,' Chino said. 'That's why you brought it here. But say hello to Pete for me.'

He walked inside and sat down at the stool again. He had a plastic glass of Jack going and he took a drink. Waiting for the fat man to come through the door, hangdog. Which he did, after a minute or two.

'Gimme the fifty.'

Chino used the loader to drag the thresher off the trailer while Digger tossed the rims and the rest in a pile by the gate. Five minutes' work winded him. When he was gone Chino poured more bourbon in the cup and wheeled his torches over to the thresher, fixing to cut it up. Before he lit the torch though, Bug pulled into the yard. He slid out of the Dodge pickup, finishing a beer as he did and tossing the can into the scrap pile along the shed, the same heap where Digger had thrown the rims. Bug was skinny as a snake and wearing the same black jeans he'd been wearing for a few years, and a T-shirt with the logo of some bar in Florida on it. Bug had never been to Florida that Chino knew. His hair was to his shoulders and he had a wispy goatee that he'd been trying to grow for years. His eyes had a permanent chemical flash to them, whether he was high or not.

Chino pushed the goggles up into his hair and set the cutting torch aside. 'You find him?'

'Said I would.'

'Where?'

'He ain't on the rez. He's over to Tareytown.'

'Let's go.'

Billy Taylor was by a utility shed behind the house, fixing the cord on a vacuum cleaner he'd picked up at the Sally Ann that morning. He'd made a work bench out of two sawhorses and a half sheet of plywood; the vacuum was sitting on top, the casing open, motor exposed. Billy was tall, an inch over six feet, and thin. The homemade bench was low and he had to hunch over to work on the appliance. His hair was cropped close to his head, making the scar along his right temple stand out, the scar he'd gotten flipping a dirt bike when he was just twelve. His stepfather had given Billy the bike, not as a gift, but because he himself couldn't get it to run. He'd told Billy that he wouldn't either but Billy had proven him wrong. It was worth the fifteen stitches to do that.

It was a hot day and Billy was working in the shade of a

crooked pine tree. Skinning the wires to the plug, he heard a
vehicle pull up out front, doors opening and closing, but didn't
think anything of it. It was a busy street, the old part of town,
mostly wartime housing turned into rental units. He heard
somebody say something and he looked up and saw Bug
Murdock walking across the lawn. Billy watched Bug as he
approached, loose as a scarecrow, the crooked little smirk on
his face that he always wore, like he was reacting to a joke
he'd just heard. Billy had no reaction to Bug's presence. Bug
was just Bug.

But there was a second guy, trailing, taking everything in.
The second guy was heavy, maybe fifty, with graying hair and
tattoos on his forearms and neck, what looked like prison ink.
Approaching, he looked at Billy with amusement in his eyes.
Or maybe it was contempt. Whatever he might call it, Billy
had seen the look before and never cared for it. Nothing good
ever came along with it.

'What's up, Billy?' Bug asked.

Billy shook his head in response. Nothing was up. Nothing
up was good.

'Mr Fixit?' Bug asked, indicating the electrical cord in
Billy's hand.

Billy shrugged. 'We'll see.'

Bug looked at the big guy, who was now standing by the
open door of the shed, taking a gander inside. 'This guy could
get anything to run,' Bug said.

Billy made no reply to that.

'This is Chino,' Bug said.

Billy nodded while Chino turned toward him, holding the
look. Billy saw now that he had a teardrop tattoo, running
down from the corner of his eye.

'You working, Billy?' Bug asked.

'Laid off.'

'Laid off,' Bug repeated, glancing at Chino. 'Looking for
work?'

'I can't get into anything,' Billy said. 'Cheryl and I are
making a go of things. Got a boy now, just turned two last
week. I can't get into anything.'

'Suspicious little fucker, isn't he?' Chino said. Talking to

Bug but still looking at Billy. 'How's he know we aren't here to offer him a job down at the Ford plant?'

'Come on, Chino,' Bug said. 'Billy's OK.'

Chino ignored him. Billy's cigarettes were on the makeshift work bench and Chino helped himself to one, lit it with the Zippo lying there. 'You don't want to listen, Billy who can fix anything?' he asked as he exhaled.

Billy shrugged.

'Maybe you should,' Chino said. 'Maybe you can make two thousand dollars for a few hours' work. Does that interest you?'

Billy fell quiet, looking at the electrical cord in his hand, the naked copper wires.

'Where else you gonna make that kind of coin in a day?' Bug asked.

'Something seems too good to be true, it usually is,' Billy said, looking at Bug now, Bug still wearing the grin.

Chino turned toward the house. The shingles were curled at the edges, some were missing altogether. Some of the windows were covered with plastic. The place was clapboard and hadn't seen fresh paint in twenty years.

'You own this place or rent?' Chino asked.

'Rent.'

Chino pulled on the cigarette. 'Looks to me like you could use a couple grand.'

The bar was called Hard Ten and it was built on the county line, four miles south of Rose City. The parking lot was nearly empty, a few cars and trucks by the front door, a half dozen Harleys parked in the back. Chino and Bug walked in at six o'clock. The place smelled of beer and chicken wings and deep fryers that hadn't had the oil changed in a while. Chino ordered two draft beers at the bar and indicated the corner table, where Tommy Jakes sat drinking coffee.

'On his tab,' he said.

The bartender was a cold-eyed blonde with a tarantula tattooed on the back of her hand. She gave Tommy a look, and when she got nothing in return she poured the draft. Chino and Bug carried their glasses to the table and sat down.

Bones Sirocco came out of the back, as if summoned, turning sideways to pass through the narrow doorway. He walked over to where the three men sat, but he didn't sit down. Stood there like a sentry, his breath wheezing in his chest. He was a big man, with huge arms like a lifter, but did not seem healthy.

'Hour late,' Tommy said.

'Taking care of business, Tommy,' Chino said. He took a drink of draft, smacking his lips.

Tommy glanced at Bones and then at Bug. 'Who are you?'

'Bug.'

'That's not a name, it's an insect.'

Bug had been watching the blonde bartender and now he looked at Tommy and shrugged.

'His name is Larry Murdock,' Chino said.

Tommy took a sip of coffee and placed the cup on the table. 'Is Mr Murdock here because he's going to make the delivery for us?'

Chino snorted. 'Bug's got a sheet as long as that bar and he's dumber than fucking dirt. They run his name at the border and the whole place would light up like a Christmas tree.'

'Then why is he here?'

'Because he set us up with the guy who's going to cross,' Chino said. He drank off a quarter of his beer, wiping his mouth after.

Tommy glanced up at Bones for a moment. The big man was impassive. Tommy leaned forward, elbows on the table, and addressed Chino. 'Johnny K tells me that you are a discreet individual.'

'Fucking right.'

'But I hear that you're into Johnny for some money. Something to do with football parlays.'

'What's that got to do with this?' Chino asked.

'I'm not sure,' Tommy said. 'It occurs to me that Johnny wants me to hire you so you can pay him what you owe.'

'And what's wrong with that?'

'Nothing, if you can deliver,' Tommy said. 'What about Mr Murdock here – is he a discreet individual too?'

'He wouldn't be anywhere near this if he wasn't.'

Tommy sat back and reached for his cup. 'So who's the third man?'

'Don't you worry about that,' Chino said. 'It's covered.'

'Who is it?'

'It's covered.'

'Tell me his name,' Tommy said. 'Or leave.'

Chino hesitated. 'His name is Billy Taylor.'

Now Tommy looked at Bones again. The big man shook his head.

'Why do we like him for this?' Tommy asked.

Instead of replying Chino nodded to Bug, who was watching the bartender once more. He seemed transfixed by her.

'Bug,' Chino said sharply. 'Tell Tommy why we like Billy.'

'Billy's got no record,' Bug said. 'He used to jack trucks and run 'em to the chop shops on the rez. Never been convicted. He was good at it. He could hotwire anything on wheels. Stole a two hundred thousand dollar Maserati once. Thing ended up in Arabia or one of them countries.'

'So he's a car thief who's never been caught.' Tommy showed his palms, as if to display just how unimpressed he was.

'There's something else,' Chino said. 'He's an Indian. And Indians get a free pass at the border, as a rule. Especially an Indian with no record.'

Tommy nodded at the information. 'How long have you known this Indian?'

'Him and Bug go way back,' Chino said. 'They were kids together. Bug's old man was banging some Indian broad on the rez and Bug used to stay out there.'

Now Tommy got to his feet, coffee cup in hand. Chino watched as he walked to the bar and got a refill from the blonde bartender. He spoke to her quietly for a time and when he turned away she laughed at whatever he'd said. When he sat down again he looked at Bug for a time without speaking.

'What's her name?' Bug finally asked. Breaking the silence.

Tommy glanced over at the bartender. 'Joni's her name. Why – you like her?'

Bug nodded, sneaking another look toward the bar.

'She'll be flattered,' Tommy said, the sarcasm thick. He leaned toward Bug. 'So you'll vouch for Billy Taylor.'

'Yeah.'

Tommy turned to Chino. 'And you'll vouch for Mr Murdock here.'

'That's right.' Chino's mind was on the laughing bartender. What was between her and Tommy that was so funny? When he looked over, it seemed that she was watching him, the smile still on her face.

Tommy Jakes sipped the hot coffee. When he put the cup on the table, he shifted his gaze to Chino.

'We'll be in touch. Pay for those beers on your way out.'

FOUR

After breakfast Saturday morning Frances carried her coffee down to the brooder house to ready it for the new arrivals. Carl had driven into town earlier to pick up the day-old chicks from the co-op. Frances swept the building out and spread fresh wood shavings on the floor. She got the heat lamps from the warehouse and suspended them from the ceiling joists, turning them on to check the bulbs. She brought in the feeders and the water troughs. She was filling them when she heard Carl pull into the drive.

Ten dozen chicks fit in two cardboard boxes, each no bigger than a large suitcase. They put the boxes in the middle of the floor and opened them, then stood back to watch the chicks find their own way out, at their own speed. Some emerged at once and began to explore the coop. Fluffy and bright yellow, the size of a person's fist, they stumbled and hopped through the shavings, awkwardly colliding with one another, falling down and getting up. They ignored the food for now but would be eating and drinking within an hour or so. By that time they had all escaped the boxes and were wandering about, already growing accustomed to their new world.

That afternoon Carl and Frances took a walk to the bush lot at the rear of the farm. Carl carried a knapsack and a ten-pound sledge hammer and Frances an armful of surveyor's stakes. The property was one of the few in the county that still had a lane dissecting it. The rest of the farms – owned or rented by cash croppers – had the lanes and fences bulldozed and cleared away. The family farm had gone the way of the dodo. What was once a patchwork of eight or ten fields was now usually a single hundred-acre piece, more amenable to the use of large-scale equipment. The bulldozing was practical but – to Carl's eyes anyway – it stole something away from the landscape, something that could never be replaced. It robbed cottontails and foxes and ground squirrels of their habitat as well. And Carl hadn't seen a jackrabbit in five years. They'd been pushed aside by modern farming.

The lane ran precisely through the center of the farm, a single dirt road with leafy hardwoods on each side, old growth oaks and maples that created an overhead canopy. Along the fence row stood a number of elm trees as well, most of them dead from disease, their bark stripped away, the revealed wood bleached nearly white by the sun.

It was a pleasant walk. Frances, freed from the television cameras for the weekend, was relaxed and loose. Carl had made her breakfast that morning and they'd eaten lunch at a diner in Talbotville.

'The crew's back here on Monday then?' Carl asked.

'Yeah,' Frances said. 'Just a couple of hours, though. We didn't get the footage of me doing my Paul Bunyan thing, splitting wood.'

'Then you're done?'

'Pretty much.' As she walked, Frances reached above her head and took down a maple leaf, rolled it between her fingers. 'But we're already talking about the Christmas special.'

'They're going to want to shoot at the house again,' Carl told her.

'That's not happening.' Frances made a tube of the leaf and blew through it before tossing it aside. 'I need to put the brakes on. This TV show is like one of those giant mushrooms in the northwest. You don't notice it at first but it just grows and grows and pretty soon it just takes over. Next thing, they'll want to shoot you and me getting up in the morning.'

'I'll have to buy some silk pajamas.'

'I'd pay money to see that.'

The lane ended at the forest. The bush lot covered roughly eight acres. Carl took a claw hammer and a box of copper nails from the knapsack and they spent an hour walking around, identifying the sugar maples and marking them each with a nail in the trunk. They counted fifty-seven in all.

'Why do we need to mark them?' Frances asked.

'Come sap time in the spring, and the trees have no leaves, it's not always easy to tell a hard maple from a soft,' Carl told her. 'The old-timers could tell by the bark but you and I are rookies. We might end up tapping an ironwood tree.'

'What would we get from an ironwood tree?'

'I don't know but I wouldn't want to pour it on my pancakes.'

When they were finished with the marking they wandered about for a bit, trying to decide where they would build the sugar shack. They eventually settled on a rise near the north end of the bush, seventy yards or so from where the lane ended. They cleared some brush away from the spot and then staked the building out, twenty feet by twelve. Afterward they sat on the rise and drank two bottles of ale that Frances had packed in the knapsack.

'When can we start?' Frances asked.

'When do you want to start?'

'Yesterday.'

Carl laughed. 'I took those pine logs over to Kendrick's this week. Should have the planks in a few days and then we can build. Depends on your schedule.'

'I have one more day and then I'm done for the time being,' Frances said. 'We've got those Cortland apples we need to press into cider. And I think I have someone who will take the rest of the acorn squash off our hands, if we can deliver it.'

'That's not a problem.'

Frances turned to him. 'Just don't get the idea you're going to be building this shack without me, Mr Burns.'

'Did I say that?'

'I know you.'

Carl smiled and drank from the bottle.

'I think it should have a cedar shake roof,' Frances said.

'Steel is good,' Carl told her.

'I like the looks of cedar.'

'It's a lot of work and it's expensive,' Carl said. 'Steel goes on quick and it'll last longer than either of us.'

'Cedar doesn't last?'

'Well . . . yeah, it does.'

She looked at the site of the future sugar shack for a moment, imagining it, and then she smiled at him.

'You think you can show me that smile and get whatever you want,' Carl said.

'How do you know what I think?'

Carl got to his feet and took a few steps. He pointed with his chin. 'That big white oak has got to come down.'

'I'd still like to know what killed that tree,' Frances said. 'Wait – are you changing the subject? We were talking about the roof.'

'You were talking about the roof.' He stood looking at the massive oak. 'Lot of firewood there. We can use it to make the syrup.' He turned. 'Those dead elms along the lane too. Elm burns hot.'

'How do you know all this?'

'I have a head full of useless information,' he said.

Frances stood now as well, finishing the ale and putting the empty bottle in the knapsack. 'I'm looking forward to this. I wish we could start building today.'

'Does the TV station know that you're going into the maple syrup business?' Carl asked. 'They're going to want to film everything.'

'No,' she said emphatically. 'They don't know and I'm not telling them. I have a feeling that my TV career will be coming to a close real soon. They keep wanting more and more. The money's not that great and to tell you the truth it really doesn't . . .' She hesitated, searching for the words.

'Turn you on?' Carl suggested.

Frances laughed. 'Yeah, I guess you could say that.' She fell silent for a long moment, looking toward the farmhouse and barns in the distance. 'The more I am on TV, the more I like being a farmer.'

'I suspected that,' Carl said.

'Well, now you know,' Frances said, turning toward him. 'And as far as this sugar shack goes, you and I are building it. Nobody else. OK?'

Carl smiled. 'OK.'

FIVE

C hino hoisted the wheel on to the tire machine and was removing the valve stem when Bug pulled up in the pickup, skidding to a stop in the gravel outside the shop. Chino glanced out the open door, first at the truck and then out to the road, expecting another vehicle. There was none. Bug climbed out of the truck and walked into the shop as Chino let the air out of the tire and broke the bead on the inner part of the wheel. He slid the flat bar under the lip of the tire and hit the foot pedal, rotating the wheel to pull the edge of the rubber up and over the steel rim. The machine was pneumatic and Chino's air compressor kicked on noisily, running for a couple of minutes before shutting down. When the racket stopped Chino cast an eye on Bug, who was now sitting on the work bench, drinking a beer he'd produced from his coat pocket.

'Where's our boy?' Chino asked.

'Thought he'd be here,' Bug said.

'Well, he's not.'

Chino walked past Bug to an old chrome and Arborite table in the corner of the shop. The dope was there, stacked in a dozen or so bundles. Bug watched as Chino opened one of the bundles and with a kitchen spoon scooped out three or four ounces of the cocaine, doling it into a baggie. There was a bag of white flour on the table and Chino replaced the pilfered coke with an equal amount of flour, stirred the contents carelessly with the spoon before resealing the package.

'You're shorting them?' Bug asked.

'You heard of shipping and handling?' Chino asked. 'Well, this is the handling part.'

Chino carried the bundles of coke to the tire machine and began to stuff them inside the wheel, distributing the packets around the perimeter of the rim. When he was finished he put the tire back on the bead and filled it with air. Lifting the wheel from the machine, he rolled it over and leaned it against the door jamb. He looked out to the road again.

'That Indian getting cold feet?'

'He was OK when I talked to him last time,' Bug said. 'I mean, he ain't what you'd call thrilled about the whole deal, but he needs the money. They got that little kid now, him and the old lady. She's working at the dollar store.'

Chino took a cigarette from the pack in his coverall pocket and lit it. He watched the road for a while longer, then turned and walked to the table where he'd left the coke. There was a cupboard overhead; he went into it and brought down a bottle of Jack, poured three fingers into a plastic cup. He drank from the cup, thoughtfully looking at the baggie on the table.

'You want a bump?' he asked.

'Shit,' Bug replied.

Chino rolled a five dollar bill and they each did a line. It was good coke. It was better coke than either of them was used to. Bug hit his first and when the drug reached his brain he jerked upward from the table, smacking his head on the cupboard overhead.

Chino shook his head and then bent to his own line. 'Oh baby,' he said when he snorted it.

They sat back then, cool and cocky under the drug. Chino drank bourbon and listened while Bug told stories, about his love life, about his adventures with the judicial system, about anything that came to mind, it seemed.

They did more coke and lost track of time. Just when it seemed that Billy Taylor wasn't going to show up, he was standing in the doorway. Chino wasn't sure if he'd been there for two minutes or two hours. Bug offered him a line.

'He can buy his own dope,' Chino told Bug.

'I'd just as soon get going,' Billy said. 'Long drive, and I don't want to do it wasted.'

Chino got to his feet. 'Let's roll.'

'Where's the merchandise?' Billy asked.

'In the tire,' Bug laughed. He pointed. 'It's in the fucking tire, Billy.'

The plan was to cross at Fort Erie. They reached town late in the afternoon and found a motel a few blocks from the bridge to the US, a low slung row of connected rooms that sat just yards away from the rushing Niagara River. Billy pulled the Pontiac up to the office and Chino went inside to register.

The room had two beds and smelled like cigarette smoke and cleaning fluids. They had picked up a bottle of bourbon and a bucket of fried chicken on the main drag coming in and now they carried everything inside, setting the chicken and the liquor on a chipped veneer bureau inside the door. Bug had been drinking beer in the car and he went into the bathroom for a leak. Chino took a drumstick from the bucket and flopped on the bed. Billy stood inside the doorway.

'You gonna eat?' Chino asked.

'No.'

'You want to get moving, don't you?'

Billy nodded.

'Christ, you're a nervous nelly,' Chino said. 'I hope you're up to this. You'd fucking better be.'

Billy stared at him, his eyes dark.

'Go, then,' Chino said, indicating the door. 'Unless you need to go over it again.'

'No.'

Chino put the chicken leg in his mouth and stripped it clean of meat. 'Make fucking sure you count it,' he said as he chewed.

'He knows,' Bug said, coming out of the john carrying two plastic drinking glasses.

'Where you gonna be?' Billy asked. 'Here?'

'Right here, son,' Chino told him. He looked at his watch. 'Supposed to be a three-hour drive. Say an hour for the deal, and whatever else crops up, that puts you back here around one in the morning. OK?'

'Yeah.'

Chino tossed the chicken bone in the general direction of a waste basket in the corner, then reached beneath his shirt and pulled a thirty-eight caliber revolver from his belt. He laid the gun on the dingy bedspread. 'Don't you be thinking about getting lost with that cash now,' he said idly to Billy.

Billy looked blankly at Chino, then turned and left, leaving the door open. Bug poured bourbon for himself and grabbed a couple of pieces of chicken from the bucket. Lifting the glass, he was aware that Chino was watching him, that shitty look he gave nearly everybody, always in judgment.

'What?' he finally asked.

'That's your buddy just left. And pretty soon he's gonna be all by his lonesome, with sixty grand in the trunk and the border between us. You're not worried he might get ambitious all of a sudden?'

'Billy wouldn't do that.' Bug gnawed at the chicken in his hand while looking over toward the TV. 'Billy and me go way back. We was kids together.'

'Sixty grand is sixty grand,' Chino said. 'You're the one brought him into this. You're the one accountable.'

'I don't figure it that way,' Bug said.

'I do,' Chino said, and turned on the TV.

SIX

The border was a snap. The line-up was long, due to the hour, but at the entry point itself things went smooth as silk. Pulling up to the gate, Billy showed his status card to the border guard, who barely glanced at it.

'Where you heading today?'

'Picking up my sister at the airport,' Billy said.

The guard nodded and Billy drove off. He took the thruway east out of Buffalo and in twenty minutes was clear of the city. The cruise control worked on the Pontiac and he set it to the speed limit. No sense in risking getting pulled over, not with the merchandise in the trunk. The car had a bit of a shimmy at that speed but Billy knew it was a bad tire and nothing to worry about. He had a spare in the trunk. It wasn't the spare he'd left home with but it was a spare. Traffic was light on the thruway. He cleared Rochester and then Syracuse. It was growing dark when he reached the exit for the town of Stoddard.

He kept punching up stations on the radio as he moved from market to market – country and classic rock and even some rap. Anything to keep his mind off the task at hand. Sometime during the previous night, lying nervously awake, he had decided to back out of the deal. When he woke up in the morning he had tried to call Bug on his cell to tell him, but the number was out of service. Then, while they were eating breakfast, Cheryl had told him that she was getting her hours cut back at the dollar store, and also that her car was making a grinding noise when she shifted gears. Billy was feeding the boy while she told him. He had been applying for work all around – both on and off the rez – and he knew it was only a matter of time before something came up. He was good with tools and he could build. He had once framed houses for a summer when he was still in high school. Something would come up soon.

But soon was just soon and now was now. And two thousand dollars wasn't something he could turn down under the circumstances. Cheryl knew about his past, jacking trucks for the chop shops, and he had promised her that he wouldn't go that way again. So he told her that he was headed across the border to see a buddy in Tonawanda about some construction work. He might stay over if it got late. So he was keeping his promise to quit stealing trucks but he was smuggling drugs across the border. He doubted that Cheryl would be all that happy with the trade-off. He told himself it was a one time thing. The money would tide them over until he found steady work. He was doing it for Cheryl and the kid. Surely she would understand that, if she knew what was happening. Not that Billy would ever tell her.

He could see Stoddard from the thruway, the lights spread out on a little rise a mile or so away. He went through the tolls and drove along the two lane blacktop into the center of town. It took less than five minutes to find the garage called Monty's Gas & Lube. There was a gas bar out front with the

lights on but the garage itself appeared to be closed. Billy
pulled up to the doors and sat there for a moment, waiting to
see if somebody was inside. He'd been told they'd be waiting
for him. After a while he got out and walked around to the
gas kiosk.

'I have an alternator for Monty,' he told the cashier, a redhead
with graying temples and a boozer's nose.

'Monty ain't here.'

Billy waited a moment. 'Well, I got his alternator.'

'Probably be here in the morning.'

'I'm supposed to meet him tonight,' Billy said.

'He ain't here.'

Billy turned and looked out at the street. It was an old
industrial town, red brick buildings, once factories or mills,
now housing stores and bars and restaurants. There was a town
square a couple of blocks in, with a statue of a man wearing
a broad-brimmed hat and carrying a rifle. Or it could have
been an axe; Billy couldn't be sure from where he stood. Down
the block an old style movie theater could be seen. The place
was dark and there was nothing on the marquee; presumably
there had been nothing there for a while.

'Can you call him?'

'I don't like to,' the cashier said. 'He gets irritable.'

'What's your name?'

The man sighed. Billy could smell the liquor on his breath.
There was a bottle stashed somewhere behind the counter.
'My name is Rainer.'

Billy nodded. 'When I talk to Monty I'll tell him that Rainer
wouldn't call him cuz he's irritable.'

'Fucksakes,' the cashier said and reached for the phone.

Twenty minutes later a black Cadillac Escalade pulled up.
Billy was sitting in the Pontiac, listening to the radio. He
watched as a round man with a shaved head got out of the
driver's side and approached. Billy rolled the window down.

'You Monty?'

'Pull inside,' the man said.

The man went through the side entrance and a moment later
the big overhead door ascended. As Billy drove the Pontiac
into the garage, the passenger door to the Cadillac opened and

another man got out. He was around forty and wore a golf shirt and creased navy slacks, a cap with a Nike logo across the front. When Billy got out of the car the man stood there, looking him over, as if Billy's appearance might inform him of something.

'You brought me what?'

'Brought you an alternator,' Billy said. 'That is, if you're Monty.'

'I'm Monty.' The man made an upward motion with his thumb, telling Billy to open the trunk. 'I was told you'd be here tomorrow morning.'

Billy didn't know anything about that and so he said nothing as he opened the trunk. The tire was secured under the carpet there, as the spare from the factory would have been. Billy pulled the mat aside and removed the wing nut that held the jack and wheel in place. When he lifted the tire from the trunk the round man took it from him and carried it across the shop to a tire machine. Billy watched as he let the air out of the tire. He could still feel the eyes of the man named Monty on him and now he returned the look.

Monty was lounging against a work bench. He was fit and tanned, somebody who spent time outside. Maybe he was a golfer, as his clothes suggested. Whatever he was, he didn't look like a guy who ran a gas and lube joint. He didn't look like a drug dealer either but then Billy wouldn't know what a drug dealer might look like. He'd never done anything other than a bit of grass. He didn't drink much either; he found that booze made him angry and then, afterward, remorseful.

'What's your tribe, son?' Monty asked then.

'Mohawk.'

'I would assume that's a good thing, with regards to the border. Tommy's getting smart in his old age.'

'Who's Tommy?' Billy asked.

Monty smiled. 'Right.'

Within minutes the other man had the tire broken from the rim and was extracting the coke from inside the wheel. He laid the plastic bags all in a row on a table against the wall. Monty went over and opened the packets, one by one, testing each by wetting his finger and rubbing the dope on his gum.

He then extracted a small amount on the blade of a pocket knife and made a line on the table. He gestured to the round man, who stepped forward to snort it. After doing so he stood straight up, motionless for maybe half a minute, before turning to give Monty a curt nod of affirmation.

'All right,' Monty said, turning to Billy. 'What's your name, son?'

'Why do you need my name?'

'I don't. But you know mine. And you know my place of business. Not only that, but I'm about to give you a gym bag full of cash. It would be nice if there was a semblance of trust between us. Don't you think?'

Billy did give it some thought. And then he told the man Monty his name. His first name anyway.

'Nice to meet you, Billy.' Monty walked to the Cadillac and opened the back door. He brought out a blue sports bag and hoisted it on to the table where the cocaine was. The money was in stacks, wrapped with elastic bands. The cash came out of the bag and the coke went in.

'Count it,' Monty said, stepping back.

There were a dozen stacks of hundred dollar bills, fifty in each. Billy counted the money while Monty and the round man watched. The bills were new and had a tendency to stick together. Twice Billy had a count come up short and both times he counted again, to find that the number was right after all. When he was finished he glanced at Monty.

'OK.'

'OK indeed,' Monty said. 'How do you intend to carry it?'

'Back in the tire,' Billy said.

Monty turned to the round man. The man's tolerance to the coke he'd snorted was obviously high; he stepped forward and began to distribute the money inside the spare, still on the tire machine.

'I assume the tire was Tommy's idea?' Monty asked.

'I told you I don't know any Tommy,' Billy said.

Monty took a moment. 'You're not kidding. I thought you were playing dumb before.' He paused. 'So Tommy told me this was a test run. Which means he's checking you out. It also means you're working for an intermediary. Is that right?'

Billy shrugged. He was keeping a close watch on the man at work at the tire machine, making certain that all of the money went inside.

'You don't say a hell of a lot, do you?' Monty said. 'Is that an Indian thing? You're like the wise old Indian in the movies, watching everything, not saying shit. Maybe you're the wise young Indian. Is that it?'

'I'm smuggling drugs across the border,' Billy told him. 'Not sure that's wise.'

'It is if you don't get caught. I trust Tommy's paying you well. What I can't figure is why he's not dealing with you directly. Who are you working for, if it isn't Tommy?'

'Like you said, intermediaries.'

'What – they don't have names?'

Billy glanced over. 'I tell you their names, then I guess it's OK for me to tell them yours.'

Monty laughed and looked at the round man, who had the tire back on the rim. 'You hear that, Jason? I like this kid. I think I might just steal him from Tommy. Especially since Tommy doesn't fucking know him anyway.' He turned back to Billy. 'Maybe you should come and work for me. We could be like the Lone Ranger and Tonto. Would you like that?'

'That all depends,' Billy said.

'On what?'

'Which one am I?'

SEVEN

C hino sat back on the bed, the pillows propped against the headboard, flipping through the channels on the TV. Bug was sprawled sleeping in a chair in the corner, his ass slid forward, boot heels dug into the rug as if to anchor himself. Before he'd nodded off he'd been telling wild tales about first one thing then another, his words slurred and mercifully unintelligible. Chino realized too late he shouldn't have

given him any coke. Bug was one of those guys who got drunk
on a six pack of beer. Give him a few lines and wash it down
with cheap bourbon and he turned into a two-year-old. It was
a wonder he hadn't shit himself. Chino had cut him off from
the coke too late. He didn't care how blasted Bug got but there
was no point in wasting good dope on him. It was no different
than throwing it out the window.

He was uneasy about the Indian even returning. Chino
didn't trust Indians in general. He'd known his fair share of
them in the joint and they had all been moody and aloof,
keeping to themselves. Try to talk to one of them and they
wouldn't say a word, like they were above everybody else,
above incarceration even. Well, they'd fucking well done
something to get themselves locked up.

This kid Billy had the same resentful way about him. Never
saying shit, as if he was bigger than Chino on some level.
Bigger than Bug. Well, he probably was bigger than Bug, who
didn't have the intelligence of a fence post.

What if resentful young Billy decided that sixty grand was
a nice enough stake to start him on a new path in life? He
wouldn't be leaving much behind, a rundown rented house
and a wife and kid that were probably, like most wives and
kids, a pain in the ass. Chino kept putting himself in Billy's
shoes. What would he do if the same chance presented itself?
Chino knew right fucking well what he would do.

The deal was that Tommy Jakes got fifty-five grand for the
coke and Chino had the five that was left to distribute the way
he was told. So Billy was getting two thousand for making
the drop and Bug was getting a grand for setting Chino up
with Billy. That left Chino with two thousand, which was
chump change when it came down to facts. He was doing all
the work and putting up the risk. And Tommy Jakes was sitting
in the Hard Ten looking down his nose at Chino and making
snide jokes to that bitch of a bartender.

Chino went back to switching channels. He settled on a
show where a big blonde-haired doofus, wearing suspenders
and a carpenter's apron, was demonstrating how to build a
back deck. Chino wouldn't hire the guy to build a fucking
doghouse but the couple he was working for – standing there

in their corduroy pants and matching sweaters – weren't capable of tying their own shoes, let alone building a deck.

Chino smoked his last cigarette and so he did a line and then stashed the remaining coke in his jacket pocket before walking out to the street to find a corner store. There was a Mac's a couple of blocks away. He bought cigarettes and lottery tickets. The cashier was a chubby girl, eighteen or so. Chino asked her when she got off work and he thought she was about to start screaming. He told her to fucking relax and left.

Before going back to the room he took a walk along the river, toward the bridge that led to the US. He smoked and watched the lights of Buffalo, wondering where Billy was right now. Heading this way, Chino hoped, chugging west on the thruway with a wad of cash in the trunk. He had better be heading this way.

Chino's phone rang. He flicked the cigarette into the river and pulled the phone from his pocket.

'Yeah?'

'I hear you're working for Tommy Jakes.' It was Johnny K on the line. There was noise in the background, what sounded like a hockey game.

'You sent me there,' Chino said.

'So I did,' Johnny said. Chino heard him tell somebody to turn the volume down. 'I expect I'll be seeing you in a day or so.'

'Yeah.'

'We can get squared away.'

Chino hesitated. 'Well, I was thinking I could make a sizable payment, keep the account current.'

'And what would you call sizable, Chino?'

'A thousand.'

'I don't think so,' Johnny said. 'I'm carrying half the fucking town these days and I'm getting sick of it. You owe me thirty-three hundred. I want it.'

'It's three grand.'

'Thirty-three with the vig,' Johnny said. 'And you can't say you don't have it because I know you're working for Tommy.'

'You don't know as much as you think,' Chino said. 'If you

did, you'd know that Tommy ain't paying me enough to get square with you. Like I said, I'll give you a grand to keep the account running.'

'Before you make another bet with me, I need to be paid in full,' Johnny said. 'This ain't the fucking bank. See you.'

The line went dead and Chino had an urge to throw the phone into the river. He stood there for a time, thinking. He knew now why Johnny had vouched for him with Tommy Jakes. It was just Johnny looking out for Johnny, as usual. And then Tommy offers Chino two grand, so Johnny gets payment, Tommy gets his delivery made and Chino is left walking a fine fucking line between the two of them. What else was new?

When he got back to the room, Bug was awake. He had crawled up on to the other bed and wrapped himself in the bedspread. He was watching TV, his hair sticking out every which way, his eyes droopy, jaw slack.

'Where'd you go?' he asked.

'Out for smokes,' Chino told him.

'Thought you left.'

'Did you start crying?'

'No, I didn't start crying,' Bug said. 'Where's the coke? I need a pick-me-up.'

'It's all gone,' Chino lied. There was plenty left but it was in his pocket and staying there. If he needed a line, he'd go into the bathroom. 'You snorted it all, you hog.'

'Well, fuck,' Bug said.

Chino sat on the bed. As consolation he tossed Bug a cigarette. Lighting one for himself, he looked at the TV. Some Thanksgiving show was on, a family on a farm somewhere. Chino really wasn't seeing the picture. He was seeing Tommy Jakes and Johnny K, sitting at the Hard Ten, working out their little plan.

'I ain't had a good Thanksgiving in years,' Bug said. 'I always loved it when I was a kid. My grandmother would have us all to her house.'

'You're breaking my heart.'

Bug, his eyes on the TV, shook his head at Chino's attitude. 'You ever see this chick? She's a sexy woman.'

'I've seen her,' Chino said. 'She bugs me. Everything she does is fucking perfect.'

'Oh man,' Bug said. 'She's fucking hot. She's gotta be, like, in her forties, but she's got a great body.' He laughed. 'I want her to cook for me.'

'You know this is all bullshit,' Chino said. 'You think she cooked any of that food?'

'Sure she did.'

'Bullshit,' Chino said. 'They got people who do that for her. It's all done someplace else, like in a restaurant or something, and then she comes in and pretends she did it. Broad probably lives in a condo somewhere.'

'She lives on a farm,' Bug said. 'They just showed it. She was chopping fucking wood, man.'

'*Bull*shit.' Chino got up and went to the dresser and splashed some bourbon into his glass.

'Lookit,' Bug said then. 'She's raking leaves, man. That's the farm.'

Chino sat down on the bed again. 'So it's a farm. It's not her farm.'

'You know everything, don't you, Chino? I'm surprised they don't give you a fucking TV show. You could tell everybody everything you know. Be on twenty-four hours a day.'

'Don't piss me off, Bug. I'm not in the mood.'

Now Chino was taking a second look at the image on the TV. 'Wait a minute. I know that fucking place. Look at the barn, says River Valley Farm. Shit, that's outside of Talbotville, on the way to the lake. I worked out at Lowville, used to run that road every day on my Harley.'

'Told you she had a farm,' Bug said. 'I wish she'd turn around, I want to see her ass.'

'You keep dreaming about all these women. She might let you check the oil in her Mercedes, that's about it.'

'She's going inside now.' Bug grinned like an idiot. 'It's turkey time.'

Chino was dozing, sitting up in bed, when the noise of the Pontiac's engine woke him. He opened his eyes to see the headlights through the blinds, then the lights went out and the engine shut down. Chino walked over to take the chain from the door and let Billy in.

The Indian stood there, looking over the mess. Bug was sleeping on the other bed, pulled up in a fetal position. There were chicken bones everywhere, on the floor, on the dresser, even on the pillow beside Bug's head. The bottle of bourbon was nearly empty.

'Well?' Chino asked.

'All good,' Billy told him.

Chino picked up the bourbon and took a drink straight from the bottle, watching the Indian as he did.

'Who were you dealing with down there?' he asked. 'Bikers?'

'He wasn't a biker,' Billy said.

'What was he?'

'Just some guy.'

'Mafia maybe?'

'I don't know what mafia looks like.'

'You don't know much,' Chino said.

Billy shut down then. Chino went into the bathroom, took a piss and did a line. When he came back out, the Indian was still standing just inside the door. He hadn't moved an inch. Chino walked over and kicked Bug in the shins a couple of times to wake him.

'Ow!' Bug blurted as he came to. 'What the fuck?'

'Get up,' Chino told him. 'We're blowing.'

Bug swung his legs over the edge of the bed and sat there for a time, rubbing his shin.

'The money's in the tire?' Chino asked Billy.

'That was the plan, wasn't it?'

'You just answer yes or no,' Chino said.

'The money is in the tire,' Billy said deliberately.

Chino walked to the bed and picked up his jacket. 'The fucking shit I put up with,' he muttered. 'I should be making ten times what I am.'

The money had been bothering him since Johnny K had called and it was still bothering him as the three of them loaded into the Pontiac. Bug sat up front with Billy and Chino was in the back seat. Pulling out of the motel parking lot, he leaned forward and pointed to the right.

'This way,' he said. 'We got a stop to make.'

'What stop?' Billy asked.

'Just do what you're told.'

They took the parkway all the way to Niagara Falls. It was two in the morning and there was virtually no traffic along the route. Chino told Billy to keep to the speed limit. The cops would be suspicious of any vehicle they saw out at that hour, particularly a fifteen-year-old Pontiac with rust on the doglegs and an Indian behind the wheel. When they got to the outskirts of the Falls, Chino indicated a hamburger joint up ahead.

'Pull in here,' he said. 'I'm hungry. Bug – you hungry?'

'I could eat something, yeah,' Bug said.

'Pull around back,' Chino ordered. 'Out of the light.'

Billy did it, parking the Pontiac in the shadow thrown by the building alongside.

'Give me the keys, Billy,' Chino said when they had stopped. 'You guys go in. Grab me a cheeseburger and fries.'

'What do you want with the keys?' Billy asked.

'I want my fucking money,' Chino said. 'You got *my* money in your trunk and I want it. Did you think it was yours? You're working for me, remember?'

Billy and Bug went into the burger place and Chino popped open the trunk. He removed the mat and the jack and then with his buck knife he cut a twelve inch slit in the tire, the air escaping in a whoosh. Chino reached into the cut and brought out one of the bundles of cash. He stuck it in his jacket and got back into the car.

They ate there in the parking lot. When they were finished, Chino pointed out the window, to the row of casinos downtown, their lights blinking and flashing in the night. Just beyond them they could see the mist rising from the Falls.

'Head over there.'

Billy looked to where Chino pointed. He took into consideration all the ramifications of what might happen, with the people involved, and the amount of cash in the trunk. None of it was to his liking. All he wanted to do was get paid and go home. To his girlfriend and his boy.

'No,' he said.

'No?' Chino repeated.

'No.'

Chino produced the thirty-eight from his jacket and pushed the barrel against the base of the Indian's neck.

'Yes,' he said.

EIGHT

L ate in the afternoon, Carl took a load of pears into Talbotville and dropped them at the whole food place in the market square. A skinny teenager with bad acne helped him unload the fruit, stacking the hampers on a wooden skid. Carl tried to engage the kid in conversation but he didn't want to talk. Maybe he was chafing at the fact that he had to work, or maybe he was pissed off about his skin. The way Carl saw it, neither situation would be so desperate that a person couldn't make polite conversation. When they finished the kid went inside, still without a word. The loading dock was less than a hundred yards from Archer's. Carl left his truck in the parking lot and walked over.

He wasn't surprised to find Rufus Canfield at the bar, drinking draft and looking at some paperwork. The place was half full, people getting off work or in for an early meal. Taking a stool, Carl ordered a beer for himself and another for Rufus.

'How are you, Rufus?'

'I'm well. And you, Mr Burns?'

Carl nodded his well-being and waited for the beer. He put a twenty on the bar and the bartender took it away to get change. She was young – early twenties – with streaks of blue in her hair. Carl had never seen her before.

'New waitress?' he asked.

'First week,' Rufus said. He drank some beer and wiped his bushy mustache. 'A nubile young thing.'

'You're not supposed to be thinking that these days,' Carl said. 'Man your age.'

'I can think it all I want,' Rufus said. 'So long as that's all I do. Matter of fact, I take the admiring of attractive women to be a sign of good mental health. If ever I stop thinking along those lines, I give you permission to drown me in the Grand River.'

'Can I finish my beer first?'

'You may.' Rufus gathered the papers together and pushed them carelessly into a leather case at his feet.

'What are you working on?' Carl asked.

'Domestic shite,' Rufus said. 'Couple divorcing after thirty-two years. They have each decided that the other is the most despicable person on earth. It took them three bloody decades to figure that out?'

Carl shrugged and had a drink. He wasn't much interested in the unhappy couple. However, he had asked, so he couldn't blame Rufus for telling.

'How are things at the farm?' Rufus asked.

'Things are good at the farm.'

'I was there last week one day, picking up some assorted root vegetables for the big dinner this weekend. Neither you nor Frances were around. A young lady served me.'

'Stacy.'

'Yes,' Rufus said. 'Another nubile young thing.'

Carl laughed. 'What day was this?'

'Thursday.'

'Thursday Frances and I were both back at the bush lot all day,' Carl said. 'We're going to build a sugar shack. We're going into the maple syrup business next spring.'

Rufus smiled at the statement. Carl had a drink, watching the lawyer in the mirror behind the bar, his flushed face posed among the bottles there.

'Is there something about maple syrup that you find amusing?'

'Not at all,' Rufus said. 'I consider it a fine breakfast condiment.'

'Then what are you grinning at?'

'You,' Rufus said. 'In the years that I have known you, you have gone from a young Marlon Brando in *The Wild One* to one half of the couple in Grant Wood's *American Gothic*. Quite a transformation.'

'I don't own a pitchfork,' Carl told him.

'In general, you and Frances are considerably more attractive than Wood's sour Midwest farmers. Well, Frances anyway. But you know what I mean.'

Carl had more beer. 'And here I thought I was just building a place to boil sap.'

'You think that because you live an unexamined life,' Rufus told him. 'That's why you seek my company. You revel in my astute observations, even though you are probably not aware of the fact.'

'You got that last part right,' Carl said. 'I came here seeking beer. Apparently a five dollar draft comes with your ten cent psychoanalysis these days. They should put that on the sign out front. It would bring in a lot of business – for the place across the street.'

'You mock me,' Rufus said. 'But I am right, you know. You have found your niche in life, Carl. Not everybody does. I hope that you are happy because you should be. And you can thank Frances Rourke for that.'

'I won't argue with you there, Rufus.'

'You'd better not,' Rufus replied. 'I'm a hell of an arguer, especially on those occasions when I'm right. How is Frances anyway? I saw her last night on the tube, the big Thanksgiving program. Filmed at the farm, I noticed. Is she enjoying her new gig as a lifestyle icon?'

'Not particularly,' Carl said. 'She's got the Christmas show coming up and then her contract expires. They're bugging her to re-sign but I think she's going to walk.'

'She'd rather make maple syrup with you?'

'I think there's a lot of things she'd rather do than play make-believe on television.'

Rufus drained the draft and signaled to the young blue-haired bartender, showing two fingers. As usual with Rufus, Carl was falling behind. He drank his beer down in two gulps and put the empty glass on the bar as the bartender arrived with the fresh recruits. Rufus told her to put them on his tab.

'So,' he said when she was gone, 'when are you going to make an honest woman of Frances?'

Carl indicated the glass in the lawyer's hand. 'How many of those have you had?'

'That's a question, not an answer.'

'Frances doesn't want to get married,' Carl said.

'When did she tell you that?'

'She didn't tell me. I know.'

'It might surprise you, what you don't know,' Rufus said. 'Of course she wants to get married.'

'You don't know what the hell you're talking about. Frances is a modern woman. She's pragmatic. She's too smart to worry about that stuff.'

'You're saying that pragmatic, smart women don't want to get married as a rule?' Rufus asked. He thought for a moment, his lawyerly mind making a case. 'What about Gloria Steinem?'

'What about her?'

'She's modern and pragmatic and smart,' Rufus said. 'And she's been married.'

'Gee, I had no idea,' Carl said. 'So you're suggesting that Frances and I get married because Gloria Steinem did? That changes everything. Is there a jewelry store nearby? I need to pick up a ring.'

'Again you mock. But now you'll be thinking about it. You know you will.'

'And I have you to thank for it,' Carl said. 'Next time I want a beer around quitting time, I'll pick up a six pack to go.'

Frances took tea and a plate of butter tarts down to the warehouse, where Stacy was alone, doing online orders and answering the phone. The pup was in the back yard, lying on its back with its feet in the air, and when the dog saw Frances it jumped up and followed her. Frances put her collar up as she walked across the lawn and down the slope to the building. The day had started out sunny and mild but had now grown cold, the wind whipping across the river, pushing the leaves across the lawn and into the field behind the chicken house.

Stacy was on the phone when Frances walked in. With her eyes she feigned great excitement at the sight of the tarts. Frances poured tea for them both, placing a cup on the counter where Stacy stood before moving over to her desk, the desk she'd seen little of lately. She went online and checked the sales figures for the month.

Stacy hung up and reached for the tea, blew into the cup and had a sip. 'Thanks, Frances,' she said. 'And butter tarts too.' She took one and looked at the pup, standing expectantly inches from the plate. 'No, these aren't for you.' She bit into the tart, closing her eyes as if in ecstasy. 'Ooh, how do you do this?'

'I possess this amazing talent,' Frances replied. 'I was in town, happened to walk by Burk's Bakery, saw those tarts in the window and went in and bought them. There are certain things you can't teach, Stacy.'

'Another illusion bites the dust,' Stacy said, her mouth full. 'Good tarts though.'

'How busy has it been?'

'The online stuff has been so-so. But a lot of people calling, wanting stuff for the weekend. We sold our last pumpkin this morning.'

'Bad time for Norah to get sick.'

'She called and offered to come in,' Stacy said. 'But she sounded terrible on the phone, hacking and coughing. I told her to stay home.'

'I'll hang around and help this afternoon.'

'I thought you were at the studio.'

'Just this morning.' The dog made a move for the tarts. 'Stop that,' Frances said sharply.

The dog ignored her. 'Sit,' Stacy commanded and the pup sat.

'Why does he obey you and not me?' Frances asked.

'I'm just around him more. He'll come back to you. You know how fickle the male animal is.'

Frances laughed.

'Well, maybe you don't know,' Stacy said. 'You have Carl.'

Frances had some tea. 'So Carl's not fickle?'

'Not when it comes to you, he's not,' Stacy said. 'I mean, he's got this taciturn thing going, but he totally adores you. You know that, right?'

'Actually, I didn't know that,' Frances admitted.

'I've known since my first week here. And so does everybody else. What did you think was going on with you two?'

Frances shrugged. 'Just that it works. Analyzing stuff is not always a good idea, you know.'

'I agree with that part,' Stacy said. 'But he adores you. Take my word for it.'

'I'm very happy to know that.'

'You can't tell him that you know,' Stacy warned.

'Why not?'

'You just can't.'

'How do you happen to know all this?' Frances asked. 'You're a kid.'

Stacy touched her fingertip to her temple. 'Yeah, but up here I'm wise beyond my years. What else do you want to know?'

'I'm good for now,' Frances said smiling. 'Just being adored has made my day.'

Stacy laughed and reached for another tart. 'I might eat this whole plate. Hey – I saw the Thanksgiving show last night. It was good.'

'Well,' Frances said doubtfully, and she drank her tea.

'What was with the hockey player though? Was he stoned?'

'Just stupid, I think.'

'Oh,' Stacy said, clearly disappointed. 'Well, it's a good thing he can skate,' she said after a moment. 'I googled him while I was watching. Dude makes five million dollars a year. Playing hockey.'

Frances looked up from her computer screen. 'And why did you google him?'

'He's really good-looking, Frances. I mean, come on.' Stacy sighed. 'That was before I found out that he's stupid.'

'Now he's not as good-looking?'

'Matter of fact, he's not. What's wrong with me, Frances?'

'Absolutely nothing,' Frances laughed. 'When are you flying home anyway? Are you good to work tomorrow?'

Stacy carried her tea to the desk across from Frances and sat down at the computer there. 'I decided not to go.'

'Why not?'

'Flights are so damn expensive at Thanksgiving. Total rip-off.'

'I can get you a flight on my air miles,' Frances said. 'I'm not using them. It's Thanksgiving. Go be with your family.'

Stacy began to type into the computer. She didn't say anything for a while.

'What's going on?' Frances asked.

Stacy typed some more numbers and hit enter before looking over. 'My dad has this new girlfriend. She's, like, a year older than me. She bothers me, Frances.'

'Because she's so young?'

'No. Because she acts as if she's his age. She talks to me like I'm her daughter, giving me advice on what to wear, who to date, makeup tips. She's my age, she should act it.'

'I wouldn't like that either,' Frances said.

Stacy shook her head. 'On top of that, my mother resents her. *Of course.* So I have to be careful how many hours I spend at my dad's, and how many with my mom. I feel like they've got a stopwatch on me, to make sure they get equal time.'

'Sounds like a lot of fun.'

Stacy smiled. 'So, I can buy an expensive plane ticket, put up with a crowded airport, and spend three miserable days in Vancouver with my dysfunctional family. Or I can hang out at my apartment, drink some wine and binge some Netflix.'

'Or you could spend Thanksgiving here at the farm.'

'No. I'm not intruding on you and Carl.'

'You're right, you will not be intruding on us,' Frances said. 'But you are spending Thanksgiving here.'

NINE

Chino's house was built beside the scrap yard, a clapboard bungalow with aluminum siding, once white, now faded in most places to the slate gray of the metal. There was a concrete patio behind the house, cluttered with lawn chairs and a picnic table and half of a forty-five gallon drum turned into a barbeque. Chino's Harley was on

jack stands beside the drum. The bike hadn't moved in nearly
a year.

Bug pulled into the yard and stopped by the open door of
the shop, his window down. He waited for a few moments
for Chino to walk out of the shop and when he didn't he
drove over to the house. He shut the ignition off and sat
there, wondering how much Chino had blown at the casino. The
night was hazy; Bug remembered sleeping on and off in
the Pontiac, waking up every time Chino came out and went
into the trunk for more cash. Bug remembered Billy too, sitting
behind the wheel, too pissed off to sleep. He had a right to
be pissed. The sun was up when they finally headed for home.

The house was unlocked and Bug walked in without
knocking. The place smelled of stale beer. A radio played
somewhere, some sports talk show. There was a cell phone
on the counter, lights blinking. Bug moved from the kitchen
to the living room, calling out for Chino. He looked out the
front window to the road and called again, louder this time.

A moment later the radio shut off and Chino came out of
a bedroom into the hallway, half stumbling, wearing just his
shorts. He glared at Bug before detouring into the bathroom,
leaving the door open while he pissed. Bug heard a tap running
then, and the sound of Chino drinking directly from it.

'What?' he snapped when he came out.

'We're fucked, that's what,' Bug told him. 'That guy Bones,
works for Tommy Jakes, was at my house this morning.'

Chino lit a cigarette and sat on the couch. 'What'd you tell
him?'

'I didn't tell him nothing,' Bug said. 'Told him I didn't
know nothing. Then he wants your address.' As he talked, Bug
went over to look out the front window again, as if expecting
company.

'You didn't give it to him?'

'I said I didn't know it. He didn't fucking believe me. I
want to know how he found out where I live, Chino.'

Chino wouldn't look at him. He sat smoking, sullen.

'You tell him?' Bug demanded.

'Fuck, I don't know. Maybe.'

'Why would you do that?'

'Because Tommy asked for it. All right?'

Bug cursed and came over to sit down on a chair beside the couch. 'How much is left?'

'I don't know,' Chino said. 'Four grand maybe.'

'How'd that happen? Why didn't you stick around and lose it all?'

What had happened was that Chino had been kicked out of the casino after accusing the blackjack dealer of cheating. Otherwise he undoubtedly would have dropped the whole wad. But he wasn't telling Bug that.

'Who do you think you're talking to?' he demanded. 'How'd you like me to hand you over to Tommy Jakes on a fucking platter?'

Bug fell silent for a time. 'Come on, Chino.'

Chino smoked the cigarette down and lit another. He went into the kitchen and found a bottle with a couple of ounces of rye left. He picked up his blinking cell phone and brought up the display before tossing it aside. He walked over to the back door and looked out the window there, toward the shop, as he drank the whisky from the bottle.

'We'd better go talk to him,' he said at length.

Tommy Jakes wasn't at Hard Ten when they got there but the snotty blonde bartender was and she got busy on her phone the moment Chino and Bug walked through the door. The Wild Lucifer clubhouse was only five hundred yards away and there was a garage out back where some of the gang worked on their bikes. Chino and Bug ordered a pitcher of beer and were sitting at a table, the same table they'd met Tommy at the last time, when Bones came in through the back. He just stood there, watching, as if making certain they weren't going to leave. Fuck him, Chino thought; if they were going to leave, why would they show in the first place?

Nervous as he was, Bug still tried to sweet talk the bartender when she brought over the beer. She looked at him like he was something stuck to the bottom of her shoe.

Tommy Jakes came in twenty minutes later, wearing a suit and tie. He was clean-shaven and had his long hair pulled back in a ponytail. When he walked through the front door,

Bug reached for his glass to have a drink; his hands were shaking. He wasn't thinking about the bartender now. Tommy got a cup of coffee from the bartender and came over to sit down.

'I was getting worried that you boys might have met with some misfortune. I've been calling your cell, Chino.'

'I got your message,' Chino said. 'Figured I'd just drive on over and see you in person. What's going on, Tommy?'

'What's going on?' Tommy repeated. He had a sip of the hot coffee. 'What is going on is that I don't see my money. Is it under the table? Did you leave it in the parking lot?'

Chino showed surprise. 'You don't have it?'

'I beg your pardon?'

'The kid never dropped it here?' Chino asked.

Tommy didn't say anything then. He drank more coffee and sat back in the chair, watching Chino. Bug was looking at Chino too now. Bug didn't have much of a poker face even under the best circumstances. Tommy waited Chino out.

'He was told to drop it here on his way home,' Chino said. 'You telling me he didn't show?'

'You're referring to our young Indian friend?' Tommy asked.

'Yeah.'

Tommy turned in his chair. 'Bones, there been any Indians around here toting a bag full of cash?'

'No.'

Tommy turned back to the table. 'Looks like you got a problem, Chino.'

'That little fucker,' Chino fumed.

Tommy held his palm up. 'Before you start going on about somebody taking you off, I'm going to interrupt you, Chino. You took this on. You – nobody else. And now you owe me fifty-five grand. Whether this Indian has it, or it's stuffed beneath your mattress or you used it to buy yourself a new Cadillac – you owe me fifty-five grand. When do you intend to pay me?'

'Soon as I track that little fucker down. I'll bring you his head on a spike.'

'You're not listening to me, Chino,' Tommy said. 'I don't care about the Indian. And I don't want to hear tough talk about somebody's head on a spike. I want my money.'

'You'll get your money,' Chino said. 'I'll guarantee it.'

'I know I'll get it,' Tommy told him. 'I don't know if it's going to be the hard way or the easy way, but I'll get it. You want to go the easy way, you've got twenty-four hours.'

TEN

Carl was on his right side on the carpet, his hands bound behind him with plastic electrical ties and duct tape across his mouth, wound round his head a couple of turns. There was blood running from his temple down his jawline and into his shirt.

He had walked right into it. When he saw the dog on the lawn, he couldn't register what might have happened. All he could think was that there'd been an accident. There were often hunters in the area, after ducks and geese on the river or deer in the bush, although Frances wouldn't allow deer hunters on the farm. Still, Carl could only think that a stray shot from an adjoining property, or from down by the river, had struck the pup.

So he'd walked in, like a sap. In the same moment that he saw Stacy, bound and gagged on the couch, he was hit, probably with the revolver the man had in his hand now. The man had to have been standing behind the door, waiting. When Carl came to, he was on the floor. His temple throbbed like an enormous toothache. Seconds ago he had watched the big man knock Frances down and pick her up again. Now he was forcing her to look at Carl and Stacy.

'You see how things are?' he was saying to her. 'Right now everybody's still alive. You're the one can keep it that way.'

Carl kept his eyes on Frances, and when she looked at him he fiercely nodded to her and waited for her to react. Finally she did, returning the nod, her eyes desperate. Frightened. Her breath was coming in gasps. Carl could see her struggling to comprehend what was happening. And why.

Carl was doing the same. He was – if nothing else – encouraged that the men all wore masks. It meant that they intended to leave them alive. There was nothing else remotely encouraging about the situation. Carl couldn't imagine what they wanted. Since coming to and gathering his senses as best he could against the pain in his head, he could only speculate that this was a case of mistaken identity. These guys were in the wrong house.

The big man, still holding Frances by the hair, propelled her past Carl, shoving her roughly into a wingback chair. The turkey she'd been carrying earlier was by the fireplace. There was a fire going there; Stacy must have lit it when she came in from work.

Using only his legs, Carl scrambled around on the carpet, determined to maintain eye contact with Frances. Now he looked quickly over at Stacy as well. She was curled on the couch, recoiled from the skinny guy in coveralls beside her. She was wearing a skirt that had hiked up, displaying her thighs. Her eyes were frantic. The skinny guy was watching the big one, who was obviously in charge. The third man was by the front window, keeping watch, it seemed.

After pushing Frances into the chair the big man pulled a coffee table over in front of her. He sat down on the table and leaned forward, the revolver dangling in his left hand while with his right hand he reached out to brush back the hair from her face. His eyes behind the mask were small, the pupils dilated. Frances was still wearing her coat and she shrank into it, away from him.

'OK,' he said. 'You gonna play ball with me?'

Frances nodded, looking away from the man to Carl, a few feet away.

'You look at me, bitch,' the man said. 'You don't look at him. I'll put a fucking bullet in his head and throw him out on the lawn with the dog. You want that?'

'No,' Frances said quickly, forcing her eyes back to the man.

'All right,' the man said. 'You see what we got here, don't you? As of this minute, we own your family. You, the hubby on the floor and the daughter over there on the couch. We *own* them. And you're going to buy them back. You're a business-woman, right? Well, this is a simple business transaction. OK?'

Frances nodded again, somehow buoyed by the suggestion.

'Now this is what you're going to do,' the man said. 'You're going to go back out that door, and you're going to drive into town to your bank. It's Friday night, the banks are open. You're going to withdraw a hundred thousand dollars and you're going to bring it here and put it in my hand. A hundred grand.' The man straightened up and sat watching Frances for a moment. 'Are you with me so far?'

'I don't know if I can—' Frances began.

'Yes, you can,' the man snapped. 'You think you have options? You go to the cops and we're going to kill your family. You come back without the money and we're going to kill your family. You do anything except what I just told you and guess what? We're going to kill your family.'

Instinctively Frances started to look at Carl again, but stopped herself. The big man saw.

'Go ahead and look at him. You want to ask his advice?'

The man got up and went to Carl. He knelt down and put the barrel of the revolver against Carl's forehead. 'What do you think the little missus should do, pal? Are you worth a hundred grand, you and the little cutie with the nice legs on the couch over there? What do you think?'

'All right,' Frances blurted out.

The big man suddenly backhanded Carl across the face, the sickly sound of the blow resonating in the quiet room. He stood up and turned to Frances.

'I don't think your hubby likes me,' he said. 'Get your ass moving now. And you had better think up a story for the bank, TV lady. Why you need that kind of coin. Tell them you're buying a Porsche or something and the dude wants cash. Make it real, whatever you come up with.' He paused, watching Frances. 'The quicker you get this done, the quicker we're out of your life. You can go back to playing pretend on the fucking television.'

Carl's eyes were watering from the blow, but he was watching the big man intently. The TV lady, he'd said. So this was not a case of mistaken identity. The farm had been the target. But why would they think they could get money here?

Carl could see Frances gathering herself. Another person

would be on the floor, whimpering. Not Frances. She glanced across the room to Stacy.

'It'll be OK,' she said quietly, holding the younger woman's eyes for a moment. She turned, gave Carl a quick look and started for the door.

'Hey, you want to say goodbye to your family?' the big man said. 'You know, in case you fuck up and never see them again?'

'I'll see them,' Frances told him.

The big man smiled. 'Tough chick, eh? Maybe I had you wrong.'

As Frances drove away, her headlights swept across the lawn and she saw the pup there, lying dead in the grass, a pool of blood beneath its head. She didn't make it a mile down the road before she had to pull over. Her hands on the steering wheel were shaking so badly she nearly struck an oncoming car. She pulled into an overgrown lane that led down to the river, drove a few yards and stopped. She sat there motionless, feeling her heart pounding in her chest.

Her cell phone was in her coat pocket. She took it out and held it in her hand. At one point she punched in 911 but then shut it off. She didn't know what to do. She had no idea what to do. In fact, there was only one person in her life who would know and that person was back at the house, bound and gagged on the carpet. She could call Rufus Canfield, but what could he do? He was a small-town lawyer with a game leg. He was hardly the type to rush the house, and he was too smart to call the police. Or maybe the opposite was true – maybe he would insist on calling the police. Maybe that was, after all, the smart move. There was a chance that the asshole with the bad breath and the gun was bluffing. Maybe a very good chance.

But not good enough. Frances was not about to take that risk.

She had to play along and hope that it worked out as the man claimed it would. He'd been right about one thing – she had no options. She took a deep breath and then she realized there was a truck parked alongside the lane, fifty yards farther in, tucked into the brush. She turned her lights on and saw that it was a white Dodge half ton. It wasn't all that unusual to see; fishermen and hunters sometimes parked there before heading down to the river. She turned on her high beams to get a look at the license plate. After another minute she put the car in reverse, backed out of the lane and started for town.

At the bank, the teller was of no help. When Frances asked to talk to the manager she was told that he had gone home. He didn't work Friday nights. Finally the teller called someone in the building and a few minutes later led Frances into the office of the loans manager, a woman named Kelly. For some reason, in the face of the teller's impotence, Frances had grown calmer. Maybe it was because she had something to do. Something she had to do.

'What is this about?' the manager asked. She was sitting at her desk, her eyes on the open laptop in front of her. Frances assumed she was looking at her account information.

'I need a hundred thousand dollars,' Frances told her.

'Yes, Steven said that,' the manager said. 'But surely you don't require cash?'

'I do.'

The manager hesitated. 'Can I ask why? I mean, we can provide you with a certified check, which is the same as cash.'

'It has to be cash.' Frances now tried the story she'd been working on. 'There's a piece of property along the river I'm buying. The owner insists on cash. He's old school, doesn't trust banks.'

'But if you tell him that a certified check essentially *is* cash,' the manager said. 'If you like, I could call him—'

'No,' Frances said quickly. 'He's very eccentric. And I need to get this done tonight. He might change his mind by tomorrow. He's done it before. Why can't I withdraw it?' She gestured toward the laptop. 'I have a line of credit.'

'That's not the problem,' the manager said. 'The problem is the vault. It's on a timer and it won't open again until Monday morning. I don't know how much cash we have on hand but I doubt it's anywhere near what you want.'

'I really need the money.' Frances felt her heartbeat racing again. How could this be happening? 'Please.'

The manager looked at her strangely but she got to her feet. 'Wait here a moment.'

She went out into the bank and was gone for ten minutes or more, while Frances's anxiety rose steadily. When the manager finally returned, she did not sit down.

'It looks as if we can put together forty thousand, possibly forty-five. Can we do that, along with a check for the balance? Or we could give you the rest of the cash Monday morning. Surely forty thousand will hold the place for the weekend?'

Frances realized she had no choice. 'All right, I'll take the forty-five. I'll have to . . . I'll have to make it work.' She hesitated, looking at the manager. 'I have to make it work.'

'We'll get you your money.'

'Please,' Frances said.

ELEVEN

Chino found a bottle of Irish whisky on a shelf beneath the island and he poured large measures for himself and Bug, who had walked over from the couch when he'd seen Chino rummaging through the cupboards. Chino had offered the fifth toward Billy Taylor, still standing by the bay window watching the road out front, but Billy had shaken his head. Probably a good thing, Chino thought. An Indian drinking hard liquor could be a problem. A prison guard had once told Chino that Indians couldn't handle grain alcohol because, historically, they had never been exposed to the stuff. Not until the white man had shown up anyway. The guard could have been full of shit; most of them were.

Bug carried his glass back to the couch and sat down by the girl there. He'd been talking to her non-stop. He probably thought he was getting somewhere with her.

Chino had made a search of the house while he waited for the woman to return. He'd pocketed some jewelry and a man's watch in the master bedroom upstairs and went into the bathroom there, looking for drugs in the medicine cabinet. Coming up empty, he did a couple of lines on the counter. He'd given some coke to Bug earlier, to get him wound up for the job, but that was all he would get. Chino didn't want him getting out of hand before they got the money.

Downstairs he searched an office looking for cash or a safe, but found nothing. Off the kitchen there was a door leading down into a stone basement. It was low-ceilinged and dark, even with the lights on. There was an oil furnace there and shelves with cans of paint and preserves. A couple dozen bottles of wine stored sideways in a rack. A work bench with some antique tools.

Now Chino sat at the counter and drank. Carl was facing away, his eyes fixed on the wall. His head had stopped bleeding and the blood along his face had coagulated, growing dark. He was quiet, barely moving since the woman had left. Still, there was something about him that bothered Chino.

The girl had retreated into the corner of the couch, as far from Bug as she could get. With her hands tied behind her there was no way she could push her skirt down and she appeared dismayed by that, constantly squirming, scissoring her legs in an effort to cover herself.

'I'll take that tape off so you can have a sip,' Bug said.

'You leave that fucking tape where it is,' Chino said. He was talking to Bug but watching Carl, who had shifted around so he could see what was happening across the room.

'You are such a sweet girl,' Bug said. 'How old are you anyway? I love a young thing.'

Only Bug would try to strike up a conversation with a woman he'd gagged, Chino thought. Carrying his glass, he slid off the stool and approached Carl, kneeling down there to block his view of the couch. He took a moment, looking at the man. He was strong, Chino could tell that when he'd bound his wrists with the electrical ties. His forearms were powerful, his hands large and callused. There was something capable about the man, and that pissed Chino off.

'What's the matter?' Chino said. 'You don't like my buddy sparking your little girl? You'd better hope the missus brings home the bacon or I might let him take her on a little date.' He drank from the glass. 'Oh, that look in your eyes. You're about ready to blow a head gasket, aren't you? I bet you're thinking about what you'd do to me. You know, if you had the chance. In your head, you're a tough guy. Real life, you're just another pussy, sitting here on your fancy farm. Probably never had your hands dirty in your life. I'd kick your fucking ass six ways to Sunday, pal. You and your attitude. Well, who's lying on the floor bleeding and who's drinking whisky and having a good old time?'

Chino saw Carl's eyes register something and he turned to see Bug running his fingers along the girl's thigh. Tickling her, Bug giggling as the girl shrank back in horror. At the window, Billy turned from his vigil to see what was going on.

'Look at those crazy kids, getting along,' Chino said to Carl. 'Must make a father happy to see that. You got potential son-in-law material right there. Dumb as a rock and couldn't spell cat, but he likes your girl.'

Bug's hand went under the skirt and the girl attempted to scream beneath the tape, the sound emerging like a frantic moan.

'Leave her alone,' Billy snapped, stepping toward the couch.

'Come on,' Bug laughed. 'I ain't hurting nobody. I just wanna touch that sweet thing a little bit.'

'Leave her alone, man,' Billy said. 'Not why we're here.'

'Shut up and watch the fucking road,' Chino said.

'Not why we're here,' Billy said again.

'Relax,' Chino said. He looked at Carl. 'Don't you hate it when people can't get along? Come on, tough guy. Give us a smile. I don't like that evil eye, boy. You best change your attitude or I'll shove that empty whisky bottle up your ass.'

Billy stared defiantly at Bug, who had backed off some, although his hand still rested on the girl's knee, his fingers drumming a little beat there. The girl was looking at Billy as if he was her last chance.

'Leave her be,' Billy said once more.

Chino got to his feet and made a move toward Billy, menace in his eyes. 'You don't tell anybody what—' He stopped as headlights swept the room. 'She's back.'

Billy moved at once to the window.

'She alone?' Chino demanded.

Billy watched a moment. 'Appears so.'

'Keep your eyes on that fucking road,' Chino ordered. 'Could be cops trailing.'

He pulled the revolver from his belt and moved toward the back door. When Frances walked in he grabbed her by the arm and propelled her past him into the living room, then stepped outside for a look around. He stood there on the patio for a full minute before walking over to look inside Frances's SUV.

When he came back into the house she was standing in the middle of the room, holding a heavy cloth bag in one hand and staring defiantly at Bug, who had now taken his hands off the girl. His eyes were on Frances and even behind the mask he appeared sheepish, as if caught in the act.

Chino pointed the gun toward the bag. 'You get it?'

Frances turned to him, taking a breath. She held the bag forward. 'There's forty-seven thousand. All I could get from the bank and the ATMs.'

'Fuck!' Chino shouted. 'You fucking cooze. What did I tell you?'

He snatched the bag from her and dumped the bills out on to the island. He stood staring at it, his chest heaving. Bug got up from the couch and walked over. He picked up some of the money as if to count it, then left off. He turned to Chino.

'It might be enough,' he said. 'I mean it's close, right?'

Chino stared at the money, his mind working. 'She's lying,' he said quietly.

He turned and slapped Frances across the face with such force she fell backwards into the coffee table and went down.

'You are fucking lying!' Chino screamed. 'A hundred grand. You're on fucking TV! You're worth ten times that.'

Seeing Frances fall, Carl tried desperately to stand, struggling to gain his balance with his hands bound behind him. As he got to his knees Chino punched him in the face, then grabbed him by the shoulder and hit him again and again.

'You people make me sick!' He left Carl alone and went over to grab Frances, jerking her to her feet and pulling her face close to his. 'I got a feeling you got it all and you're trying to fuck me. Seeing if you can save yourself a few dollars. You don't want to spend a dime, even to save your stinking life.'

'No,' Frances said. 'The vault is on a timer. I swear.'

Chino hit her again, closing his fist and driving it into her mouth. Carl was on his side a few feet away and he swung his legs around and drove his heavy work boot into Chino's knee. Chino screamed in pain and collapsed. Bug jumped forward and began to kick Carl.

'Jesus Christ,' Billy said. He headed for the money. 'Let's take this and get out of here.'

Chino got slowly to his feet. Reaching up, he removed the balaclava and limped over to where Carl was lying, his head turned away from Bug's wild kicks. Chino pushed Bug aside and grabbed Carl by the neck and shoulder, lifting him to his feet and dragging him to the door leading to the basement. He put his face inches from Carl's.

'I gave you a chance. Both of you. And you fucked it up.'

When Bug saw Chino without his mask, he removed his own. He stepped to the basement door and opened it. 'Get rid of him,' he urged. 'We got the women.'

Chino shoved Carl through the door and into the basement.

Carl, without his hands to break the fall, hit the steps head-first and then continued down, his left shoulder crashing onto the steps, one by one. At the bottom, his head slammed into the concrete floor of the basement and he went out.

Chino turned back to the others.

'Jesus, let's get out of here,' Billy said again.

'Not yet,' Chino snapped, approaching Frances. 'They broke the deal. I warned them. Go get the truck, bring it up to the house. Wait for us.'

'Let's just go,' Billy said. 'There's fifty grand.'

Chino pointed the gun at Billy's head. 'Get the truck and wait for us.'

When Billy was gone, Chino gestured toward the girl on the couch. 'Make it quick,' he said.

He watched while Bug led the girl down a hallway, then turned to Frances.

'One last time,' he said. 'Where's the rest? I know you got it.'

Frances had gone from watching Carl disappear down the stairs to seeing Stacy being led off. She was barely able to speak.

'I'm telling you. Please—'

'You think I'm trash, don't you?' Chino said. He spread his

palms. 'But look where we are. Not so snooty now, are you? Now you're going to have to beg.'

He put the gun barrel against Frances's forehead. 'In case you didn't know, you beg on your knees.'

When Bug came out of the bedroom, Chino was stuffing the money back into the bag. The woman was nowhere to be seen.

'Go out to that garage and find a can of gas,' Chino said. 'We're leaving nothing behind.'

'Where's the woman?'

'With her hubby,' Chino said. 'Do it.'

When he had the money stowed, Chino went beneath the island for three more bottles of liquor. He put the bottles on top of the cash as Bug returned with a gas can.

'Billy waiting?'

'Yeah,' Bug said.

Chino handed Bug the bag. 'I'll be two minutes.'

Bug waited in the truck with Billy, who sat sullenly, saying nothing. Chino came out the front door on the run. He jumped into the passenger seat and they drove off. As they hit the river road, the interior of the house exploded.

TWELVE

It seemed to Carl that the sound of the fire woke him – the snapping and crackling of the flames, like miniature fireworks, from somewhere above him. When he opened his eyes it was pitch black. His cheek was against the cold concrete floor. Behind the duct tape that gagged him, his tongue felt swollen and his mouth was dry. The pain in his left shoulder was excruciating, shooting from his neck down into his biceps. He smelled the smoke then. Looking up, he could see the flames dancing beneath the door at the top of the stairs.

When he moved, he felt the warm body beside him. He couldn't see her and he couldn't touch her, but he knew at once it was Frances. He knew her scent, her being. He lowered his face next to hers, hoping to feel her breathing. He could not.

Pushing his back against the newel post at the base of the stairs, he managed to get to his feet. He worked his wrists against the plastic ties that held them behind his back. They would not give. He knew that the shoulder was separated, and badly so. There was a light switch at the bottom of the stairs. He moved to it, feeling the wall with his right shoulder, his good shoulder. When he found it, he crouched and flipped it on with his chin. Nothing. The fire must have blown the breakers.

Standing there, he could now feel the heat from above. The house was burning down. He wondered about Stacy. Was she down there with them? In the dark it was impossible to tell. He moved around, feeling with his feet, but couldn't find her.

He stopped for a moment, looking again at the fire beneath the door above him. Going up was not an option. He told himself to slow down. To think. At the back of the cellar there was a storm door that led outside. Carl had never known it to be opened and he thought it was padlocked. He needed to get his hands free.

He moved away from the stairs to the wall opposite, where the wine rack was built. Finding it in the darkness, he turned his back to the wall and reached out to grab a bottle. He pulled it from the rack and dropped it on to the concrete floor, smashing it. Slowly he knelt down, feeling for the broken glass on the floor behind him. The pain in his shoulder was making him nauseous and he stopped for a moment, thinking he would be sick. Searching again, he found the neck of the bottle, turned the jagged edge upward in his hands, seeking the ties that bound his wrists. He sawed away clumsily, felt the broken glass slice into his skin. Still he moved the bottle neck around, working it back and forth, finally feeling it against the plastic ties. He screamed as he drove the shard upward, into his flesh and through the plastic. His hands came free.

He pulled the duct tape away from his face, feeling it tear at his hair. Both wrists were bleeding profusely, the blood running from his fingertips to the floor as he made his way in the darkness to the storm door. There was a hasp there, and a padlock. The heat from above grew stronger, the noise of the fire louder. Carl turned and followed the wall to the work bench, his hands before him, reaching for it in the dark. He felt frantically along the bench and then the pegboard above it. Screwdrivers, pliers, pipe wrenches. Finally his hand closed on the claw hammer. He went back to the door in the dark and began to hammer at the lock, the lock he couldn't see. He pounded away, missing more than connecting, the blood from his wrists coating the hammer handle, making it slippery and hard to grip. As he swung futilely, the panic inside him grew. When he stopped and reached for the padlock, it was still intact.

Above him something collapsed, hitting the floor with a deafening crash. The staircase, Carl thought. Soon the whole house would fall into the cellar. The floor was burning above his head and the heat descended on him like a sauna. He was drenched in sweat. He reached for the lock, running his bloody fingers along the hasp itself. The wood there was old and cracked. Turning the hammer over, he attempted to drive the claw between the clasp and the wood. He missed, and missed again. The hammer slid from his bloody fingers and fell to the floor. He dropped to his knees to find it. He began again and on the fifth attempt the claw caught. He jerked the handle upward, felt the hasp break loose a little. And then the hammer slipped. He did it again and again, gaining an eighth of an inch each time. Finally he drove the full length of the claws behind the hasp and ripped it out of the door, the wood splintering. He jerked the door open, swinging it wide on the rusting, complaining hinges. Cool night air greeted him, like an angel's embrace.

When he turned away from the door there were flames at the top of the steps leading upstairs, illuminating the stairwell. He could see Frances now, crumpled on the floor, legs drawn up. She was still wearing her coat. Moving to her, Carl looked desperately around for Stacy but didn't see her. He knelt beside Frances and ran his fingers along her throat, feeling for a pulse. It was there. He attempted to lift her and when he did the pain raced through his shoulder like a shot. He thought he would pass out. He released her, allowed her to slump back on to the floor. He couldn't carry her.

There was another crash from above. The sound of the blaze was incredible, like a firefight. Carl reached down with his right hand and, taking Frances by the collar of her coat, he dragged her across the concrete floor, through the open storm door and into the stairwell. She was dead weight and she didn't make a sound. It was all he could do to move her. His back to the stairs, his heels dug in, he moved her upward, one step at a time. When he got to the top, he had to stop. His heart was pounding, his breath coming in ragged gasps.

He could rest for only a moment. The heat was vicious there, the walls above him on fire. He took her again by the collar and pulled her away from the house, across the grass of the yard. Twice his feet went out from under him and he fell. The second time, he took Frances in his arms and just sat there, watching the inferno that was the house. The place was fully engulfed now, the windows blown out, the roof ablaze. The heat came after him again where he sat. With an effort, he got up and again began to pull Frances along. When he was fifty yards from the building, he stopped. He couldn't go any further and so he hoped they were safe. He kept thinking of Stacy and praying she had somehow escaped.

His hands and arms were sticky with the blood that still flowed and he began to feel weak. In the distance, he thought he heard sirens.

THIRTEEN

There were trucks and tankers and rescue units parked everywhere, in the drive and in the yard and along the road out front. A news team from Rose City was on the scene, wandering around the periphery of the ruined house looking for footage and soundbites.

The fire crew was pumping water from the river, keeping a steady flow on the house, but it was obvious there was little to salvage at this point. It was an old farmhouse and the substructure would have been tinder dry. They had soaked the garage to prevent it from catching fire as well. The wind was gusting, flaring hot spots here and there in the ruined house, showering the garage roof and vehicles with sparks illuminating the dark sky.

Dunbar parked the SUV along the road, a hundred yards or so away, and walked up to the scene. He had been at home when he got the call. He and Martha had had a late dinner, roasted chicken and potatoes and salad. They had drunk most of a bottle of wine with the meal and were watching a movie that he had little interest in when the phone rang.

'Why are you being called to a house fire?' Martha had asked.

'Good question. Dispatch didn't know, other than to say the fire marshal had requested it.'

So he'd left the boring movie and driven out to Talbotville. The marshal's name was Jason McLean. Dunbar had never met him before. He was young, maybe thirty or thirty-five. Dunbar wasn't certain that thirty-five was considered young these days, but it was certainly young to him.

'So what's going on?' he asked.

'Something not right about this one,' McLean said. 'Looks to me like a murder/suicide gone wrong.'

'Oh?'

McLean pointed to the back yard. 'When first response got here, a man and a woman were on the grass over there. Both unconscious. Neighbor confirms that they live here. Looks like the woman took a pretty good beating and the man's wrists were slashed. I'm thinking he beat her up, got all remorseful and tried to off himself. Set the house on fire and then changed his mind about the whole thing and got him and her out of there in the nick of time.'

That was a fair amount of calculating for a young fire marshal, Dunbar thought. And pretty premature to boot. 'Where's this neighbor?'

McLean looked around for a moment before spotting the woman, standing with a group of others in the lee of the garage, out of the wind. 'There,' he said. 'In the green jacket with the hood.'

Dunbar nodded. 'The couple – you have their names?'

'Not yet, but the property belongs to a Frances Rourke.'

'You say they were both unconscious?'

'Yeah,' McLean said. 'Paramedics said in his case it could have been from lack of blood, although his face was banged up too, like from a fall or something.'

'What were her injuries?' Dunbar asked.

'Blunt trauma to the head.'

Dunbar stood looking at the house, where the firefighters were moving about, hitting hot spots with the hoses. There was a lack of urgency in their movements, as would be expected with a lost cause. Dunbar turned to take in the numerous vehicles in and around the property. By the garage, dripping with water from the hoses, there was a Lexus SUV, a Ford pickup and an older hatchback of some kind.

'Do we know if anybody else was home?'

'Not definitely,' McLean said. 'But the neighbor said it was just the two of them lived here.'

'Those three vehicles by the garage,' Dunbar said. 'Were they here when your men showed, or are they part of the circus that came afterward?'

'Well . . . I don't know,' McLean said.

'Let's find out.'

Dunbar walked to the three vehicles in question and as he took down the plate numbers he asked McLean to direct him to the first responder. It turned out to be a captain named Pollard. He was standing by one of the tankers, drinking a cup of coffee. He was tall and heavy, with a walrus mustache.

'So far as I recall, those three cars were parked there when we arrived,' he said. 'We wouldn't pay a whole lot of attention to that. We're looking at the fire.'

'I suppose it's too early to speculate on cause,' Dunbar said.

'Not too sure about that,' Pollard said. 'Come here.'

He led Dunbar around to the front of the house, where a large bay window had blown out. The heat was fierce even yet and they couldn't get any closer than forty feet or so from the building. Pollard pointed inside, to the water-soaked living room. Most of the floor had collapsed into the basement but a portion of it, alongside a stone fireplace, was still intact.

'See there, by the hearth? Looks like a gas can. One of those old steel cans. You know anybody keeps a can of gas in their living room?'

Dunbar allowed he did not. McLean had been trailing and now he stepped forward. Apparently he was feeling left out.

'Why wasn't I told about this?'

'We just spotted it,' Pollard said. 'The building was on fire previously.'

'You'll hang on to that for me when you can get to it,' Dunbar said.

The captain assured him of it. Dunbar left them there and continued to walk around the house. The walls were caved in along the far side but the rear wall was still partially erect, held upright by the stone fireplace. Stopping in the back yard, Dunbar saw stairs leading to the basement through a storm door. He attempted to get near for a closer look but the heat drove him back. Stepping away, he skidded on the slippery ground and almost fell. He knelt down and ran his fingers over the grass. They came up bloody. Taking his flashlight from his pocket, he followed the blood trail to the storm door, or at least as close as the heat would allow. Then he turned to retrace his steps. Several yards out into the yard he came upon a spot where the grass was matted down and there was a considerable amount of blood. Presumably that was where the couple was found.

He tracked McLean down by one of the tankers, talking to the reporter from Rose City. Dunbar recognized her. She was young and very pretty and tonight was wearing a trench coat. Old school. Dunbar waited until McLean finished talking to her and then approached.

'Looks as if the couple came up from the basement,' he said, gesturing to the yard.

McLean glanced over. 'I wouldn't know.'

'There's a trail of blood from the storm door.' Dunbar indicated the house. 'I count three exit doors above ground. Why would they leave from the basement?'

'Who knows? Maybe they were trying to get away from the fire.'

'You said she was unconscious,' Dunbar said. 'He carried her downstairs and then up again?'

McLean shrugged. 'You wouldn't think so.'

'Where did they take them?' Dunbar asked. 'Which hospital?'

'Talbotville.'

Before he left, Dunbar walked over to talk to the woman in the green jacket. She was maybe seventy, wearing duck boots and corduroy pants. He told her who he was, then asked where she lived.

'Next place over.' She pointed to the west. 'I was walking my dog down by the river and coming home I heard the fire. I could see the flames through the trees. I went in and called nine-one-one, but somebody else had already called it in.'

'And you walked over?'

'Yes,' she said. 'I put my dog inside first. He's funny around fire.'

'And you saw two people on the lawn?'

'Frances and Carl,' the woman said. 'They were both lying over there. She was kind of in his lap but they were both unconscious. I didn't get too close because the rescue trucks were just pulling in.'

'Can you give me their names?' Dunbar asked.

'Frances Rourke and Carl Burns.'

Dunbar wrote in his notes. 'How well do you know them?'

'Frances I know real well. This is her family farm. She's a good person. She has a big heart but she doesn't take any guff from anybody.'

'And him?'

'Him – well, the last couple of years I've got to know him. Some thought at first like maybe he was a bit of a hoodlum, maybe taking advantage of her. You know, with it being her farm and all. Not that Frances would be easy to take advantage of. But I don't figure that's how it is. He's a real good worker, and I know he treats her fine.'

'What do you mean by hoodlum?' Dunbar asked.

'He's been in jail.'

Dunbar started to ask more, but it was then that he recognized the name.

'Did you see anything earlier, when you were out walking?' he asked. 'Strange car in the driveway or anything like that?'

'I never walked past here. I always make a loop down along the river to the side road up yonder and back.'

'You see any strange cars on the road?'

The woman shrugged. 'The usual traffic, I guess. What would you call a strange car?'

'Good point,' Dunbar admitted.

'Oh, there was a truck parked on the lane leading to the river,' she said.

'Where was this?'

She pointed. 'A couple hundred yards or so past my drive. But people park there quite frequently. They fish off the old stone dam down below.'

'Was this after dark?' Dunbar asked.

'Just, I'd say.'

'And you didn't see it leave?'

'No.'

'I don't suppose you'd have any idea what kind of truck it was?'

'It was a white Dodge.'

'You're certain of the make?'

'That's what was written on the back,' the woman said. 'My father always drove a Dodge. He claimed Henry Ford was in cahoots with Hitler.'

Dunbar wrote down what she'd told him, aside from the father's political theories. He got the woman's name and phone number before indicating the three vehicles by the garage.

'Do you know who owns those?'

'Frances drives the SUV,' the woman said. 'The pickup is Carl's and the little red car belongs to the girl that works here.'

Dunbar walked over to the vehicles. None of them were locked and he looked inside all three. There was a cell phone on the console of the SUV. Dunbar put it in his pocket, got into his car and headed for the hospital.

Billy stayed home the following day and the day after that, watching the news and reading the papers. After they had left the burning farmhouse he'd driven Chino and Bug back to Chino's house at the scrap yard. In the truck they were both drunk, pulling from the bottles they'd stolen. They were high on adrenaline and what they had seen. What they had done. Billy had tried to close his ears to it; he didn't want to know.

When they got to Chino's, Billy left them staggering around the yard and got into his car and started for home. As he drove he wondered if this time Chino would give the money to Tommy Jakes. The only reason that Billy had gone along tonight was that Chino told him that Tommy Jakes was under the impression that Billy had ripped him off. It didn't take much to figure out where he'd gotten that idea. Billy didn't know Tommy Jakes, other than by reputation, but he knew that he was nobody to cross. Not that Billy had crossed him, but all that mattered at this point was that Tommy thought that he had. According to Chino anyway. Billy wondered if Tommy Jakes would believe whatever Chino told him. Billy was in no position to think otherwise.

Chino had said that the woman who owned the farmhouse was rich and that the robbery would set them square with Tommy and net them a few thousand apiece to boot. Apparently she had her own show on television. Billy didn't care about the money anymore; all he wanted was to be free of Chino and Bug. He should never have agreed to the border run to begin with. He knew when Chino and Bug had showed up in his yard that day that nothing good would come of it. He'd been right but he'd gone along anyway.

Just as he'd gone along tonight. And tonight was going to stay with him forever. As he drove he tried to convince himself that the three people had escaped from the house. Out a window or back door, some way. It didn't seem likely, though. The state of the house as they'd driven away, it really didn't seem possible.

Cheryl and the boy were asleep when he got home. Billy looked in on them in the bedroom and then walked outside. He sat there in a lawn chair, smoking, until it was nearly daylight in the east.

The next morning he watched the news as he fed his son cereal. Cheryl had already left for work. Billy was elated to hear the reporter say that the man and the woman were found on the lawn. They were both in the hospital, in critical condition. But alive. There was no mention of the other woman though, the scared girl huddled on the couch beside Bug. Maybe she had gotten away and was too frightened to come forward. Maybe the cops had her and weren't saying anything. Because if there was one thing that Billy knew, it was that the cops were involved. The news said that the cause of the fire was unknown at this time, but they knew. Arson was hard to hide, especially arson by amateurs. Not only that, but the couple would have told the cops everything by now. And they had seen Chino's face, and Bug's too. But they hadn't seen Billy's.

Billy kept the TV on the news channel all day and late in the afternoon they announced that a body had been found in the house. No identification as yet. The boy was sleeping and Billy shut off the TV and went out on the back step and lit a cigarette. He sat there for a long time, watching the neighborhood. It was a sunny day and in the park down the way a mother was playing on the slides with her daughter. A couple threw a tennis ball for their dog and beyond them an older man was casting a line out into the river. Billy had talked to the man before; he fished there nearly every day.

Billy hadn't even wanted to go into the house, thinking the less he knew the better. He'd said he would wait in the truck, which they'd parked a half mile away, near the river. But Chino said he was coming along. Chino kept acting as if it was Billy who had pissed away the money at the casino, as if it was somehow his fault. Chino seemed to be living in a world of denial. Everybody was against him. Most of what he believed was just false.

When the three of them had walked into the house wearing the masks the girl had been standing in the kitchen preparing a salad. There'd been a glass of wine on the counter. She didn't speak when she saw them. It appeared that she was too frightened to say anything. Chino had grabbed her in a choke hold and dragged her to the couch, where he and Bug had tied her hands with electrical wraps and wound the duct tape around her head. She was a pretty girl, maybe twenty,

Billy had thought, watching her scared expression. He had wanted to leave then.

But he hadn't.

When Chino got up, it was noon. He made instant coffee and then went to check on the money, which he'd stashed in the cupboard in the back porch when they'd come home. It was gone.

Chino got his revolver and went into the living room. He lifted Bug off the couch and threw him on to the floor. Bug came awake scrambling for cover, his hands above his head.

'What?'

'Where is it?' Chino demanded.

Crabbing his way backwards toward the wall, Bug looked up at him through bloodshot eyes. 'Where's what?'

'The money, you little cocksucker.'

'I didn't touch it, Chino.'

Chino saw Bug's brain slowly come to life, washed as it was in the fog of the booze and the drugs. He could see him begin to know what he already knew.

'Where is it?' Chino asked.

'I moved it,' Bug realized.

Chino pointed the gun at Bug. 'Where is it?'

'Fucksakes,' Bug said. It took him another few moments to remember. 'I put it under the sink.'

Chino turned and went into the kitchen. The money was there. 'Why the fuck would you do that?' he shouted into the living room

Bug stood up. 'So you wouldn't get drunk and gamble it again.'

Chino shook his head and went to the sink for a glass of water. He had some pills in his pocket and he took two. 'Do me a favor, Bug. Don't think.'

Chino pushed the flyers and mail off the kitchen table and on to the floor. He dumped the cash out and began to count it. With what he hadn't lost at the casino and the money from the TV lady, it amounted to a little over fifty-one thousand.

In the other room Bug sat huddled on the couch, shoulders hunched, sucking on a menthol cigarette. He was shivering like a dog coming out of a cold bath. Things were coming back to him.

'Oh man, we fucked up,' he said.

'What are you talking about?' Chino asked calmly. He was stacking the money, putting it back in the bag.

'Last night was bad,' Bug said.

Chino shook his head. 'We were never there. Anybody asks, you say you were home alone, watching football. Michigan and Nebraska.'

Bug silently mouthed the words. *Michigan and Nebraska.*

'We were never there,' Chino said again.

At the bar called Hard Ten, Tommy Jakes leaned back in his chair and watched as Chino walked over and put the bag on the table in front of him. Chino's partner Bug skulked along behind, his eyes darting left and right. Tommy didn't look in the bag but turned toward Bones, who came over to grab it. He went out the back door, presumably heading for the clubhouse across the way. It wouldn't look good, counting that much money in front of the few customers who were in the bar.

'It's short,' Chino said when Bones was gone.

Tommy Jakes raised an eyebrow. 'How short?'

'Four grand.'

'And why is that?'

'Because like I told you, the fucking Indian made off with the original score,' Chino said. 'I had to raise this on my own. Fifty-one is what I came up with. On pretty fucking short notice too.'

'But you owe me fifty-five thousand,' Tommy said. 'Why would you bring me fifty-one? And I told you that I wasn't in the mood for stories about thieving Indians.'

Chino exhaled, exasperated. 'I'll get you the rest.'

'When?'

'Soon as I can,' Chino said. 'I got some scrap to move. I was waiting for the price to go up. But if you're in a hurry—'

Tommy shook his head in disbelief. 'You want me to wait until the price of scrap goes up? You cheat me and then you want me to wait for the price of scrap to go up?'

Chino began to speak but then, looking at Tommy Jakes,

thought better of it. He shook his head. They sat there in silence until Bones came back a few minutes later.

'Fifty-one thousand,' he told Tommy.

Tommy didn't reply. After a moment he looked over at Bug, who'd been sitting quietly, nursing his substantial hangover and trying to keep out of Tommy Jakes's crosshairs.

'What about you, squirrel?' Tommy asked. 'You got four thousand dollars?'

'No, sir.'

'Tell me,' Tommy said. 'What's your name again – Larry? Tell me, Larry, what happened to the money you guys brought across the border?'

Bug began to sweat. Chino turned in his chair. He had a feeling that Bug was about to tell Tommy Jakes anything Tommy wanted to know. And, for a moron, Bug knew a lot.

'He doesn't know,' Chino cut in. 'He wasn't there. It was just me and the Indian. Bug set me up with the guy and that was it. He wasn't there.'

'I wasn't there,' Bug said. He grabbed at the story like a drowning man reaching for a rope.

Tommy Jakes had heard enough. He didn't believe any of it.

'Get me the rest of my money,' he said as he stood. 'You think I won't kill you both for four grand? You just try me.'

When the two had gone Tommy asked Joni to bring him a couple of ounces of the good Buffalo Trace. He and Bones sat at the corner table and watched the pool players in the back room. There were four of them, kids in their twenties. They'd been hanging around the bar for a few months now. They all owned Harleys and wanted to join the Wild. They were too eager and wouldn't get in, not at that age, but they came in handy when there were errands to run. Errands that might result in police involvement. Tommy had a doctor on the hook, a middle-aged dermatologist with a thing for strippers and coke. He wrote scripts for Tommy whenever he was told to and Tommy got the kids to fill them at the various pharmacies in the city. It was a good gig but it wouldn't last. One of these days the good doctor would get found out and the kid presenting the prescription that day would go down with him. Until then, it was a profitable scheme.

Tommy sipped the Kentucky bourbon and glanced over at Bones, who was drinking soda. Bones never drank in the bar. Something about losing his edge. Alone in the clubhouse he would sometimes get stupid drunk, but never out in public.

'So Chino shows up here one day, claiming he's been ripped off,' Tommy said. 'Two days later he's carrying a bag with fifty grand in it. You figure he had it all along, Bones?'

'No.'

'Why not?'

'The money today, a lot of it was brand new bills,' Bones said. 'Monty always pays with used hundreds.'

'Maybe this time was different.'

'I called him after I counted it,' Bones said.

'What did he say?'

'It was used hundreds.'

Tommy had another drink. 'So where does a fucking loser like Chino come up with fifty large in two days? And what's with the new bills? It's not counterfeit, is it, Bones?'

'I don't think so. That's out of Chino's range.'

Tommy laughed. 'I had this image of him and that other nitwit printing money in a basement somewhere. Except they would have walked in here with ink all over their hands.' He watched the pool players for a full minute, thinking it over. 'Where do you get new bills? You get them at a bank. Maybe Chino robbed a bank. But if anybody robbed a bank around here it would have been on the news. So what else – maybe Chino sold something and whoever paid him got the cash from a bank. Chino's got property over in Markham County some-where. Maybe he sold it. He's always saying some farmer wants to buy it.'

Bones shrugged. 'Do you care where he got it?'

Tommy considered the question. 'No,' he decided. 'What else did Monty have to say?'

'Said he liked the Indian. Called him Tonto. Wonders why he's not working for us directly.'

Tommy Jakes lifted the bourbon to his lips. 'That's a good question, Bones,' he said before he drank.

FOURTEEN

Carl was eating rice pudding when the cop Dunbar came into the room. This time he had a woman with him, a lanky redhead wearing jeans and a blazer. She had a badge clipped to her belt and her jacket flared above her hip, where her gun was. Dunbar introduced her as Detective Rachel Pulford.

'Hello, Carl,' she said.

Carl nodded, his mouth full. He swallowed and pushed the plastic bowl away from him. He'd had little appetite since being admitted. His left arm was strapped against his body, keeping the shoulder immobile. He had eight stitches in his scalp above his temple and a couple dozen more in each of his wrists. The doctor who had sewn him up said that he had come very close to bleeding to death and that they'd given him ten units of blood. He'd told Carl that he was a lucky man. Carl wasn't feeling particularly lucky.

'How are you doing?' Dunbar asked now.

'All right,' Carl said. He had met Dunbar earlier. He was a big man with a bit of a gut, maybe early sixties. His graying hair was worn slightly long, giving him the appearance of a shaggy bear. His voice was even and quiet. In fact he appeared to be a quiet man.

'The doctor tells me your shoulder surgery is scheduled for tomorrow.'

'That's what I hear,' Carl said. 'You know – unless I try to kill myself again.'

Dunbar gave Pulford a glance.

'I guess you've been watching the news,' she said to Carl, nodding toward the little TV screen suspended by the bed.

Carl just looked at her.

'We can't control what a fire marshal says to a reporter,' Dunbar said. 'For what it's worth, we don't think you tried to kill yourself, Carl. Moreover, I believe everything you told me yesterday. That's why Rachel is here. This is now a murder investigation. On top of robbery, arson, home invasion and assault.'

Carl sat silently for a moment, looking at the wall across the room. 'I asked the doctors about Stacy and they said they didn't know anything. She died in the fire?'

'Yes, she did,' Dunbar said. 'They got a positive ID from her dental records.'

Carl exhaled. 'What happened to her?'

'In the fire?'

'No. I mean afterward.'

'Her parents are here. They're taking her remains back to British Columbia.'

'What about a funeral?'

'I don't know anything about that,' Dunbar said.

'I want to go to the funeral,' Carl said.

'The doctors might not be in favor of that,' Pulford told him. 'We can try to find out the details.'

Her voice was low and even. She was trying to be reasonable, Carl knew. It wasn't a practical idea, him getting out of bed and flying across country to go to a funeral. A funeral where nobody would even know who the hell he was. But there was nothing in him that felt like being reasonable.

'I talked to one of your neighbors the night of the fire,' Dunbar said. 'She said she saw a truck parked in a lane about a half mile west of your farm. A white Dodge truck.'

Carl nodded. 'There's a dirt road there, leads down to the river.'

'You know the vehicle?'

'I don't think so,' Carl said. 'Lot of people park there to go fishing. It was a pickup?'

'That's what she thought. She didn't think anything of it at the time. Probably nothing, like you say.'

'They had to have wheels somewhere,' Carl said. 'There were no vehicles around when I went up to the house. It was planned.'

There were two chairs along the wall and Pulford pulled one over beside the bed and sat. 'You're right, it doesn't appear that this was a random thing,' she said. 'From what you told Detective Dunbar, Frances Rourke was targeted. Do you agree?'

'I have no idea.'

'But you said the leader called her the TV lady,' she said.

'Yeah.'

'So who do you think did this?'

Carl stared at her. 'I don't know.'

'You saw their faces,' Pulford persisted. 'Two of them at least. You're absolutely certain you never saw them before?'

'If I'd recognized them, I would know who they were. I just told you I don't.' Carl looked over at Dunbar. 'What is this?'

Pulford looked at Dunbar as well, as if waiting for him to explain. But he gave her nothing. Apparently it was her show.

'Here's the thing, Carl,' she said. 'You've had some problems with the law before. And you've served time in the past. You were in Wellington Detention for fourteen months a couple of years ago. We have to assume you associated with some bad people in there, the kind of people who might commit an act like this.'

'I've gone from being an attempted suicide to an accomplice?' Carl asked.

'No,' Pulford said emphatically. 'But do you recall anyone at Wellington who might have seemed overly interested in the farm, or in Frances? Somebody asking questions? It's obvious that these people were under the impression that Frances had easy access to a lot of money. Do you recall anyone like that?'

'I never talked about Frances in there,' Carl said.

'Did you talk about the farm?' Pulford persisted. 'How successful it was?'

'If I talked about it, it wouldn't have been like that. I wouldn't have made it out to be a place where somebody could score big. What is this about – what do you know?'

'We don't know anything, Carl,' Dunbar said. 'We need to make a connection of some sort. If we can figure out the connection, maybe we can find out who did this.'

'You ever read *In Cold Blood*?' Pulford asked. 'Somebody told a story in prison about a farmer with a lot of cash on hand and a few months later two guys showed up and murdered the whole family. It has happened.'

Carl thought back to his time at Wellington. He never talked about Frances, or money, or even the farm in general. And there had been nothing familiar about the two men who'd removed their masks.

'Never happened with me,' he said.

'Did Frances have enemies?' Pulford asked.

'Nobody who would do this.'

'What does that mean? Who were her enemies?'

'I don't know if enemies is the proper term,' Carl said. 'She's pissed off a few politicians and some local farmers, the ones using GMO seeds and feeding their livestock steroids and stuff. Those people didn't raid the house the other night.'

'I suspect not,' Dunbar said.

'Have you seen her?' Carl asked.

'Frances? I haven't seen her, but you know she's not . . . responding.'

'She's unconscious, pretty much all they're telling me.'

'They told me that too,' Dunbar said.

Carl looked down at the sheet covering him. His right hand opened and closed by his side, the fingers flexing. His eyes were dark and he seemed to be fighting himself over something.

'What else did they say?' he asked finally.

'What do you mean?'

'Was she assaulted?'

Dunbar looked at Pulford.

'They did a vaginal swab and found nothing to suggest she'd been raped,' Pulford said.

Carl exhaled, looking down at the sheet that covered him. It seemed that he relaxed, just a little. After a few moments he looked up at Dunbar.

'Something I remembered after you left. When Frances gave them the money, the forty-seven grand, one of them said something. He said maybe it was enough.'

'Enough for what?' Pulford asked.

'I don't know,' Carl said.

'Which of the three said it?' Dunbar asked.

'The skinny one with the bad teeth,' Carl replied. 'The one bothering Stacy.'

Pulford took a notebook from her pocket and wrote in it. 'Enough,' she said softly, as if turning it over in her head.

'So what if there is no connection?' Carl asked. 'What if it's just somebody who saw Frances on TV and assumed she had money? It wouldn't be hard to find the farm.'

'That obviously makes it more difficult to catch these guys,' Pulford said. 'The hardest crime to solve is one where there's no common ground between the victim and the perpetrator.'

'You telling me you're not going to catch them?'

'We'll get them,' Dunbar said. 'Right now, you're our best lead. You saw two of them. We want you to look at some pictures. Mug shots.'

'Bring them in,' Carl said.

'We can wait until after your surgery, when you're feeling better,' Pulford said.

'I can look at pictures right now.'

'The doctor said you lost a lot of blood,' she said. 'It will take a while for you to bounce back. Let's give it a couple of days.'

Carl started to protest further, then stopped. Maybe they were right in this. He'd been lightheaded since coming to in the emergency ward that night, with the IV in his arm and only a foggy memory of what had happened. Details had been coming back to him slowly ever since.

'Are you confident you'd recognize them?' Pulford asked.

'I will recognize them,' Carl said.

'Sorry, but we have to ask this,' Pulford said. 'Will you testify against them in court?'

'I will. You don't need to ask me that again.'

'I was hoping the Wellington angle might have panned out,' Pulford said as they walked across the hospital parking lot.

Dunbar shook his head. 'Burns had a good look at two of them,' he reminded her. 'If they were men he'd done time with, he'd have remembered.'

Pulford unlocked the car. 'I was thinking more along the lines of six degrees of separation. He talked to somebody who talked to somebody. That kind of thing.'

'He looks to be a man who keeps his own counsel,' Dunbar said. 'And probably more so when locked up.'

'I got that from him.' Pulford put the car in gear and they drove out of the underground and into the bright autumn sunlight. 'To tell you the truth, he doesn't seem the jailbird type in general.'

'He shot a guy who raped his daughter. Before you got here.'

'Really?' Pulford said. 'Is there something there? Somebody looking for revenge? Maybe they were after him and not Frances Rourke.'

'Given the principals of the case, I doubt it,' Dunbar said. 'And keep in mind they weren't exactly after Frances Rourke. They were after the money. Things went south when she couldn't raise the hundred grand. They showed up wearing masks, which means they intended to leave everyone alive. But they got to drinking and maybe drugging and then the money was short. And the shit hit the fan.'

'That's an understatement,' Pulford said. 'What about the one saying that maybe it was enough? What is that?'

'I've been thinking about that,' Dunbar replied. 'It suggests they needed the money for something specific. They wanted a hundred thousand but maybe fifty was enough? That's odd. And what do you buy for fifty grand?'

'Drugs.'

Dunbar shook his head. 'But not for personal use. That much money, there had to be something else.'

They drove in silence for a while.

'I have another question,' Pulford said at length. 'Frances Rourke is roughly my size. Five seven, maybe five eight. I'd say about a hundred and thirty pounds. Carl Burns claims he carried her up those stairs and out of the house when she was unconscious. That's dead weight. You're buying that?'

'Yes.'

Pulford glanced over. 'Keep in mind he had a badly dislocated shoulder. Yet he still managed. I have my doubts.'

'I don't.' Dunbar gave Pulford a long look. 'You've never been in love, have you?'

They drove into Rose City to the RCTV studio on Front Street. Pulford had called ahead and they were met in the foyer by a woman named Christina. She was forty-something, tall and attractive, although she looked drawn and stressed, her eyes red. The three of them went up a floor, to an open studio, where they were joined by a pudgy kid who introduced himself as Shawn. They were both producers of some kind. Shawn wanted to be in charge, even though he was obviously years younger than the woman.

'What do you need from us?' he asked.

Dunbar left Pulford to do the talking as he wandered about the room. The set was built as half a kitchen. There was a faux granite counter with gas burners and a grill. A refrigerator and a wine rack, fully stocked. Dunbar expected the bottles to be empty but when he checked, they weren't. He realized now that, although he knew of the show in passing, he had never actually watched it. He would have to ask his wife if she had seen it.

'What kind of feedback does the show get?' Pulford asked the two producers.

'You mean the ratings?' Shawn asked.

The woman Christina gave him a look before turning to Pulford. 'We get comments all the time, usually by e-mail. You're wondering if there's been anything negative?'

'Yeah,' Pulford said. 'Anything that could be construed, even in the broadest terms, as threatening?'

Christina shook her head. 'We get indignant e-mails about – I don't know – gluten, or the improper use of paprika. That kind of thing.'

Pulford nodded. 'What about mash notes, somebody out there with a crush on Frances?'

'She's been asked out by viewers in the past, I do know that,' Christina said. 'She has a standard polite rejection she uses, almost a form letter. Says that she's involved with somebody and thanks for watching the show.'

'So there's been no one who might have approached stalker status?'

'No. And she would have told me. We're pretty close.'

'There's been nothing that I was made aware of,' Shawn said. He seemed anxious to be a part of things.

Dunbar walked over. 'Did she use a work computer?'

'Just her laptop,' Christina said. 'She carried it back and forth.'

'Which means it burned up in the house,' Pulford suggested.

Christina thought about that. 'She was picking up a turkey on her way home. She'd carry that inside before her laptop. Maybe it's in her car.'

'We can check that,' Pulford said.

'I can't imagine you're going to find anything on there,' Christina said. She'd been holding things in up until now. 'She had a cooking show, for God's sakes. How does that lead to this?'

Pulford shook her head. 'I can't answer that.'

'Have you guys talked to her doctors?' Christina asked.

'Yes,' Dunbar said.

'What's going on?' Christina asked. 'They won't tell me anything.'

'She's in a coma. They're not telling us much more than that.'

'There was something on the news,' Christina said. 'Some bullshit about a botched murder/suicide.'

'You're right, it was bullshit,' Dunbar told her.

'I know that,' Christina said. 'If there's one thing in this world I know, it's that. So what did happen out there? Everything's a secret.'

Dunbar glanced at Pulford, as if giving her permission.

'It was a home invasion,' Pulford said. 'We can't say much more.'

'And you don't know who did it?'

'Not yet,' Pulford said. 'That's why we're here.'

'What did they want?'

'It appeared they were after money.'

'They were after money,' Christina said. 'So they beat Frances and Carl and killed that poor girl Stacy. For money. What is wrong with this world?'

'I can't answer that either,' Pulford said.

Next stop was the bank in Talbotville. It was a newer style brick building, one story, as banks tended to be these days. The detectives met with the manager – an athletic man named Calhoun – in his office. Before they began he called in the loans manager, Kelly, to join them. Pulford asked that she give her version of events from Friday night.

'We basically gave her almost everything we had on hand,' Kelly said in finishing. 'I mean, we had to hold back some cash for our other customers.'

'Did you know Frances Rourke from before?' Dunbar asked.

'Just from seeing her here.'

'How was her demeanor Friday night?'

'Oh man,' Kelly said. 'She was wired. I actually thought she was on something. She's usually – well, that's not her.'

'She was flustered?' Pulford asked.

'Yeah,' Kelly said slowly. 'Although I'm not sure I would say flustered. I'm trying to think of a way to describe her.' She looked at the two cops, squinting as she thought. 'OK – she was desperate. I mean, she had to have that money. And I remember thinking, why does it have to be tonight? But then, like I said, she kept saying that the deal might fall through. The deal to buy the land.'

'Did she say anything that might be construed as a hint as to what was happening?' Pulford asked. 'You know – like maybe she was trying to alert you?'

'No. Absolutely not. She just wanted the money as quick as she could get it.'

'And you gave her how much?'

'Forty-five thousand exactly,' Kelly said. 'But when she was leaving she asked about the nearest ATMs. So I assume she got more.'

Pulford made a note of that. 'Is there anything else you can remember? Anything she might have said that could help us?'

Kelly shook her head. 'No. She just wanted the money.'

'There is something,' Calhoun said. 'Purely by accident, she ended up with one of the security packs. A thousand dollars in hundreds. The bills are marked.'

When the detectives left the bank, they headed back to the city.

'Forty-five grand,' Pulford said. 'So out of the blue these guys just invaded a home and demanded a ransom. You have precedence for that?'

'No,' Dunbar said.

Pulford pulled up to a red light and stopped. 'This is a fucking mess.'

'It's all of that.'

Carl was dozing off when a nurse came in carrying a telephone, which she plugged into a wall jack.

'You have a phone call from Scotland. Someone says she's your daughter?'

Carl hesitated. 'What did you tell her?'

'We're not allowed to tell her anything. She said she heard there was a fire at the farm and when she couldn't get in touch with anybody there she started calling the local hospitals.'

Carl took the phone. 'Hey there,' he said.

'What's going on, Dad?' Kate asked. The line sounded hollow. She was probably on her cell.

'We had a fire,' Carl said.

'I know that,' Kate told him. 'I've been getting e-mails. I was looking for news online. Are you OK?'

'I'm good. Fell down the stairs is all, banged up my shoulder.' Carl wondered if the online reports had mentioned Stacy, or if the cops were keeping that quiet for the time being. Kate and Stacy had never met; Carl couldn't see the point in telling Kate what had happened. He didn't think he could talk about it yet. She would hear soon enough.

'What happened?' Kate demanded. 'Is Frances OK?'

'We're both good. How are things in Edinburgh?'

'Things are fine here,' Kate said sharply. 'My friend said there were rumors about a home invasion. What's going on there?'

'They're still sorting things out,' Carl said.

'What the hell does that mean? Do you want me to come home?'

'No,' Carl said quickly. 'You just started the new job, you can't leave. There's nothing for you to do here, Kate. Things are up in the air. Nobody really knows what happened yet.' At least that part was true, to an extent, he thought.

'Why are you in the hospital?'

'I might have dislocated my shoulder. No big deal.'

'No big deal,' Kate repeated. 'Why do I get the feeling you're not telling me something?'

It was obvious now that she hadn't heard about Stacy. 'Listen, everything is still foggy here. Let's talk in a couple days. Do not get on a plane, Kate.'

'God, but you are a frustrating man.'

'But you knew that.'

'Don't make jokes,' Kate said.

Just then the doctor entered the room, saving Carl from making up a story about a doctor entering the room.

'The doctor's here.'

'I'm going to call you back,' Kate said, and she hung up.

The doctor checked Carl's chart, took his pulse and his temperature. A nurse had done the same thing thirty minutes earlier. Carl asked about Frances.

'She's been moved to St Michael's in Rose City,' the doctor said. 'At the trauma center.'

'Is she awake?'

'She hasn't regained consciousness. That's why we sent her there. Hopefully they can pinpoint the problem.'

'She has brain damage?' Carl asked. 'The other doctor wouldn't say one way or the other. What's his name – Lauzon?'

'Yes, Dr Lauzon,' the doctor said. 'She has a head injury, and there has been trauma to the brain. To characterize it as brain damage at this point is premature. Sometimes the brain shuts down, almost as a defensive action. We're told she fell down some stairs? It seems as if she hit her head at the time.'

'She didn't fall, she was pushed.'

'Well, it appears that's when the injury occurred.'

Carl was quiet for a time. 'When do I get out of here?'

'Your surgery is in the morning. You have a bad tear in the rotator muscle, as well as the separation. But you should be able to leave tomorrow night, or Wednesday morning at the latest. You're going to be operating with one arm for a few weeks.'

Carl nodded. 'I want to see Frances.'

'I'm not sure if that's possible right now. I can ask.'

'I want to see her.'

'I completely understand,' the doctor said. 'Don't worry,

she's at one of the best trauma centers in the country. They'll do everything they can to help her wake up.'

'She's going to wake up.'

The doctor started to respond but instead he just nodded, hooked Carl's chart to the foot of the bed and went on his way.

FIFTEEN

Chino spent the morning getting the Freightliner dump truck to run and when it finally fired he drove it around to the yard and parked it there. For months now he'd been stockpiling farm machinery and assorted parts from backhoes, bulldozers and loaders, waiting for the price of scrap to go up. Now he set to work with the torches, cutting everything into small enough chunks to toss into the box of the dump. When it was full he'd lift a set of plates off one of his junkers and drive the Freightliner to the recycling center and sell it all, truck included. The price was still down, due to the fucking Chinese screwing with the market, but it might fetch enough to see him clear with Tommy Jakes.

He'd told Bug that he should be there helping him to clear the debt, but Bug was of the opinion that the debt was all Chino's doing. For a retard, Bug sometimes did too much thinking. If Chino didn't get square with Tommy, Bug would be in as deep as he was. Chino would see to that. Still, Bug hadn't shown up that morning. Halfway through the afternoon he finally did, wheeling into the yard in the Dodge, skidding to a stop.

'Fuck,' he said when he got out.

'What now?' Chino said. He was changing the acetylene tank on the torches, the goggles pushed back on his head.

'They got out,' Bug said.

'Who got out?'

'The woman and the dude,' Bug said. 'They fucking got out of the house.'

'Where'd you hear this?'

'It's on the fucking news, man.'

Chino put the torches aside. 'So they're alive?'

'Yeah.'

A diesel motor fired up in the distance and Chino glanced across the road to see the farmer who lived there pulling into the field with a tractor, trailing a seven-furrow plow. The tractor was half the size of Chino's house and probably cost a hundred and fifty grand. Chino had talked to the man, whose name was Vanhizen, a few times and – like all farmers – he always claimed that he wasn't making any money. Then he'd climb into his sixty thousand dollar pickup and drive off. The only reason the man talked to Chino at all was to try to buy Chino's place. Chino knew he considered it an eyesore, although he never had the balls to say it out loud. He wanted to buy it and bulldoze everything – house and shop and yard. Chino would sell eventually but for now he liked saying no to the prick. The guy kept claiming he was broke and then in the next breath offering to buy the place. They were all the same, just like the bitch that night at the farm, saying she couldn't raise a hundred grand. Now Chino watched as the tractor started across the field, the gleaming shares cutting into the sod like knives.

'Nothing puts us there,' he told Bug. 'Why do you think I torched the place? That means no prints, no DNA.'

'They fucking saw us, man.'

'I don't know what they saw,' Chino said. 'They were so fucking scared, you think they could pick us out of a line-up? And we're not gonna be in a line-up anyway. You gonna talk, Bug?'

'No.'

'Neither am I,' Chino said. 'There's nothing to connect us to this. Nothing.'

'What about Billy?'

'What about Billy? You're the one said he could be trusted. You better be sure about that, Bug. Because I'll go over there today and slit his fucking throat.'

'He wasn't happy that night,' Bug said. 'All that shit went down, he didn't want nothing to do with it. On top of that, he never got paid for running the border to begin with. You remember that, Chino?'

'What are you saying, Bug?'

'I'm saying neither one of us got paid.'

'Things didn't go like I planned,' Chino said.

'Seems like they never do.' Bug indicated the box of the dump truck, half filled with scrap. 'There gonna be any extra cash from this here?'

'I would be real surprised,' Chino said. 'Market's gone to shit. I'd prefer to hang on to it, wasn't for Tommy being such a hardass about certain things.'

'Right,' Bug said. 'And I work for free again.'

'I don't recall you doing a whole lot of work,' Chino said. 'I do remember you filling your fucking nose full of free cocaine, Bug. And sucking bourbon like it was your mother's tit. And if I'd had a run of luck at the casino, you would have made out real good. So that's the chance you take.'

'The casino wasn't supposed to be part of it.'

'I had no choice, the way Johnny K and Tommy Jakes planned it,' Chino told him. 'So quit your fucking whining.' Chino went back to his torches, tightening the fitting on the acetylene. 'You'd better head over to Tareytown and talk to your Indian friend. Make sure he knows that so long as he keeps his mouth closed, nobody's got a problem. But if I see a cop pull in my driveway, I'm going to know it was him. Got it?'

Bug nodded unhappily.

'I got work to do, Bug,' Chino said. He fired the torch and began to cut the front axle out from under a loader. Bug watched for a minute, then got into his truck and left.

Billy wasn't home when Bug got to the house in Tareytown. His car was gone but Bug knocked on the door anyway. When nobody answered he drove down the street to a bar he knew about, a beer and wings place called Roosters. Bug figured he could sit by the front windows and drink draft while he waited for Billy to drive past.

It was nearly dark when he did. Bug chugged his beer and got into his car and followed. Billy didn't go home, though;

he drove past his place and a couple of blocks along he pulled up in front of a white two story frame house with green shutters. He went inside and came out a minute later, carrying a little kid. Bug was parked behind Billy's car and he got out when Billy came down the walkway. Better to talk to him here than back at his place, where his old lady might be hanging around, all ears.

'Hey, Billy.'

Billy's eyes went flat when he saw Bug and it seemed as if he held the kid tighter to him, as if to shield him from whatever Bug represented. He didn't say anything, just stood there staring at Bug.

'You watch the news?' Bug asked.

Billy nodded.

There was movement from the house and Bug glanced over to see a woman standing in the open doorway, watching them. Watching Bug more than anything. She would already know who Billy was, if she was looking after the kid.

'Ain't no problem if everybody keeps their mouth shut,' Bug said, turning back to Billy. 'The fire and all took care of any prints or whatever. You know what I'm saying?'

Billy didn't move a muscle. He didn't even blink. The kid in his arms was squirming now.

'Anyway,' Bug went on. He was pissed that Billy wouldn't respond. 'Chino figured I should come talk to you. Make sure we're all thinking the same thing.'

Still nothing.

'Chino says he might have some money for you,' Bug lied. Anything to get a reaction. 'He's squaring things with Tommy Jakes and says he might have something left over for you.'

'I don't want any money,' Billy said.

'Why the fuck not?'

'I don't want anything to do with it. I don't want you coming around either, Bug.'

Bug shook his head. 'I know things got fucked up there, Billy. Wasn't supposed to be that way. But fucking Chino, man, that's the way it goes with him. Bad shit always happens.'

'Wasn't just Chino.'

'I know,' Bug said. 'I get into that powder and I'm fucked.

I need to get into a program. Maybe you can help me find a program. Indians know that shit, right? You got problems with substance and all that.'

'Stay away from me,' Billy said. He and the kid got into the car and drove off.

SIXTEEN

Carl was obliged to ride in a wheelchair down to the front entrance of the hospital, something about policy. Rufus Canfield was there to push the chair. He had shown up with a bag containing Carl's clothes from the night of the invasion. Apparently the nurse had given them to Rufus earlier to take home and launder. By the front doors, Carl stood up and walked outside. Rufus had parked his car, a fourteen-year-old Volvo, in the hospital lot. Carl got into the passenger side carefully, mindful of his left shoulder which was heavily bandaged and strapped to his side after the surgery.

'Where to?' Rufus asked as they drove out of the lot.

'Rose City,' Carl said.

They parked a block away from St Michael's and walked over. When Carl told the receptionist that he was there to see Frances Rourke she immediately got on the phone and five minutes later a man approached, wearing scrubs. He said his name was Dr John Harkness.

'What's this about?' he asked.

Carl indicated the receptionist. 'She told you what it's about.'

'You want to see Frances Rourke?'

'That's it.'

'And what is your connection to her?'

'She's my wife.'

Harkness hesitated. 'Her chart says she's single.'

'They've been together for years,' Rufus said. 'Don't be obtuse, man.'

The doctor turned an arrogant eye on the little lawyer before glancing back at Carl. 'You realize she's unconscious.'

Carl nodded.

'I might need to clear this with the police.'

'Then do it. Please.'

Harkness moved off to an office down a corridor. After a couple of minutes he appeared in the doorway. Talking into a cell phone, he described Carl to the person on the other end, mentioning the heavy wrap on Carl's left shoulder. Then he walked over to hand the phone to Carl. 'Detective Dunbar wants to talk to you.'

'Yeah?' Carl said into the phone.

'OK,' Dunbar said. 'I wanted to make sure. I didn't realize you'd been released.'

'Half an hour ago.'

'How are you feeling?'

'I'm OK.'

'Did you remember anything else?'

'No.'

'OK then. Put the doctor back on.'

Harkness listened on the phone for a bit, then hung up. 'OK,' he said.

Frances was in a room on the third floor of the hospital. Rufus remained in the hallway with the doctor and Carl went in alone. She was on her back, her arms straight down at her sides. Other than the purplish bruise along the right side of her face she appeared normal, as if she was merely asleep. Carl watched her for a time, then knelt close and spoke to her. He watched closely, hoping for a sign that she'd heard him. A change in her breathing, a flutter of an eyelid. The familiar smile.

He thought about her that night in the house, staring down the man with the tattoo. Inside she had to be scared but she wouldn't show it to him. She wouldn't give him the satisfaction. And Carl knew she would also be thinking of Stacy, of how frightened she had to be, how young she was. Frances would want to show her there was nothing to be afraid of, even though Frances knew there was. Carl, on the floor, had been of no use to either of them. He couldn't stop thinking about that. He couldn't stop wondering how things would be if he had handled things differently. He wished he could talk to her about it, about how sorry he was. But it wouldn't happen today, it seemed.

When he left Frances, he found Harkness and asked about her condition.

'She has what we call a brain bruise,' he said. 'It is exactly what it sounds like. There's some swelling, which we expect will go down fairly quickly. When the bruise has healed, we can re-evaluate.'

'Why isn't she awake?'

'Frankly, we don't know,' Harkness said. 'There is no reason for it. The brain is a complicated organ. The good news is that she could wake up at any moment.'

'I'll be back tomorrow,' Carl told him, and left.

'Now where?' Rufus asked when they were in the Volvo again.

'The farm,' Carl said.

Rufus drove a while in silence. He was a particularly bad driver, hunched forward over the wheel, constantly speeding up and slowing down for no reason. 'You do know that the house is no longer there.'

'I want to see it,' Carl said.

The police had encircled the wreckage with yellow tape and sometime after that the insurance company had erected a temporary chain link fence around the perimeter. Rufus stood by the car while Carl walked around the ruins. It was a cold day and Rufus shivered in the wind. Carl wore just a jacket – the same coat he'd been wearing when he walked in on the thugs – but didn't seem to notice the cold. At the rear of the building he stood for a long while, looking at the storm door that had been his escape hatch. Their escape hatch. It had rained in the past couple of days and the smell of the wet soot hung heavily on the air.

Continuing the circle, he walked over to his truck, parked by the garage alongside Frances's SUV and the hatchback that Stacy had driven. Carl's keys were in the ignition. Since moving out to the farm he had never bothered to remove them. He had always considered the place to be immune from any criminal activity. Not that crime didn't exist in the rural areas, but it was just that the farm felt as if it was of a different era. A more innocent time. Well, he had learned the folly of that.

Walking back toward Rufus, he glanced down the hill to the warehouse. There were no vehicles in the parking lot out front.

'Where's Norah?' he asked.

'Who?'

'There's nobody at the warehouse,' Carl said. 'Who's running things?'

'I would assume,' Rufus said slowly, 'that things have been shut down these past days, given the circumstances.'

Carl nodded. 'I'll call her. Thanks for the ride, Rufus.'

'What will you do?' Rufus asked.

'Get things up and running, first of all,' Carl said. 'Frances will want things to keep moving.'

'Where will you stay?'

Carl looked around, as if considering the question for the first time. 'I'll figure that out later.'

'Why don't you come home with me?' Rufus said. 'We have a spare room. You can stay as long as you like.'

'Thanks, but I need to stay here.'

'But *where*?'

'Thanks for the ride, Rufus.'

He called Norah from the warehouse. She'd been watching the news and right away she asked Carl about Frances. He told her what he knew, which wasn't a hell of a lot. She didn't ask about Stacy and Carl had to assume she'd heard. They had been close. She probably didn't need to hear what she already knew. It would be hard enough just knowing it.

It took some talking on Carl's part to persuade her to come back to work. He finally half convinced her that it was safe, even though he had no right to say that. He had thought it was safe there before and he couldn't have been more wrong. But he didn't think that the three men would be returning. On the one hand, he hoped that they had crawled back into their holes. On the other, he wished for them to be out and about, someplace where the cops would track them down.

Norah reluctantly said she'd come in the next day. Carl didn't want to press her, but he didn't know what else to do.

Other than Norah, the only people who knew how the business end operated were Frances and Stacy.

When he got off the phone Carl sat in the warehouse by himself for an hour, staring out the window to the farm, and the bush lot in the distance. He thought back to when it had happened, the day he'd spent the afternoon back in the bush, cutting down the ancient white oak. By the time he came back to the house, things were already in motion. Past the point of no return. What if he hadn't decided to cut the tree that day? What if he'd found something else to do, something closer to home? Things might have turned out differently. He thought of Stacy, all alone with the three men. She was just a kid. She would have been terrified. She had probably clung to the hope that Carl would return before things got out of hand. Well, Carl had returned – and he did nothing to save her life.

He got to his feet and walked outside. He stood there for a time, looking at the burned remains of the house. The building was a hundred and twenty-two years old. And gone in a flash. The last time Carl had seen Stacy she'd been playing in the yard with the pup. The dog that could fly. Carl had told her to keep the pup there, that the animal might have gotten hurt back in the bush. And they had shot the dog dead on the lawn. Carl wondered if Stacy had heard the shot. It didn't matter now, whether she did or not. Carl needed to stop thinking about it. He didn't know what to do next but he knew he had to do something. His head was going bad.

He walked to the garage and got into his pickup. He drove into Talbotville, to a place on the north side that sold house trailers and RVs and accessories. The business was owned by a man Carl had known for twenty-five years or more. They had once worked construction together. He knew what had happened at the farm – the bare details anyway – and he let Carl have a thirty-foot motorhome on credit and arranged to have it delivered the following morning. Carl slept that night in the warehouse, on a blanket atop some folded cardboard boxes used for shipping produce. With his arm incapacitated and the makeshift mattress, he had a fitful night. At two in the morning he finally swallowed two of the painkillers the surgeon had given him and fell asleep.

In the morning he was making coffee in the office when he heard a vehicle pull into the parking lot. Carl looked out the window to see Norah getting out of the passenger side of a Chevy Tahoe. Her father was behind the wheel and now he got out as well. Carl had met him a couple of times in the past; he was a mechanic at a garage in Talbotville and he had to be pushing seventy. He was short and squat, built like a Mack truck. From his expression Carl was pretty sure that he was there to tell Carl that Norah would not be working there anymore. Carl couldn't say he blamed the man. Norah and Stacy had become friends. They went out together on the weekends sometimes and once did a weekend trip to New York City.

'Hi, Norah,' Carl said when they walked in. 'Ben.'

Ben looked at the heavy wrap on Carl's left shoulder. 'Goddamn,' he said.

To Carl's surprise, Norah went to her computer, removed her jacket and logged on. Carl glanced from her to her father.

'You go on about your day,' Ben said.

'What are you going to do?' Carl asked.

'I'm going to hang around here.'

'What about work?'

'I retired two months ago,' Ben told him. 'Been bored to tears ever since.' He gestured around the office space. 'I'll keep myself busy. I'm not much for computers but I can answer a phone and change a light bulb.'

'I appreciate it,' Carl told him.

'You go on and do whatever you got to do,' Ben said. 'That coffee fresh?'

Carl said that it was. He turned to Norah.

'Thanks for coming in.'

She was looking at the screen, typing something. 'I want to put something on the website about Stacy.'

'That's a nice idea,' Carl said.

'OK, I'll write something and then show it to you before I post it.'

Carl shook his head. 'You write it the way you want and put it on.'

'OK.'

Carl started to leave and then came back.

'They're delivering a motorhome here this morning,' he told Ben. 'I was going to wait around, but if you're going to be here—'

'No problem.'

'Ask them to leave it in the yard behind the garage,' Carl said. 'I'll do the water and hydro hookup when I get back.'

Pouring the coffee, Ben nodded.

On the drive to Rose City, Carl realized he should have called ahead. He drove to the police station anyway and asked for Dunbar. He wasn't there but the other detective – Pulford – was. Carl would have preferred to talk to Dunbar. The woman seemed somewhat negative in her approach and even her attitude, as if she was skeptical of Carl in general. She came down to the front desk directly. She was wearing jeans again, with a department hoodie this time, and had her glasses pushed up into her thick hair.

'Carl,' she said. 'What's going on?'

'Came to look at those pictures you mentioned.'

'Of course,' she said. 'I tried to get in touch with you. I talked to somebody named Norah out at the warehouse earlier. She said you'd just left. You don't have a cell phone?'

'No.'

Carl sat in a windowless room for an hour, looking at mug shots Pulford had put together based on the descriptions Carl had given her. None were familiar. He wondered just how dependable his memory was regarding that night. He'd only had a quick glance at the two men, and even that was after having his brains rattled from the beating he'd taken. Everything was somewhat fuzzy. The men in the photos he was looking at were all of a kind – unkempt, unshaven, mean. Some had teardrop tattoos, like the big man at the house. But none was that man. Carl was certain of that. As for the other man, the one with the lank blond hair, Carl had just seen him briefly but he remembered him. He didn't come across a photo resembling him either.

'Mug shots are always iffy,' Pulford told him. 'Some of these are fifteen, even twenty years old. You might have seen a younger version of the big guy, before he got the tattoos. People change over time, especially people who abuse themselves, which might very well be the case with these men.'

'What have you found out?'

'Not much,' Pulford admitted. 'We went through Frances's laptop and her cell phone and couldn't find anything that would suggest she'd had a problem with anyone. Nothing in her e-mails. You don't use e-mail?'

'No.'

'I didn't think so,' Pulford said. 'There were none from you.'

'Where's the phone?'

'In my office,' Pulford said. 'Why?'

'I'll take it if you're done with it.'

'Actually, that's a good idea. We can use it to contact you.'

'Frances is going to need it.'

'Oh – is she awake?'

'Not yet. But she will be.'

Pulford made no response to that.

'What else are you doing?' Carl asked.

'Right now we're watching for the money. Close to fifty thousand – these guys will be spending it is my guess, and possibly indiscriminately. They could be addicts, which means they'll be buying drugs. We have informants out there.'

'What about the white pickup?'

'We'll watch for it, but all we have is what your neighbor said,' Pulford told him. 'You said yourself it was probably a fisherman.'

Carl got to his feet. 'If I can get that phone, I'll be going.'

'Of course.'

Carl went from the police station to the hospital. There was no change in Frances's condition. He sat with her for half an hour. He told her that Norah was back to work and that her father was helping out. He didn't mention Stacy. There would be a time for that later. As he was leaving a nurse came into the room. Carl asked if Frances had responded at all and the nurse said she had not.

'We have her clothes here,' the nurse said then, indicating a locker along the wall. 'Would you like to take them?'

'She'll need them,' Carl said.

'We thought you might want to have them cleaned,' the nurse said. 'They smell of smoke.' When Carl agreed to take them, the nurse handed him a bundle wrapped in plastic.

On his way back from the city Carl stopped to see Rufus Canfield in Talbotville. Rufus was in his office on Maple Street, drinking coffee and eating a bulbous donut filled with jelly. If he was working, he was hiding it well. Carl didn't sit when Rufus asked him to.

'The police say they're watching the local druggies in Rose City, to see who might be spending lots of cash.'

'I'm not so sure about that line of thinking,' Rufus said.

'Why not?'

Rufus took a moment. 'You said they were after a hundred grand. Typical addict is only after whatever he can get his hands on. Twenty dollars, fifty, a hundred. This seemed very specific. Why a hundred grand? Why that much?'

'I don't know,' Carl admitted. 'But then the one guy said that maybe fifty was enough. What was that?'

'Very puzzling,' Rufus admitted.

'Do you know the two cops?' Carl asked.

'I know Dunbar. He's been around forever. I would have thought he'd be retired by now. Who's the other one?'

'A woman named Pulford.'

Rufus shook his head. 'I have never heard that name. But Dunbar is a good man. An avuncular type, as opposed to some of the Neanderthals the job attracts. I'd say he's a plodder.'

'A plodder?'

'Yes, and that's a good thing,' Rufus said. 'You have concerns?'

'Not sure about the woman,' Carl said. 'She's said a couple of things – maybe suggesting they won't find the guys who did it. That was after she suggested that it could have been somebody I did time with.'

'Really?' Rufus said. 'She must be imagining an *In Cold Blood* situation.'

'She mentioned that.'

Rufus considered the notion. 'Well, if nothing else, that means she's thinking. And you say they're monitoring the Rose City lowlife population? Looking for leads on the money?'

Carl nodded. 'What about Talbotville? These guys might have been local. They knew how to find the farm.'

'They did at that,' Rufus said. 'Keep in mind the farm had been shown on TV a few days earlier.'

'You must know a few of these guys. Or at least you've been around them. You spend a lot of time at the courthouse.'

'I do.' Rufus gave it some thought. 'I see where you're going. There's a bar over by the river called Cork's. Popular with those types. I'm still not convinced that these men are your typical druggies but I could make a point of stopping in and asking some questions. I have been known to partake in happy hour there so I can be relatively inconspicuous. A man can sometimes buy a lot of information with a free round or two.'

'Let's go right now.'

'First of all, it's not happy hour,' Rufus said. 'I'm working here. And second, *we* aren't going anywhere. The people who did this know you by sight. If you walk in the front door, they walk out the back.'

Carl knew the lawyer was right. 'But it sounds like a rough place.'

'I can take care of myself, Carl. I'm not tough but I'm smarter than most people. Didn't I ever mention that?'

Carl forced a smile and left.

When he got back to the farm the motorhome was parked in the driveway by the garage. It had been leveled and someone had run electricity from the machine shed to it, and the same person had connected a water line to the RV. Carl carried the bundle containing Frances's clothes inside and stowed it on a shelf before walking down to the warehouse to thank Ben.

'Not a problem,' Ben said. He was sitting at a counter leafing absently through an organic farm magazine when Carl walked in.

'I'll pay you for that,' Carl said.

'No, you will not.'

Ben didn't look at Carl when he said it but he made it clear that the matter was closed. Carl let it go for now. He walked over to Norah.

'How's it going?'

'Pretty busy,' Norah said. 'Thanksgiving's over and everybody's thinking about Christmas already. Lots of e-mails about Stacy and a bunch wondering how Frances is. Not sure what to say, Carl.'

Carl hesitated. 'I guess just say she's in stable condition. We don't need to say she's still unconscious. By the time they got the message she'd be awake, and then we'd have to untell them.'

Norah nodded her agreement. 'Your daughter called from Scotland.'

'Oh.'

'She is not very happy with you,' Norah said. 'She . . . um . . . she knows what happened. Did you think she wouldn't find out?' She handed a slip of paper to Carl. 'She wants you to call her.'

'It's late there,' Carl said, glancing at the number and not looking forward to the call. 'I'll call in the morning.'

'Don't forget.'

Carl took Frances's cell phone from his coat pocket. 'Speaking of phones, I need you to teach me how to use this.'

Taking the cell from him, Norah gave him a long look, as if she thought he was joking. 'What do you need to know?'

'How to make a call and how to take a call.'

'Geez, Carl. Even the old man over there has a cell phone.'

'The old man can hear you,' Ben said, still looking at the magazine. 'I have a phone but I don't use it for much. It does have a good flashlight in it.'

Norah gave Carl a quick lesson. He told her that he wasn't interested in e-mailing or taking pictures. He just needed a phone.

'The battery is nearly dead,' Norah said.

Carl gestured toward the burned-out shell of the farmhouse. 'Frances always charged it on the kitchen counter.'

'My charger will work,' Norah said, and she plugged it in. 'Frances should have a charger in her car too, if I'm not around.'

Carl stood there looking at the phone on the counter, as if waiting for it to charge. As if waiting for something. Norah watched him.

'What are you going to do, Carl?'

Carl exhaled, looking around. He didn't know what he was going to do – and then he did. 'We have a sugar shack to build. I'm going to start it tomorrow.'

He felt Ben's eyes on him.

'You'll have to hire somebody,' Norah said. 'You only have one arm.'

'No,' Carl said. 'I can start laying it out. Frances was looking forward to this. She'll help me. As soon as she comes home, she'll help me.'

SEVENTEEN

Dunbar spent the day talking to people who might have some knowledge of the home invasion at River Valley Farm. He had a pocket full of fifties and, aside from the bill he'd given to Pink Stallwood for a story that turned out to be a load of horseshit, he never spent a dime. Nobody had heard any rumors about the fire and nobody seemed to have any theories on it. More significantly, nobody had noticed anyone buying coke or meth or oxi or anything else in the manner of someone who had just come into a windfall.

With Pink Stallwood, Dunbar should have known better. He'd run into him in a diner along the lake front. The man was obviously jonesing, sitting huddled at the counter slurping coffee, his hands shaking. He told Dunbar that he'd heard a story about what had gone down at the farm, and the reasons behind it. Dunbar, having struck out all day long, had taken a chance. He met Stallwood in the alley a few minutes later. The crackhead slid into the passenger seat and sat there shivering until Dunbar turned the heater on full force. Stallwood wouldn't speak until he got the money.

'OK, spill,' Dunbar said. He wanted to hear the story and then be done with the little creep. On top of everything else, he smelled as if he hadn't bathed in a month.

'I heard this from a good source,' Stallwood began. 'Think about it, man. You got yourself a rural property there. Nice and private, out of the way. Got some business where they're selling vegetables and shit. There's your front. They ain't making no money selling fucking potatoes.' He glanced over to Dunbar. 'You got a smoke?'

'No.'

'Can we get us a pack?' Stallwood gestured to a corner store a half block away.

'Buy your own,' Dunbar said. 'You got money now.'

'All right,' Stallwood said unhappily. 'So what was I saying? Oh – there's your front. Pretty obvious what was going on out there. They're cooking fucking meth, man. They're cooking and the fucking idiots blew themselves up. There wasn't no home invasion. That's a story they made up after the fire. What else are they gonna say – that they were cooking? They're lucky they got out.'

Dunbar looked out the window. The day cook from the diner had walked out into the alley and was now standing by the dumpster there, smoking a joint. Dunbar sighed; it had been a long and pointless day.

'Where you getting this, Pink?' he asked.

'Buddy of mine,' Stallwood said without hesitation. 'He's been buying meth from these fuckers all along. There was no home invasion. I can't believe your department fell for that shit.'

'And where is this place again?'

'What place?'

'Where it happened,' Dunbar said. 'Where your buddy buys the meth.'

'Aw, it's out in the country,' Stallwood said, flipping his hand in the air. 'You know where.'

'Get out,' Dunbar told him.

'You want me to find out more?'

'No,' Dunbar said. 'Get out.'

He stopped back downtown before he went home. Pulford was at her desk, working at her computer. Dunbar stood inside the door, leaning against the jamb.

'A meth lab, eh?' she said when she'd heard.

'Yeah,' Dunbar said. 'Anything at all with the money?'

'I haven't heard a word,' Pulford said. 'I'm beginning to feel like maybe this wasn't local. I've been looking into the TV show. Turns out it airs on some smaller markets here and there across the country. If the show is what attracted these guys, they could be from anywhere.'

'Maybe,' Dunbar said.

'You sound doubtful.'

Dunbar walked over and sat down opposite her. 'Something about it feels local.'

'Why aren't they spending the money?' Pulford asked.

'It's barely been a week,' he reminded her.

'A week is a long time for your standard druggie to sit on a pile of cash like that.'

Dunbar nodded. 'But we don't know they're sitting on it. Could be they're spending it in dribs and drabs and we don't know where. Or the money was for something bigger. Keep in mind they wanted a hundred grand.'

'Eventually those marked bills will come back into circulation,' Pulford said.

'If they change hands too many times, they're no good to us anyway.'

'True.' Pulford closed the laptop and leaned back in her chair. 'So what are you thinking?'

'All we've released so far is that it was a home invasion,' Dunbar said. 'Let's do a press conference, tell them about the money and give them the descriptions of the two men Carl Burns saw. Maybe that will shake something loose.'

Pulford nodded in agreement.

'Keep this in the news a little while longer, if nothing else,' Dunbar added.

'I'll set it up.' Pulford made some notes as she spoke. 'You hear the latest on Ken Hubert?'

'What did he do now?'

'Same stuff he's always been doing.' Pulford finished what she was writing and smiled up at Dunbar. 'This time he got caught. He's been taking bribes from a construction company that got the contract for the new sewer lines downtown. He chaired the committee that accepted the bids. They got him on a wire.'

'That's my ward,' Dunbar said. 'I guess we'll be getting a new councilor.'

'I would think so. They busted him this morning at his house. They're serving warrants all over the city today. Do you know him?'

Dunbar shrugged. 'I've shaken his hand once or twice, when I couldn't avoid it. One of those guys, you'd like him if you met him. But you walk away afterward feeling like you need to be power washed.'

Pulford laughed. 'Hey, I was talking to the sergeant earlier. He tells me you're retiring in the spring?'

'That's the plan.'

'You must be looking forward to it.'

'I think I am,' Dunbar said. 'I'm a little nervous about getting bored. But we'll see.' He got to his feet. 'I'd really like to solve this one first, Rachel. This one bothers me. I have a daughter, you know. Just two years older than the girl who died in the fire.'

'I didn't know that.'

Dunbar nodded. 'Besides, a man wants to go out a winner. A man wants to go out like Ted Williams.'

'Who's that?'

'I'll see you tomorrow,' Dunbar said. In the doorway, he glanced back just as she opened her laptop. 'I knew you'd google it.'

'Up yours,' she laughed.

Carl spent the night in the motorhome. He got up at dawn and had a shower, the washing made difficult by the wrap on his shoulder and the tiny size of the stall. He dried himself with a roll of paper towels he found in a cupboard, presumably left by the previous owner. Sitting naked in the trailer afterward he realized that he had no food, no extra clothes, no razor or toothbrush. No anything. He dressed in his stale clothes and walked down to the warehouse to make coffee. It was a cold morning, with frost glistening on the garage roof and across the lawn. It was early and Norah hadn't arrived yet. Using the business phone, he called Kendrick's Lumber and asked if they had finished milling the pine logs he'd dropped off. They said the planks were ready and Carl told them he'd be there that afternoon.

He drove his truck to the TSC store outside of Talbotville. He went inside and bought pants and shirts and socks and underwear. Mindful of the coming weather, he also bought insulated Carhartt coveralls and new work boots. As he got into his truck in the parking lot he had a thought and went back inside to buy an air nailer and two cases of nails. There was a good Yamaha compressor at the farm that would run the nailer, and a Wisconsin generator to provide power.

From there he drove to a grocery store in Talbotville and stocked up on canned soup, cereal, milk, cold cuts and bread. He bought whatever toiletries he needed and some towels at the dollar store. He stopped at the beer store for a case of Wellington lager and headed for Rose City. Several people had asked after Frances and Carl had told them that she was still in the hospital but coming along. Driving in to see her, he told himself it was true.

It appeared that she hadn't moved since he'd been there the previous day. Her breathing was even but her color was bad. There were dark circles beneath her eyes, as if she hadn't slept in days. But sleeping was all she'd been doing. The doctor was not around so Carl talked briefly to one of the nurses. All she said was that there had been no change, that Frances's vital signs remained good. When she left, Carl told Frances that he was starting the sugar shack that afternoon.

'I could use some help,' he said.

He waited for some reaction, a twitch of an eye or a flick of a finger. There was nothing but the steady breathing. Her dark hair hung lankly. Carl asked a nurse for a brush and she found one somewhere. He sat by Frances for half an hour longer, softly brushing her hair as her chest rose and fell almost imperceptibly. He tried to talk to her but he couldn't think of what to say, he couldn't come up with the words she needed to hear in her condition. He wished he could.

Back at the farm he carried his purchases into the trailer and stowed everything away. He heated some mushroom soup on the electric range and ate it over the counter in the dinette, looking out the window there, watching the farm. Ben's truck was again parked by the warehouse. Norah would be inside, working. On the surface, anyway, things were getting back to normal. Beneath that was a different story. Normal wasn't a word Carl could ever imagine using again.

He had been putting off the call all morning. Now he took the number from his pocket and smoothed it out on the counter. He looked at it for a full minute before punching it into the cell phone. She answered on the third ring.

'Well, slow but sure,' she said.

'Sorry, Kate. Things have been . . . hectic here.'

'I know how things have been there,' Kate said. 'I have heard how things are. I want to know why I didn't hear about it from you. How's Frances?'

Carl sat down on the bench beneath the trailer window. 'She's in a coma. I really can't tell you much more than that because I'm not being told any more than that. She could wake up at any time.'

'Where is she?'

'St. Michaels in Rose City.' Carl waited for a moment. 'I don't want you flying home, Kate.'

'I've already booked my flight. I'll be there tomorrow morning.'

Carl had been afraid of that. He didn't want Kate to come home. There was nothing she could do there but, more to the point, he didn't want her close to the situation. He didn't know where the culprits were but he had to assume that by now they knew they had left eyewitnesses. Maybe they were of a mind to do something about that and Carl didn't want his daughter anywhere near if that was the case. He wouldn't tell her that, though.

'You can't just pick up and leave. You have your job.'

'Dad, a woman was killed,' Kate said. 'And Frances is in the hospital. My job will either be here or not. But I'm coming home.'

'Things are a mess here,' Carl said. 'The house is gone. I'm living in a trailer. Seriously, there's nothing you can do right now.' He had a sudden notion. 'I wish you would wait and come home when Frances gets out of the hospital. She'll need you then.'

'What about you?' Kate said. 'I heard you were injured too.'

'Dislocated my shoulder. I'm fine.'

'You're not fine,' Kate said. 'Either you're bullshitting me or you're bullshitting yourself. That girl Stacy was killed and I know you and Frances thought the world of her.'

Carl got to his feet and glanced down toward the warehouse, where he knew that Ben was sitting, flipping through magazines or doing crossword puzzles. Keeping *his* daughter safe.

'What are you going to do when you get here?' he asked. 'There's nothing you can do. There's nothing I can do right now either. We just have to wait for something to happen with the cops. Stay there for the time being. You have your job.'

'I shouldn't have answered the phone,' Kate said. 'I should have just gotten on the goddamn plane.'

'You know I'm right.'

'I don't know anything of the kind.' She was beginning to waver. 'What's the doctor's name at St Mike's? I want to talk to him.'

'Harkness.'

Carl could hear her exhaling heavily. 'All right. I'll stay put for now. At least until I talk to him. But you need to keep me in the loop.'

'I will.'

'You *will*,' she repeated.

When Carl got off the phone, he pulled his jacket on and headed down the hill. The GMC stake truck was inside the machine shed. There were empty hampers and bushels stored in the back. When Ben saw Carl unloading them he came out to help.

'How you figure to put up that building with one arm?' Ben asked when Carl told him he was going to pick up the lumber.

'I bought an air nailer,' Carl said.

Kendrick's had the pine boards ready, stacked in the yard in sixteen foot lengths, as Carl had requested. He also bought enough two-by-six spruce boards for the floor joists and rafters.

Back at the farm, Ben helped again as they transferred the lumber from the truck to a hay wagon. Carl set his tools atop the boards – generator, saws, nailer, level, square, chalk line and sawhorses. He backed the Ferguson tractor to the wagon tongue and Ben dropped the pin in place.

'I could come back and help you unload,' Ben said.

Carl glanced at the warehouse. 'I think Norah is more comfortable having you here, Ben.'

Ben nodded. 'Any news from the police?'

'No.'

When he got to the bush, Carl pulled the wagon alongside the site he and Frances had staked out. He fired up the generator and in the couple of hours of daylight he had remaining, he built the frame for the cabin floor. With one arm the work went slowly. Without the air nailer he couldn't have managed.

By the time he drove up to the farm it was nearly dark. He backed the wagon into the shed for the night, to keep the tools out of whatever weather might come. In the motorhome he turned the electric heater on and made a sandwich. After eating he sat in the semi-darkness, drinking beer, waiting for the fatigue he knew wouldn't come. He would have to work harder tomorrow. He needed to be tired. He needed to be so tired that his brain would shut down, at least for a few hours. He wished he'd picked up a bottle earlier; the beer wasn't going to cut it.

It was a clear night and from inside the motorhome he could see the ruins of the farmhouse. He realized it would be up to him to speak to the insurance company about cleaning up the mess. When Frances came home, she would be anxious to rebuild the house. He supposed he would have to get the cops to sign off on the investigation before anything could happen. He would call Dunbar in the morning about that. Then he could contact the insurance company, if he could find out who it was. Frances would have had that information, probably stored in the rolltop desk in the study. The paperwork would have gone up in the fire. But maybe there was something on it in the files down at the warehouse. Norah might know.

Carl would check it out in the morning. He had a lot to do, if he could put his mind to it. He opened another beer and waited for sleep.

EIGHTEEN

Saturday morning Billy drove over to Chum's Service Center in Milton. He'd stopped at the Savoy Hotel Friday afternoon for a beer and Hog Simpson had told him over a game of eight-ball that Chum's was looking for a mechanic. Billy pulled on to the side lot a little past nine. There were at least a dozen vehicles parked there, customers' cars, he assumed. The garage itself had four bays and three hoists. The business had been around since Billy could remember.

There was a woman wearing blue overalls at the front desk when he walked in. When he told her what he was there for she looked him up and down and then went out into the garage to tell somebody. Five minutes later a man came out, heavyset with gray hair, wearing a windbreaker. The woman never returned. Billy saw her later when he was leaving, standing under a van on a hoist, draining the transmission.

'Come in here,' the man said, indicating a small office to the side. He never introduced himself. Billy wondered if he was Chum.

'Name?' the man asked when they were seated.

'William Taylor.'

'You licensed?'

'No.'

The man changed somewhat. 'No apprenticeship or anything?'

'Not really,' Billy said. 'I'm good with cars.'

The man looked at Billy for a moment, as if wondering why he was even there. 'Most of the stuff we do nowadays involves computers. You need some training.'

'I can learn.'

'That doesn't make you unique. Where do you live anyway?'

'Tareytown.'

'Family?'

'Girlfriend, and I got a boy. He's two.'

'And you're not working now?'

'No.'

The man got to his feet. The interview was over. When he reached the doorway he had a thought and turned back. 'You do any brake work?'

Billy nodded. 'Quite a bit.'

'Leave your name and number on the pad on the desk. Anything comes up, I'll call you.'

Cheryl went in at noon and worked until eight that night. Billy fed Seth leftover mac and cheese from the night before and afterward the two of them took a walk in the woods beside the park across the road. There was a creek there, running through the trees down to the river, and they liked to hike up the stream, looking in the water for frogs and minnows. Sometimes they would see bigger fish, bass and crappie, coming up from the river.

There was an ancient wooden bridge farther up the creek, constructed of oak timbers and cedar planks, the structure mostly collapsed now. Today Billy and Seth sat on the span crossing the creek and dangled their feet above the water.

'Frog,' the boy shouted, pointing.

There was a small leopard frog squatting in the mud along the bank, its back shiny, front feet twitching.

'Catch him,' Seth said. He began to pull off his rubber boots.

'The water's too cold today,' Billy said.

'I want to catch him,' the boy pouted.

'He's getting ready to go to sleep for the winter,' Billy said.

'He's going to sleep?'

'He sleeps all winter long.'

'No, he doesn't.'

'He does. We'll come back in the spring and see him. We'll see tadpoles too. Remember the tadpoles?'

'Little and wiggly,' Seth said.

They spent a couple of hours in the woods, walking further upstream where the water was shallow enough that they could wade across in their boots. They spooked a horned owl from some pine trees and Seth asked a couple dozen questions about the bird. Where did he live? Why did he hoot? What did he eat?

When they got back to the house Billy put Seth down for

a nap and then opened a beer and sat in the living room, thinking of the money they would owe at the end of the month. They had enough to meet the rent but they were going to be short on both the electrical and telephone. Billy was supposed to replace some brake lines on a Mustang next week but other than that he had nothing lined up.

He stopped thinking about it, for a while at least. He opened a second beer and watched part of a movie. It was a Western, made in the 1950s, where the Indians spoke perfect and awkward English. *The white men are as many as the stars in the sky.*

Billy fell asleep on the couch. When he woke up he wondered if he would ever hear from Chum's Service Center.

In the Wild clubhouse down the road from the bar, Tommy Jakes sat watching the NASCAR race on the big screen. The newspaper was on the table beside him, folded to the page he'd just read. Tommy was drinking Buffalo Trace. Across the room Joni was cooking chicken wings in the deep fryer, bringing them over a half dozen at a time, each serving in a different sauce. Honey garlic, buffalo style, ranch. So far Tommy liked the chipotle the best. When he'd had enough, she came to sit with him. She'd been smoking weed and drinking vodka on the rocks all afternoon and she was loose and easy, her lipstick smeared. She smelled like pot and hot sauce.

'Come here,' Tommy said, pulling her toward him and kissing her. 'You taste good, baby.'

'I'm horny,' she said. 'Take me in the back and taste me proper.'

'After the race.'

'Fucking asshole,' she said, flopping on to the couch beside him. 'There's guys would jump at that offer.'

'There's guys who have.'

'Fuck you. Get your wife to cook wings for you.'

Tommy reached over and slid his hand beneath her skirt. 'I'm not with her. I'm with you.'

Joni smiled and drank from her glass. She could drink a lot of vodka. Tommy kept his hand on her thigh while he turned back to the race. It was under a yellow again. It was going to take a half hour to run the last five laps.

Bones walked in a few minutes later. He looked at Tommy and Joni, sitting cozy side by side on the couch, and walked over to the bar for a glass. He poured a couple of ounces from the bottle beside Tommy and had a drink.

'How did it go with the councilor the other day anyway?' Tommy asked.

Bones shrugged. 'He's always the same.' He tipped back the rock glass again. 'He's getting careless though.'

'Careless how?'

'Wanted me to hand him the envelope right there in the bar at Angelo's,' Bones said. 'Place is half full of people. He thinks he's Teflon or something.'

'What did you do?'

'Told him I'd be waiting in the parking lot,' Bones said. 'You want the money, walk your ass outside.'

'And he did?'

'Yeah. Made me wait for twenty minutes, as if he's teaching me a lesson. One of these days I'm going to put his head through a wall.'

'Wait until he's out of office,' Tommy said.

'Another thing,' Bones said. 'When he got out of the car, he asked if I knew a good lawyer. Like he was joking, but maybe not. What's that about?'

'Fucked if I know,' Tommy said, dismissing it. 'What about our boy Tonto – you find him?'

Bones nodded as he finished the bourbon. He'd needed a drink. 'Wasn't easy. He doesn't live on the rez.'

'No?'

'He lives over in Tareytown.'

'What's he got to say?' Tommy took his hand out from under Joni's skirt and reached for the remote to turn the volume down.

'He doesn't say a hell of a lot of anything. But he's not interested.'

'You tell him that Chino is out of the picture?'

'Yeah,' Bones said. 'First he claimed he didn't know Chino. Or the other one neither. I had to explain things to him, brought up Monty and Stoddard and all that. He still didn't want to talk about it.'

'That's a positive,' Tommy said. 'Man knows to keep his mouth shut. He finally admit that he made the trip?'

'Yeah, and he never got paid.'

Tommy looked up. 'Chino stiffed him?'

'So he claims.'

Tommy laughed. 'So Chino's telling us the Indian ripped him off and really it's the other way around. Fucking Chino – how did he ever live this long?'

Bones poured more bourbon in his glass and then came over to sit in the leather recliner. He had a drink, looking up at the race.

'Did you ask him about the money from before?' Tommy asked. 'Where it went?'

'At first he said he didn't know shit,' Bones said. 'I pressed him on it some. We were out behind his house and he didn't like me being there. Had a wife and kid in the house and I could tell he just wanted me to leave. So I suggested we go inside and talk.'

'And?'

'He loosened up,' Bones said. 'According to him, Chino lost the money at the casino that night.'

Tommy thought about it. 'Yeah, I could see that happening. Chino's got problems in that area. Which is why Johnny K sent him my way to begin with.'

'But then how does Chino come up with the cash two days later? That's the mystery.'

'Maybe not.' Tommy picked up the newspaper and handed it over to Bones, showing the page in question. 'Remember that fire out along the river last week? The cops are releasing more info. It wasn't just a home invasion, Bones. It was a robbery. Three suspects. They got descriptions of two of them. Read it.'

Bones read the paper as he drank the whisky. 'You think it was them?' he asked, looking over at Tommy. 'It doesn't say how much they got.'

'I'm goddamn sure it was them,' Tommy said. 'Look at the timing. Thursday they say they lost the money, Friday they pull off this robbery arson deal and Saturday Chino shows with the cash. And the descriptions fit.'

Bones considered it. 'What about the new bills?'

Tommy shrugged. 'Sounds as if this farm was a business, organic food and whatever. Could be they deal in cash sometimes.'

'Fifty grand worth?'

Tommy waved his hand. 'Doesn't matter about the bills. What matters is that this changes the conversation with our Indian buddy. The cops didn't mention an Indian but I have to figure he was the third party.'

Bones put the paper aside. 'How do you want to do this?'

'Let me think about it,' Tommy said after a moment. 'There was a dead girl in that fire. Doesn't matter who lit the match, you're talking capital murder for all three of them. And the other two would roll over on the Indian in a heartbeat.'

'You want me to talk to him again?'

'I might go this time,' Tommy said. 'Relax and watch the race. I'd go right now but I made a promise to this woman here.'

'Yes, you did,' Joni said.

'I always keep a promise,' Tommy said. He had a drink before glancing at Bones. 'I might just mention that to the Indian.'

Dunbar got up early and by the time Martha came downstairs he had breakfast ready. Saturday mornings he liked a good old-fashioned breakfast. Eggs and home fries and either sausage or ham, with lots of coffee and toast and preserves. He had become a bit of an egg snob in recent years, after reading an article about the inhumane treatment of laying hens in factory farms. Dunbar hadn't bought eggs in a supermarket since. He and Martha usually hit the farmers' market in the city once a week, or bought from the roadside stalls outside the city.

Dunbar suspected it was a sign of approaching old age, his concern for unknown hens on unknown farms. In his younger years, an egg was just an egg. But he'd noticed that his heart was getting softer with the years. A couple of weeks ago he'd struck a squirrel with the squad car while driving past Oakland

Park and it had bothered him all day long. He wondered if any of his peers felt the same way. He didn't know and he wouldn't broach the matter with them. How could he?

Martha came down the stairs as he was scrambling the eggs, dressed in jeans and a Bahamas T-shirt she'd bought on their vacation the previous winter. It was cool in the house and she was pulling on a sweater as she came into the kitchen to sit at the counter. Dunbar served the breakfast as she sipped her coffee. It was the one morning in the week when he cooked and he knew that she luxuriated in it.

'We have frost,' he told her.

'Oh?' She glanced out the window to the back yard.

'Your basil is done.'

'No.'

Dunbar nodded, sitting down opposite her. 'I saw it when I went out for the paper. The flowers out front too.'

'I was going to pick the basil and dry it.'

'A day late,' Dunbar told her as he tucked into the meal.

They ate in silence for a time. Oliver came in and jumped up on the stool beside Martha. He sat there, whiskers flicking, as if contemplating making the move to the countertop. He knew better, though. After a while he thumped to the floor and walked over to his dish by the back door. He looked at his food for a few seconds before flopping on his side, where he began a cleaning of his face with his paws.

Martha poured more coffee for herself. Replacing the pot, she noticed the empty egg carton there and picked it up.

'Look.' She turned the carton to show Dunbar what was written. 'I knew that name sounded familiar.'

'River Valley Farm,' he read. He took a moment. 'That's right. We bought these at the farmers' market a couple of weeks ago.'

'It wasn't from Frances Rourke, though,' Martha said. 'I would have recognized her from the TV show.'

'It was a kid that day,' Dunbar remembered. 'A girl.'

As he said it, he realized that it might have been the girl who was killed in the fire. He knew that Martha was thinking the same. She pushed the carton aside and poured cream into her cup.

'What's going on with that anyway?' she asked. She almost never did that. She knew that most of the time he'd rather not discuss things. Especially things of a certain nature.

'Not a whole lot,' he admitted. 'We basically have nothing so far. The girl's parents were here for a couple of days. They had all sorts of questions we couldn't answer. They went back to British Columbia last night.'

'I suppose with the fire, there's no evidence,' Martha said.

Dunbar took a forkful of eggs and nodded. 'We have to assume that was the reason for the fire. Whatever they did, they wanted it covered up. No fingerprints.' He paused, not looking at his wife. 'And no DNA.'

'Do you think the women were sexually assaulted?' she asked.

'I don't know,' Dunbar said. 'It's a possibility, based on what Carl Burns saw before they threw him down the stairs. He said that one of the thugs was manhandling the young woman. Maybe there was more. He asked if Frances Rourke had been raped.'

Martha shook her head.

'They were pretty loaded,' Dunbar said. 'Two of them anyway. Sounds as if the third was some kind of sentry. He tried to keep the other two in check, according to Burns. It was almost as if he didn't want to be there.'

'But that's just what Burns assumed,' Martha said. 'He wouldn't be used to these types.'

'No, he's been around,' Dunbar said.

Martha ate the last of her breakfast. 'What's the prognosis on Frances Rourke?'

'She's still in the coma. No response.'

'How is Burns doing? I suspect he's catatonic.'

'No,' Dunbar said. 'But he might be in a bit of denial.'

Martha got up and carried her plate to the sink. She began to clean the mess always created by Dunbar when in cooking mode.

'Leave that,' he said. 'Come and drink your coffee with me.'

She did as he asked.

'How are you going to find the people who did it?' she asked as she sat down.

'I don't know. If it turns out that it was completely random, it will be tough. We need somebody to talk. And so far, nobody's saying anything. There's nearly fifty thousand dollars out there that doesn't seem to be moving.'

'Why would they target that farm?'

'I wish we knew,' Dunbar said. 'It might help with the investigation. The place is kind of in the public eye, because of the TV show. Maybe that's all it was, these people thinking it was a place they could score.' He sipped his coffee. 'My partner thinks there's more to it.'

'Such as?'

Dunbar shrugged. 'Carl Burns has done time. She thinks there's something there that's connected. I'm not so sure.'

'Burns shot Mayor Sanderson, didn't he? Wasn't he protecting his daughter?'

'Yeah,' Dunbar said. 'He saved her. I'm sure he thinks he should have done the same in this case. He didn't, and I get the sense that it's weighing on the man. But what could he have done? These guys are bad. As bad as I've ever seen.'

'You'll get them.'

'I hope so,' Dunbar said. 'And when we do, I hope Burns can ID them. Because without him, we have nothing.'

NINETEEN

Carl fell into a routine of sorts. He was up early and ate cereal and drank coffee, then did whatever jobs needed doing around the farm. The chicks he and Frances had started had doubled in size already and needed tending. There were the larger hens to feed and eggs to gather. Manure to shovel and bedding to spread. All with one arm. They were well past the first frost and everything had been harvested and stored in the warehouse and barns. A truck left daily with the online orders; Norah and the part-timer Josh took care of that.

Around nine each morning Carl got on the phone. He called the insurance company first, asking when they would send a bulldozer to clean up what was left of the farmhouse. They were being difficult. The policy – and the property itself – were both in the name of Frances Rourke and they kept insisting that they speak to her. They couldn't seem to grasp the concept of a person being in a coma.

There seemed to be a gray area regarding Frances and the insurance policy. Technically she was the only one listed in the paperwork. The company didn't know what to do, or at least they were pretending that. So far, Carl had gone through two agents and the office manager. After a certain amount of doublespeak, they eventually all maintained that things were moving forward.

Next he would call the two detectives, first Dunbar and then Pulford. Dunbar always took time to talk, and stayed on the line for as long as Carl wanted. He didn't, however, have much to report. He said more than once that they were waiting for a break.

'In cases like these, someone almost always talks,' he told Carl one morning.

Almost always, he'd said.

Pulford was less accommodating. She was polite but to the point and after a few minutes on the line Carl was usually left with the distinct impression that he was bothering her.

'We'll call as soon as we have something to tell you,' she'd say. When she said it, Carl knew that the conversation was at a conclusion.

The media was still covering the story, even though there was little to report after the initial deluge. The police weren't saying much, which was only natural since there was nothing new to say. Reporters and news teams showed up at the farm off and on for the first couple of days, seeking comments from Carl, or Norah in the warehouse. Neither had much to tell them, for the same reasons that the cops didn't. Carl in particular wanted nothing to do with them. They seemed determined to make a soap opera of the incident, to have him talk about himself and Frances. One reporter even asked pointed questions about Carl's possible involvement with Stacy. Carl had asked the man to leave and ended up escorting him to his car by the scruff of the neck. That made the paper.

Virtually all of the neighbors within a couple of miles had been interviewed, or at least given a chance to comment on what they'd seen or expound upon whatever theory they might have about the incident. There was a prevailing feeling of both fear and outrage in the community. However, as the days passed, it was replaced at least in part by a sense that the perpetrators had flown the coop. Nobody seemed to be of the opinion that they might be next in line, although most of the older farmers in the area had their shotguns loaded and ready in case they were wrong.

One of the newspapers, a tabloid from Rose City, ran a piece in its weekend edition focusing on Carl and his past. The piece went on about his troubles with the law, the Sanderson case and the fact that he had spent time in prison on two occasions. It suggested somewhat cryptically that the police were concentrating on Carl's history while investigating the home invasion. The theory was reinforced by a statement from Pulford that they were 'not ruling anything out'. The tabloid did not bother to try to get a comment of any kind from Carl before running the piece. Not that he would have given them anything. After reading the story and tossing it in the trash, Carl had a notion to call Pulford to ask her if she wanted to expand on what she had said. He decided against it though; it wouldn't accomplish a thing.

Every few days he would call Kate in Scotland. She'd ask about any developments and Carl would have to tell her there were none and then hear the disappointment and frustration in her voice. He considered not calling as often but he was afraid that she would then fly home, suspecting something was the matter. He still didn't want her near, not while the three men were at large. It was unreasonable to think they would go after her, but in this Carl chose to be unreasonable.

Mid-mornings he drove to Rose City to see Frances. There was no change in her condition, although it seemed that each day she had more tubes and lines running into her. IV feeding, saline solution, electrolytes. The bruise on her face was fading while her skin was growing paler. Some days Carl would sit close to her, holding his breath, staring at her closed eyelids as if willing them to open.

It was surreal, seeing her like this. She was the most capable person Carl had ever known. The most alive. Nothing fazed her, in work or play. She had an analytical mind when it came to the business and seemed to know instinctively what would work and what would not. On the more impractical side, she and Carl had made love in nearly every room of the old farmhouse as well as in the hay mow several times, and once in the warehouse atop some cardboard cartons. Just a month ago she had mentioned that they would need to 'break in' the sugar shack as well, once it was built.

For that reason, and others, he would tell her daily about the progress on the cabin, and give her whatever news Norah had about the business. In Carl's mind he could see her, at any moment, getting out of the bed and returning to the farm, to work, to play. To her life, and his. It was impossible that she would not.

Before leaving he would talk to the nurse on duty, or Harkness, if he was available. They had nothing more for him than did the cops. Everything was wait and see. Carl felt as if he'd been waiting too long for too little development. Close to two weeks had passed. Carl was by nature an impatient man. Sometimes that impatience had served him well but most times it had not. In this case, it didn't really matter. His level of patience would not impact the investigation. Or so he thought.

The only time he relaxed was when he got back to the farm, drove the tractor and the wagon with the tools to the bush lot and went to work on the cabin there. At first he was able to get by using just his right hand. Nailing the joists and the boards for the floor was easy enough; he had gravity to keep it all in place. The walls were a different story. A few days after his surgery he ditched the heavy wrap on his shoulder and made do with a sling that enabled him at least to use the fingers of his left hand, which helped considerably. He could put the planks in place and then prop them there with his left hand and knee while using the nail gun with his right hand. It took twice as long as it normally would but he didn't mind. What else was he going to do?

By the end of the week he had the floor finished and the

four walls up. He roughed in a door and two windows, all on the south side. Earlier that fall Frances had shown him some windows she'd stored in the machine shed, left over from a project her father had started years earlier, and Carl now hauled them back to the shack and installed them. Coming home from Rose City on Thursday morning he'd picked up hinges and a latch and that afternoon he built a plank door for the cabin and hung it.

Friday afternoon he finished the double plate atop the walls. Next up were the rafters. They would be tricky, handicapped as he was. He considered asking Josh to help him out on the following day – the Saturday – but he decided against it. This was his project. His and Frances's actually, but until she was better, it belonged to Carl.

He nailed two-by-fours on a vertical on each end of the building, then calculated the pitch to get the height for the ridge board. He cut the board from a length of two by eight and tacked it approximately in position on one end, then moved the ladder to the other to do the same. Checking the height and the level, he went back and forth, moving the board slightly each time until he had it right.

It was time-consuming climbing up and down the ladder, moving the ridge board with one hand, but Carl was fine with that. It gave him purpose, and purpose was all he had for now. It was nearly dark when he finished. With the board in place he took a measurement and cut the first rafter. He tried it on either side of the board and it fit perfectly, the birdsmouth tight against the plate. He would cut the rest in the morning. Before leaving he determined how much steel he would need for the roof, using the cut rafter for reference. It would take a few days for the steel to arrive and he needed to order it. After making his notes, he loaded his tools on to the wagon and headed for home.

As he entered the motorhome, he took the cell phone from his coat pocket and saw that there was a message waiting. The phone must have rung while he was driving the old Ferguson up the lane; he wouldn't have heard it over the noise of the tractor. The number on the display was Dunbar's. Carl's pulse quickened at once. They'd found something.

But they hadn't. Dunbar was going away for the weekend, up north on a hunting trip, and he wanted Carl to know that he wouldn't be reachable by phone. Carl appreciated the call but he was disappointed at the lack of news. He opened a beer and sat in the trailer, drinking and thinking about his reaction at the mere sight of Dunbar's number on the phone. Thinking of how it was all out of his control, this thing that had happened to Frances and Stacy, and everything that had happened since. Or conversely, all that had not happened since. Maybe the police were making progress but not saying anything. Maybe they had suspects they were following. If so, Carl was out of the equation. His job was to wait, the one role he was most unsuited for. Wait on the cops, on the insurance company. Wait for Frances to wake up.

Wait for something to happen.

The waiting would be easier if Carl knew for a fact that something eventually *would* happen. But he didn't know that. There were crimes that went unsolved forever. That was just a fact. But it was something he couldn't bring himself to consider in this case. He felt as if he should be out there doing something to preclude that possibility, but he had no idea what that something might be. In truth there was nothing he could do, and so he spent his hours in the bush, trying not to dwell on that nothing.

When he got up the next morning he drove to the lumber yard in Talbotville and ordered the steel for the roof. He had to choose a color and he settled on red. Frances would like a red roof, he thought. It would have to be cut to length at the fab shop and he was told it would take a week or so to come in. He also bought a new blade for his circular saw and a spare extension cord to use at the shack.

From the yard he drove to the hospital, where he visited with Frances for a half hour. He was feeling strangely guilty about ordering the steel. Frances had been adamant about cedar shingles. But steel was the best way to go, Carl had told her. In the end, Frances was a pragmatist. Today he didn't mention it to her. He didn't say much at all, in fact, just sat there, watching her on the hospital bed, seeing her chest rise and fall, the movement so slight it hardly seemed to be there.

He wondered if she was thinking in her state. Did she dream of waking up? Did she know how desperate Carl was for her to awake?

As Carl was leaving, Norah came in. Carl was surprised to see her; she hadn't mentioned that she was planning to visit.

'I was in the city,' Norah said.

Carl glanced at Frances. 'She doesn't really respond, you know.'

'I know.'

'You were here before?'

'A couple times,' Norah said. 'At night. I don't stay long. Just, you know . . .' – she hesitated – '. . . to say hello.'

Back at the bush lot that afternoon, Carl cut the rafters – thirty-two in all – and nailed them in place one by one, awkwardly climbing the ladder clutching a rafter in one hand, with the air nailer clipped to his tool belt. It was mid-afternoon when he finished and there was thunder to the southwest, the clouds building there, stacking up like a great gray abutment atop the horizon. There would be rain by nightfall. Carl cut the fascia boards for the end rafters and nailed them and afterwards sat on the wagon to look at the building, which now actually resembled just that.

Next he needed to nail two-by-four strapping along the rafters at two foot intervals. The steel roofing would be screwed to the strapping. It began to drizzle and as he sat there he thought back to the day when he and Frances had staked out the building site. How they had gone back and forth about the particulars. How many windows were required, where would the doorway face? Carl remembered how excited she was about the project, not just the making of maple syrup but the actual building of the cabin. He knew that she'd been looking forward to being back here, just the two of them. And so had Carl.

And she had wanted a cedar roof. The fact was, she had never really asked anything of Carl. She had never asked anything and yet there was nothing Carl wouldn't give to her. Then and now, there was nothing. So why would he deny her the roof she wanted? And why would he deny himself the chance to see her face when he finally brought her here to show her?

Carl began to cry, and as he did the rain started to fall in earnest.

He drove the tractor through the downpour up to the farm and parked it in the shed. He went into the motorhome and after changing into dry clothes he picked up the cell phone and punched in the number for the lumber yard. He needed to cancel the steel and order a couple of skids of cedar shingles. The phone lit up and then went dark. The battery was dead.

Norah had been charging it for him in the warehouse every now and again. But it was Saturday and Norah wasn't there. The yard would close in half an hour. Carl recalled that Norah had said that the phone could be charged in Frances's car. He went out the door and trotted through the rain to the vehicle. Since the night of the fire Carl had not, for reasons he didn't quite understand, gone anywhere near the car. The keys were in the ignition. Frances wouldn't have thought to remove them the night she'd returned from the bank. Inside, Carl couldn't locate the charger. He didn't know what it looked like anyway. He knew that the police had searched the vehicle and found the cell phone along with Frances's laptop. Maybe they'd taken the charger as well.

Running back through the rain to the trailer, he suddenly remembered the bundle of Frances's clothes that the nurse had given him at the hospital. Carl had stowed them in an overhead bin in the trailer, thinking he needed to have them cleaned, and then forgotten. He wondered if Frances might have kept the charger in her coat pocket.

It turned out there was no charger there. There was some chewing gum, lip balm and a sales receipt. It was the receipt that drew Carl's attention. It was from Fred's Custom Meats in Talbotville for the Thanksgiving turkey Frances had bought. Scrawled across the paper in black marker was a number. A license plate number.

Carl sat in the trailer for several minutes, holding the scrap of paper in his hand, considering it. Frances had picked the bird up on her way home that night. There were just two possibilities with regards to the plate number. The first was that she'd written it down at some point on her drive home from the butcher shop. That seemed unlikely. It seemed more plausible that she'd written it later, between leaving the house for the bank and returning with the money. Carl folded the paper carefully and put it in his shirt pocket.

He walked over to his truck and headed for town.

He had faith in Rufus Canfield being a creature of habit and that trust was duly rewarded. It was just past six as Carl walked into Archer's bar to find the little lawyer propped on a bar stool at the far end of the room. It was happy hour on a Saturday and Rufus was drinking dark ale and talking basketball with a guy wearing a Toronto Maple Leafs jacket. Carl settled on a stool a few feet off and ordered a beer. His expression must have given him away because within minutes Rufus had concluded his conversation with the Leafs fan and moved over to sit beside Carl.

'What's going on?'

Carl put the receipt from the butcher shop on the bar. Rufus picked it up and examined it while Carl told him of how he'd found it, and of his theory about the number.

'What are you thinking?' Rufus asked.

'I'm thinking about the Dodge pickup parked down by the river that night,' Carl said. 'Lucy Bronson next door told the cops about it. Remember?'

Rufus nodded. 'The assumption was it belonged to a fisherman.'

'Yeah.'

'And it probably did belong to a fisherman,' Rufus said. 'Keep in mind, Carl, there are probably a million reasons for Frances to take down a license number. Maybe she spotted a reckless driver. Maybe somebody backed into her car and drove off. Maybe she – oh, I don't know.'

'You said a million but you only came up with two,' Carl said. 'I don't see Frances writing down a number for a reckless driver. And if somebody backed into her, she'd chase them down. Besides, there's no damage to her car.'

'You have talked yourself into something here,' Rufus warned. 'Probably due to the lack of anything happening with the investigation.' He looked at the slip of paper again. 'I agree, though. You should have the police run the number. Leave no stone unturned. Have you called them?'

'No,' Carl said. 'Dunbar is away.'

'What about the other one? What's her name again?'

'I'd rather deal with Dunbar.'

'And when is he back?'

'Not sure. He left a message and said he was going hunting for a few days.' Carl watched Rufus for a moment. 'You don't have any way to run a plate number?'

Instead of replying, Rufus signaled for the bartender to bring a round. Carl waited until the fresh draft arrived before asking the question again.

'That's something for the police to handle,' Rufus said. 'Not you or me. For a couple of reasons. One, they are the police. Two, there are issues here relating to invasion of privacy statutes.'

'Invasion of privacy?' Carl said. 'I can't believe you said that.'

'I'm sorry. That was bloody stupid of me.'

'You didn't exactly answer the question,' Carl said.

'I believe I did.'

'I asked if you have any way of running a plate number,' Carl reminded him.

Rufus had a long drink of ale. 'Legally I do not have any method for running a plate number.'

'We're getting closer to an answer.'

Rufus started to say something but then stopped. Getting to his feet, he drained his glass in three gulps and placed it on the bar. He put the receipt in his coat pocket. 'I swear, one of these Saturdays I am going to head straight home at the end of the day.'

The office was walking distance from the bar. They entered through a back door and Rufus turned on an overhead light. Carl remained on his feet while the lawyer went to sit behind the cluttered desk by the bay window that looked out over the street. He logged on to a computer and hit a few keys.

'Well,' he said after a moment.

Carl walked over. Rufus pointed to an entry on the screen.

'We have a Dodge pickup truck registered to one Larry Murdock.'

'That's the truck,' Carl said.

'It would appear so.' Rufus paused, looking at the information on the monitor. 'A rural address north of Tareytown. Keep in mind, this tells us nothing. It could be that Mr Murdock is merely the fisherman we've been supposing all along.'

'Maybe,' Carl said.

Rufus turned in the chair to look at him. 'You've convinced yourself that there's something here, Carl. Take it slow. You are the one who said that fishermen and duck hunters use that lane.'

'I did say that,' Carl replied. 'People park there frequently. But as far as I know Frances never took down a license plate before. Why this time, Rufus?'

'She was never in a situation like this before, Carl.'

'That's my point.'

There was a scratch pad on the desk. Carl picked up a pen and began to write down the address on the computer screen.

'You're not going to the man's house,' Rufus said.

Carl shrugged. 'The police will want the info.'

'The police will run the plate number themselves. How are you going to explain being in possession of this information?'

'I'm not going to throw you under the bus,' Carl said. 'You know that.'

'They are going to ask.'

'I'll just give them the plate number.'

'Then why are we sitting here in front of my computer screen?' Rufus asked. 'What are you thinking, Carl?'

Carl moved away from the desk. He stood by the bay window, looking out into the town. The scrap of paper was clutched in his right hand. 'I'd like to get a look at him,' he said after a time. 'Like you said, it could be nothing. At least I'll know.'

'You need to turn this over to the police, Carl.'

'I will, Rufus.' Carl put the address in his pocket and left.

'Shit,' Rufus said to the closing door.

TWENTY

Heading there, Carl had no intention of getting close. All he really wanted was a glimpse of the guy who owned the white truck. And preferably at a distance. If the owner was one of the two men he could recognize from the farmhouse that night, Carl would call the police. If not, then it was probably a dead end. Of course, there existed a third possibility – that the truck's owner was the third man in the house that night, the one who had not removed his mask. Carl knew only that he was tall and thin. If that description matched, he would still call the cops.

He had made himself wait until morning, resisting the urge to drive there directly from Rufus Canfield's law office. The next day was Sunday, a good time to catch somebody at home, he reasoned. The address was the village of Bonwick, a crossroads roughly halfway between Rose City and Tareytown. It was nearly an hour's drive for Carl.

He spotted the Dodge truck from a quarter mile away, parked at an angle in a driveway. To be sure, he drove by, slowing down to get a look at the license plate. The house was on the edge of the village, a story and a half stucco with faded paint and a collection of junk scattered in the yard, lawnmowers and rototillers and car engines. A steel utility shed in the back yard had collapsed in the wind. The grass was so long it was lying flat on the ground, like prairie grass after a wind storm.

The village had just a dozen or so homes and a gas station that did double duty as a coffee shop. Anxious in his task, Carl hadn't eaten or drunk anything when he got up that morning and now he went inside and ordered coffee, choosing a table that gave him a view of the house down the road. He sat there for the better part of an hour, asking for refills he didn't want. His stomach was turning; he couldn't eat and so he ordered no breakfast. When he became aware that the woman serving him was looking at him suspiciously, he paid his bill and walked out to his truck. He sat in the parking lot for a few minutes, knowing he was still under the eye of the woman inside as well as the other few Sunday morning patrons of the diner. Small towns and strangers, he knew.

Pulling out, he drove to the first side road west of town and parked there. After a moment he got out and opened the hood, where he made a pretense of looking at an engine problem, all the while watching the white Dodge truck a quarter mile away. Even that, he knew, was a ruse that would only last so long.

After twenty minutes he closed the hood and as he did he saw a man walk out of the house, get into the Dodge pickup and drive off. At that distance Carl couldn't see anything about the man he might recognize. He was wearing a coat and moving quickly; he might have been skinny or heavy or anywhere in between. Carl got into his truck and followed.

The white truck was headed for Rose City, on the two lane blacktop. Carl, his knuckles white on the steering wheel, had to force himself to hang back. His pulse was racing now and he wished he'd gotten a better look at the driver when he'd had the chance. Maybe he should have parked closer. He had to remind himself that there was a high likelihood that the man had nothing to do with the trouble at the farm. Yet the mere possibility had Carl's blood on the rise. He tried to calm himself, to no avail.

The man drove fast and at one point Carl had to run a yellow light to keep the Dodge in sight. On the outskirts of Rose City was a mile long stretch of strip malls, bars, gas stations and box stores. The road opened up to six lanes. There was a succession of stoplights and the traffic was heavy, delivery vans and cargo trucks. The Dodge swung across the traffic to the right lane, pulling in front of a tanker as it went through a green light. When Carl reached the intersection, the Dodge was gone. He'd lost it.

Carl, in a panic now, went through the light, watching the traffic ahead. Then he glanced to his right and saw the Dodge cutting diagonally across a mall parking lot there. The truck had turned at the intersection. There was a Home Depot in the mall and a Staples, as well as some smaller businesses. Carl, caught in traffic, kept looking until the Dodge disappeared behind the first row of stores.

Carl took the next right and circled around behind the block. There was a rear entrance to the mall and he took it, driving across the back lot past loading docks and dumpsters, in the direction of where he'd last seen the Dodge. As he made a turn to swing in front of the stores, he nearly collided with the white truck. It went past him and parked in front of a bar named Diablo's. The driver got out.

Carl was less than thirty feet away. There was no question it was him. The man Carl had last seen at the farmhouse, the man who had tormented Stacy, and maybe worse. Carl knew the greasy hair, the wispy goatee, the bad teeth. All of it was etched in Carl's memory; he would remember it until he died. Seeing the man at close range Carl felt his breath catch in his chest, and for a split second he was fearful, although he didn't know of what. The man didn't look his way.

And then he did. For some reason, heading into the bar, the man stopped and turned directly toward Carl, sitting in the Ford, the engine idling. And he recognized him, there was no doubt of that. The look on his face was one of abject fear and panic. He jerked his head sideways in a violent motion, as if in the hope that Carl hadn't seen him. But he knew.

They both knew.

Even realizing it was too late, Carl put his hand up to shield his face and hit the gas, moving past the row of stores. Watching in the rear view, he saw the man stop in front of the bar and hesitate for just a second before turning and hurrying back to his truck. He jumped inside and drove off, heading out of the mall the way Carl had come in.

Carl made a U-turn, tires screaming, and followed. Behind the mall the Dodge went right, moving fast along the narrow side street, away from the city. Carl powered after it. As he drove, he fished the cell phone from his pocket and found Pulford's number. It went straight to voice mail. Carl turned it off.

He cursed himself for being careless. Leaving the farm that morning, he'd told himself that all he wanted was a look at the man. He needed to know if the license plate number meant anything. But he had gotten too close and now he had blown it. The man in the Dodge knew that he'd been made. If he got away today, he might not ever be found. Rufus had been right; Carl should have left it to the cops.

Up ahead the white pickup was flying. Carl gunned the Ford after him. They hit the main highway heading west, passing vehicles. When the road reduced to two lanes, there were several vehicles between Carl and the Dodge. He lost sight of it for a moment at a hill and then, cresting the rise, he saw the truck heading south on a gravel side road. Carl took the turnoff, nearly skidding into the ditch before roaring after it.

Soon they were entering an area of pine forest on both sides of the road, with the Dodge a half mile ahead. Carl saw the brake lights flash briefly and the truck turned to the left and disappeared into the trees. It seemed the driver knew where he was going. Carl was already hitting sixty on the stone road and now he sped up. Reaching the turnoff, he found it was a dirt road which snaked into the pines. The recent rain had made the lane impassable. The white Dodge sat fifty yards away, mud flying from its rear wheels as the axles sank into the quagmire.

Carl pulled on to the lane and stopped. He saw the driver look into the rear view mirror at the Ford, his foot on the gas pedal yet, the tires still throwing mud. The man let off the throttle and shut the engine down. He got out and stepped away from the truck. Carl climbed out of the Ford awkwardly, reaching across his body to open the door. The man half turned as if to run but in that instant he saw that Carl's left arm was in a sling. He showed his teeth as he went into a stance that suggested some martial arts training. 'Come and get it then,' he said.

Face to face with the man after these futile weeks, Carl felt a deep rage rising inside of him, a thing he could neither recognize or quantify. As he drew near the man lunged at him, throwing a weak right hand, the punch grazing Carl's cheek. Carl turned away from the blow and then put all of his weight behind a crushing right cross that landed squarely in the man's face. The man dropped to his knees and Carl took him by the hair and drove his knee into his face. The man went limp.

He called Pulford again on the drive into Rose City. This

time he left a message with enough details that she called back within two minutes. It seemed she had been screening her calls. When he pulled up in front of the police station she was waiting for him, wearing track pants and sneakers, her hair tucked beneath a baseball cap. The driver of the Dodge pickup was in the box of Carl's truck, bleeding profusely from his nose and trussed hand and foot with the extension cord Carl had bought in Talbotville the day before.

As Pulford hurried down the front steps, Carl dropped the tailgate and dragged the man out of the truck, dropping him with a thud to the concrete. The man screamed in protest as Carl turned to Pulford.

'This is one of them,' he said.

TWENTY-ONE

'He hasn't asked for a lawyer?' Dunbar asked as he and Pulford walked along the corridor to the interrogation room.

Pulford shook her head. 'He doesn't think he needs one. I have advised him otherwise but he's not much of a listener.'

Bug was already in the room, sitting at the scarred Formica table. He had scrapes on his cheekbone and forehead where he'd hit the concrete out front of the station and his nose was mashed where he'd taken the knee to the face. He was still wearing his street clothes – jeans and a T-shirt with some rock band's logo across the front. It was warm in the room and his leather jacket was on the back of the chair. He regarded Dunbar blankly.

'Mr Murdock,' Dunbar said, and he introduced himself.

Bug leaned back in the chair, looking up at the two detectives. 'So what's up – you gonna try and tag team me before you cut me loose?'

Dunbar pulled a chair over to sit opposite Bug. Pulford remained on her feet.

'It's going to be a long time before anyone will even think

about cutting you loose, Larry,' Dunbar said. 'I need you to tell me about your actions on the Friday night two weeks ago, the night of the tenth.'

Bug pointed his damaged nose toward Pulford. 'I already told her.'

'Now you can tell me.'

Bug shook his head. 'I was home alone. Drank a little whisky and watched the football. Went to bed around midnight maybe. Can I go now?'

'What football game?'

Again Bug looked at Pulford. 'You didn't tell him nothing? Why do I gotta keep saying it?' He turned to Dunbar. 'Michigan, I think.'

'Michigan and who?'

'Fucked if I know.'

'Who won?'

Bug laughed. 'Either Michigan or the other team.'

Dunbar nodded and waited. Bug said nothing else.

'Where was your truck that night?' Dunbar asked.

'In my driveway. Where else would it be?'

'Where else?' Dunbar repeated. 'Well, it might have been parked in a lane by the river east of Talbotville. In fact, it was parked there.'

'No,' Bug said. 'You got a smoke for me?'

Dunbar didn't respond for the moment. He stood looking at the man at the table. There wasn't much to Larry Murdock. He was all bluster and false bravado, a little scared boy talking tough in the school playground. He couldn't have weighed more than a hundred and fifty pounds. When he'd first heard what had happened, Dunbar had wondered how Carl had managed to subdue the man using only one arm. He wasn't wondering it now. Dunbar was pretty sure that even a one-handed Carl Burns could eat a half dozen Larry Murdocks for breakfast.

'Why was your truck parked there?'

'It wasn't.'

'It was. It was there because you were involved in a home invasion that night at a farmhouse a few hundred yards away,' Dunbar said. 'You and two other men. Who were they?'

'I got no idea what you're talking about, bud.' Bug glanced at Pulford, who was watching quietly by the door. 'Hey – did you lay charges against that asshole that attacked me yesterday, like I asked?'

'That man's name is Carl Burns,' Dunbar said. 'Have you ever seen him before?'

'Nope. Fucker chased me down for no reason and sucker punched me. Tied me up like a damn animal. That's assault *and* kidnapping. I want him charged.'

'He's seen you before,' Dunbar said. 'He is one hundred per cent certain that you were one of the men who broke into his house and assaulted him and two others. One hundred per cent. And we know that your truck was parked nearby. The indictments are coming down this afternoon. So far you're looking at first degree murder, home invasion, armed robbery, arson and felony assault. You're as good as convicted on all counts. If you want any chance at leniency, you'd better name your two partners right now.'

'I was watching football that night, bud.'

'Stick with that story, see where it gets you.' Dunbar paused. 'The nature of these crimes, you'll never get parole. How long do you think you're going to live, Larry? Because that's how long you're going to spend in prison. You OK with that?'

Bug shrugged. He looked from Dunbar to Pulford and back to Dunbar. 'You got nothing to hold me on. You're talking shit right now but you gotta let me go.'

'We have an eyewitness,' Pulford told him. 'Don't you get that?'

'I've never seen that guy before.'

Dunbar leaned back in the chair. He had driven most of the night after getting word about the unorthodox citizen's arrest. Pulford had called the hunting lodge and someone from the lodge had arrived at the camp on a snowmobile with the news. Dunbar and his hunting buddies were drinking scotch and playing euchre at the time, after a fruitless day in the woods. Apparently the hunting had been better back in the city.

'You've been locked up in the past for dealing dope and stealing cars,' Dunbar said to Bug now. 'You've been a small time nuisance and nothing more. But all of a sudden you make this leap to murder and arson and robbery. What would cause you to do that? Are you just addled by drugs?' Dunbar waited. 'Or was somebody else calling the shots that night? Your record suggests to me that you're a follower, Larry.'

Bug wouldn't look at either of them now. He stared at the scratched surface of the table. 'I was watching the football that night.'

'Where's the money?' Dunbar asked. 'Are we going to find it at your place? Some of it? All of it?'

'No.'

'So where is it?'

Bug shrugged. 'What money?'

'You know what money,' Dunbar said. 'The seventy thousand dollars you stole from Frances Rourke.'

The amount took Bug by surprise and for a split second he wasn't able to hide it. He jerked his gaze upward toward Dunbar before looking quickly away.

'I got no idea about any money. You got to let me go. You can't hold me without no charges.'

Dunbar nodded toward Pulford now and she opened the door and spoke to someone down the corridor.

'You go back to your cell and think about things, Larry,' Dunbar said. 'If it's charges you want, by tomorrow morning you'll have all the charges you could ever dream of.'

The uniform took Bug back downstairs to the holding cells. By that time the search warrant was prepared and signed. Dunbar and Pulford got a car from the garage and drove to the crossroads of Bonwick.

'You get anything from his phone?' Dunbar asked as they drove.

'We haven't found his phone,' Pulford said. 'He didn't have one on him.'

'In his truck maybe?'

'I didn't see one,' Pulford said. 'Forensics is giving it the once over.'

'Any chance that it could have gotten lost in the scuffle out in the woods?'

'I went there with the towing company,' Pulford said. 'I didn't see anything and I had a pretty good look around.'

She was driving. They were out of the city now, running the country road heading west. It was a clear day, the afternoon autumn sun bright in their eyes. Dunbar flipped down the visor on his side.

'Tell me again how it went down.'

Pulford repeated the story as she knew it.

'How the hell did he run the plate number?'

'He's not saying,' Pulford said. 'Anyway, he went to the house to have a look, and somehow Murdock spotted him. They did a cat and mouse and ended up in the woods, stuck in the mud. Next thing you know, Burns is dropping Murdock on his head in front of the precinct. Signed, sealed and delivered.'

Dunbar chuckled. 'Making us look bad.'

'Well, if he'd given us the license plate number like he should have, we would have accomplished the very same thing. I would hope that we would have done it with a little more finesse. You saw Murdock's face. We're going to hear about that when he finally smartens up enough to hire a lawyer.'

'I'm having trouble finding much sympathy for Murdock,' Dunbar told her. 'Did you notice his expression when I gave him the bogus amount on the money?'

'I did,' Pulford replied. 'He's not much of a card player.'

'And he's guilty as sin.'

The address was a little bungalow hard on the edge of the village. The forensics van was already there. Bill Valder was leaning against the front fender, smoking a cigarette.

'Been inside?' Dunbar asked.

'Waiting on the warrant,' Valder said.

Dunbar showed him the paper and Valder nodded.

'What about the truck?' Pulford asked.

'We gave it a good going over,' Valder said. 'Nothing of interest. Found a couple of roaches, some residue, appears to be coke or meth or both. Beer caps. No prints other than Murdock's though. Kinda strange. You figure there were three of them in the truck that night?'

'They must have wiped it,' Dunbar said. 'Cell phone?'

'Nope.'

Valder and his men knocked the front door in and went inside. The place was a dump, smelling of garbage and unwashed laundry. The bathroom was disgusting. There was no computer and no cell phone and nothing at all that was connected to the robbery at the farmhouse. The television was twenty years old, hooked to an antenna on the roof.

'Not exactly teched up, was he?' Valder said.

There was some mail on the kitchen table. Mostly flyers and a hydro bill. Dunbar walked outside and had a look in the shed in the back yard. The building was partly collapsed and was filled with car parts and junk. He asked Valder and his crew to sift through it all on the off chance there might be some of the money stashed there, even though Dunbar thought it unlikely. When he and Pulford left, they headed east toward Talbotville.

They stopped at the narrow lane where the Dodge pickup had been parked and spent twenty minutes looking around. There was nothing there. They found Carl Burns at the farm, driving a tractor with a hay wagon behind, the wagon loaded with saws and squares and various other tools, as well as an air compressor and electrical generator. As they parked and watched, Burns backed the wagon and tractor into a large machine shed. He shut the noisy engine down and walked over to meet them as they got out of the car. He had a carpenter's pencil behind one ear, and a makeshift sling holding his left arm. It was growing dark, the temperature dropping.

'I hear you had an eventful Sunday,' Dunbar said.

'Wasn't the way I planned it,' Carl said. 'Things got out of hand.'

'How'd you run that plate number, Carl?'

Carl exhaled heavily, taking a moment. 'Is that important?'

'I suppose not,' Dunbar said after a pause of his own. 'There is such a thing on the books as a citizen's arrest. And I don't feel like asking you a question you're not about to answer. So let me ask you this one – are you one hundred per cent certain that Murdock was one of the men in the house that night?'

Carl did not hesitate. 'Yes.'

'All right,' Dunbar said. 'And to be clear – he's the guy you said was more like the second in command? Not the leader?'

Carl nodded. 'The leader was the big guy with the teardrop tattoo.'

Dunbar nodded. 'I didn't figure Murdock to be any kind of a mastermind.'

'What's he saying?' Carl asked.

'Nothing so far,' Pulford replied.

'He doesn't seem to understand what he's in for yet,' Dunbar said. 'After the indictments come down and he lawyers up, he might have a better grasp of what's going on. Maybe then he'll be willing to talk to us.'

Hearing that, Carl fell silent for a moment, as if something in the statement bothered him. Pulford watched him closely, waiting.

'Does that mean you'll offer him a deal?' Carl asked.

'We need the other two names,' Pulford said. 'Sometimes concessions are made.'

'But he's not going to walk.'

'He's not going to walk, Carl,' Dunbar assured him. 'Absolutely not.'

'When are the indictments?'

'Tomorrow morning.'

Carl offered them a beer and Dunbar was about to accept when Pulford said she needed to get back to the city. They left Carl Burns standing in the lane beside the burned-out shell of the farmhouse. They drove in silence for a few miles, following the river.

'It would be nice if Frances Rourke woke up,' Dunbar said.

'Why is that?' Pulford asked. 'Aside from the obvious?'

Dunbar was quiet for a few moments, gathering his thinking. 'Burns can ID Murdock, and the leader when we find him. But other than that, you know what a defense lawyer is going to say. He didn't actually *see* what happened to the two women. He didn't *see* anybody start the fire. He was in the basement when that all happened. A defense lawyer is going to say that it's all speculative, and that he has to confine his testimony to what he saw. And a judge might agree.'

'But he saw the robbery go down,' Pulford said. 'He can provide the details on that. And we have the bank to back him up.'

'He didn't see them take the money. They might say it burned in the fire.'

'Shit, maybe it did,' Pulford said. 'That's why it hasn't turned up. These guys are such fuck-ups they started a fire and left without the cash.'

'You don't believe that,' Dunbar said.

'No, I guess not.'

Dunbar sighed. 'It would be nice if Frances Rourke woke up.'

TWENTY-TWO

Carl arrived at the courthouse shortly before nine the next morning. To get inside he had to bypass a considerable media presence – TV crews, newspaper reporters, radio station remotes. Carl was grateful that they didn't know who he was – not yet anyway – or of his role in the case. There were more cameras in the corridor outside the main courtroom but none inside, where they were not allowed. Carl slipped past them and went in.

The indictments were first up on the docket. Carl remained on his feet, standing just inside the rear door to the large courtroom. He spotted both Dunbar and Pulford, sitting on a bench near the empty jurors' box. A few minutes before the judge arrived, a uniformed officer led Bug in through a back entrance and deposited him in the prisoners' dock. He was wearing the same clothes he'd had on when Carl had knocked him unconscious in the pine forest. The judge was announced. He was a fat man in his sixties with curly gray hair and heavy jowls. Carl missed his name.

Bug sat slumped in a wooden chair and watched the prosecutor as she read off the litany of charges. The judge had called her Mathews. She was a tall blonde, maybe fifty, and she wore black horn-rimmed glasses. She took her time detailing the indictments, nine charges in all.

Bug glanced around the room as she did, his eyes flicking over Dunbar and Pulford before taking in the people in the gallery. He seemed to be looking for a familiar face, one that he didn't find. When he spotted Carl his expression grew hard and he glared at him before looking away. Carl kept his eyes on him, watching for a reaction to the charges as they were read. There was nothing there. When Mathews was finished, the judge told Bug to stand.

'Do you understand the charges against you, sir?'

Bug shrugged. 'Yup. And I'm saying not guilty to the whole lot.'

'You're not required to enter a plea today,' the judge told him. 'These are indictments.'

'I'll enter it anyway.'

The judge spoke louder, leaning forward as if in an effort to penetrate the oblivious nature of the man he was addressing. 'I see you are without representation.'

'What is that?' Bug asked.

'You don't have a lawyer.'

Bug looked around as if expecting to find a lawyer standing beside him. 'I don't.'

'Get one,' the judge told him. 'Or the court will appoint one for you.'

'Yes, sir.'

The sarcasm did not escape the judge, who stared at Bug for a long moment before nodding to the uniform to lead the prisoner away.

'Hold on,' Bug said. Speaking to the judge.

'Yes?'

'I would like to be released on my own . . . recognition, or whatever.'

'Your own recognizance,' the judge corrected. 'You are charged with first degree murder, arson, robbery and home invasion, among other things. And you would like to be released on your own recognizance?'

'Yes, sir.'

'You are a dreamer.' The judge turned to prosecutor Mathews. 'Next case.'

As the officer led Bug to the holding cells, Dunbar and Pulford left by the back entrance. Pearce Walker caught up to them in the parking lot. He was there representing a client on a drunk driving charge and had been in the courtroom for the indictments.

'Ted,' he called across the lot, causing Dunbar to stop.

Walker was wearing his standard pinstripe, with the carnation in the lapel. His 'costume', as the staff around the courthouse called it.

'What's the story on the Murdock charges? Didn't I hear there were three people involved?'

'That's right,' Dunbar said. He glanced at Pulford, who was watching Walker with interest.

'But just one collar so far,' Walker said. 'The other two are still in the wind?'

'So far.'

Walker made a show of straightening his tie. One of his theatrical courtroom moves. 'Any discovery yet?'

'The arrest was two days ago,' Dunbar said. 'How could we have discovery at this point?'

Walker smiled. It had been a stupid question. 'What about the arrest? I'm hearing it was some sort of vigilante deal and Murdock got the shit kicked out of him. By the looks of his face, I believe it.'

'I was up north at the time,' Dunbar said.

'Right.' Walker smiled. 'You don't know anything about it. But I heard it. I have to say, that's pretty unorthodox.'

'As opposed to murder and arson?' Pulford asked.

'Spare me that, detective.' Walker turned toward the court-house. 'But I think I will have a little talk with Mr Murdock. I'm going to assume that the vigilantes neglected to read the man his rights.'

'I read him his rights,' Pulford said. 'Sunday morning, on the sidewalk in front of the precinct.'

'Well, whether that is true or not, he's going to need a lawyer,' Walker said.

Pulford was fuming at the suggestion she had lied. Dunbar stepped in.

'Tell him the smart move would be to give us the names of the other two. It can only help him down the road.'

'Thanks for the advice, Ted,' Walker said. 'But I've done this before. And I wouldn't make any such suggestion until I find out if you even have a case against the man.'

He walked away. Pulford and Dunbar watched and when Walker was inside the building she spoke.

'What does he want with that? He doesn't think Murdock can afford him?'

'No,' Dunbar said slowly. 'But he knows this is going to be a big case, with lots of media. Walker will do it on the court's dime just to get his face on TV.'

'He's a pig.'

'Sometimes even pigs get to be famous,' Dunbar said.

Carl went from the courthouse to the hospital where he sat with Frances for a half hour. He talked to her about the farm, of how well sales had been leading up to Christmas, and he told her that the sugar shack was coming along. He said that he needed her help with the interior details – tables, chairs, the equipment for making syrup. He decided not to mention what had happened with the license plate number and Murdock, or the arrest afterward. He was concerned it might upset her, even hearing about it. He still trusted she could hear him.

When he was leaving the hospital he spotted Harkness talking to somebody in the foyer, a woman in a tight skirt and sweater. Harkness was smiling, charming her. She was smiling back. Carl went over and stood off to the side until the woman moved away, heading for the elevators. Harkness was aware of his presence and now turned a cool eye on him. It seemed he would walk away if Carl didn't call to him.

'Anything new with Frances?'

Harkness took a moment. 'I'm not sure how to answer that. The bruising is nearly gone but now we suspect there is fluid on that part of the brain.'

'What's that mean?' Carl asked.

Harkness shrugged. 'It might be affecting the situation or it might be nothing. It could gradually dissipate as her condition improves.'

'Is her condition improving?'

Harkness had misspoken and he didn't like the question. 'We'll continue to monitor it,' he said after a moment. 'There is a possibility that we do surgery at some point, to drain the fluid.'

'When would that be?'

'Not now,' Harkness said. 'As I mentioned, we're hoping the fluid disappears on its own. Now I have to finish rounds.'

'Keep me in the loop,' Carl requested.

Harkness nodded and walked away without another word. Presumably he was running late, although he hadn't seemed overly rushed while flirting with the woman in the skirt.

On the drive home Carl stopped at the lumber yard and picked up the cedar shingles he'd ordered. Frances would get the roof she wanted but when would she be able to see it? It was over two weeks since she'd been injured, since she'd lost consciousness after being hurled down the stairs into the cellar. Carl had been certain she would have awakened by now. He wondered for the first time if she was getting the best medical care. There were other hospitals, other doctors.

His mind went back to Murdock, standing in court earlier and asking to be set free without bond. Was he that stupid? It seemed likely that he was. Even so, he had refused, so far anyway, to cooperate with the police. Maybe Carl should have tried to get the names of the other two from the man before turning him over to Pulford.

As he approached the farm he had a thought and slowed down to pull on to the lane where Murdock had parked his truck that night. Carl got out and walked up and down the roadway for a time, looking in the long grass for something, anything, that might be a clue. He was aware that Dunbar and Pulford had been there yesterday yet still he felt compelled to look. It happened in movies all the time, where someone returns to the scene and finds a key piece of evidence everyone else has overlooked. Carl spent the better part of an hour walking the lane and then the road between there and the farm, the route the three men would have taken to get to the house. He found nothing.

Life wasn't a movie.

Chino spent the morning burning the insulation away from two hundred pounds of copper wire he'd bought the night before from Digger Bagley. He was in the yard just past dawn, starting a fire from some half-rotted fence posts and hardwood skids, getting it good and hot before tossing the coils into the flames.

Bagley had stolen the wire a couple of nights earlier from a railroad compound along the tracks somewhere up west. The price for scrap copper was high but the yards preferred it to be clean. Not only that, but clean made it impossible to trace. Bagley wasn't ambitious enough to burn the insulation away so he'd shown up at Chino's at two in the morning, half bagged, rousting Chino from bed and haggling for twenty minutes before selling the coils for a hundred dollars. Burned clean, it would be worth six or seven times that.

The insulation was rubber-based and it sent up a thick black plume when burned. Tending the fire, Chino had seen the farmer Vanhizen standing out in his yard staring at the smoke which was drifting his way, billowing black against the blue sky. Even from that distance Chino thought he could see the expression on the farmer's face. Who was Chino to be fouling his air? Arrogant fucker.

Shortly before noon, Chino left the smoldering coils and walked out to the mailbox to see if his pension check had arrived. He got four hundred a month from his trucking days, for a back injury he'd invented after falling from a tractor trailer in a yard in Dearborn. The check wasn't there. He went inside to catch the news at noon from the Rose City affiliate. It had been on his mind all morning.

Bug made top of the hour. There was no footage of the little bastard, but the reporter standing outside the courtroom described him and his reactions as the indictments had come down. There were nine in all, and they were pretty much what Chino had expected. The reporter ended the piece by saying that two suspects were still at large. She did not know at this time whether or not Mr Murdock was cooperating with the police. Which meant that the cops weren't telling the reporters anything.

Chino clicked the set off. Mr Murdock had better fucking not be cooperating with the police. Since hearing of the arrest early Monday, Chino had been back and forth on that. He was pretty sure that Bug was too scared of Chino to talk. He was glad now that Bug's cell phone server had cut off his account months ago for non-payment. If that hadn't happened, the cops would already have connected him to

Chino. They would have been knocking on Chino's door Monday morning.

But they were working on it, Chino knew. They'd be telling Bug all sorts of shit to get him to roll over. What they were going to do for him if he did, and what it meant for him if he didn't. Chino had no idea if Bug had the guts to hang in. He didn't have the brains of a mouse. If the cops promised him a truck load of ice cream he might tell them he was Jesse James.

If Bug was the joker in the deck, then the Indian Taylor was the wild card. Bug wasn't afraid of the Indian, so he might be tempted to give him up. Chino was pretty sure the Indian would talk to save his hide. He hadn't wanted to be at the farmhouse in the first place and Chino could see him spilling everything to get himself a deal. There was no trail between him and Chino – no calls or texts – but he knew where Chino lived. And that would be enough. Of course, that was *if* Bug gave the Indian up. Chino guessed that Taylor was watching the news himself right now, and shitting his pants in the process.

He'd been hoping that his check would be in the mailbox. He could sell the copper in the yard, cash the check and take off somewhere for a while. Head north and rent a cabin under a false name. Wait and see if the cops fingered him. It would be all over the news if they did, and at that point he'd have to make a real run for it. He wasn't going down on this.

It was a matter of time, he knew. He was lying to himself if he thought Bug would keep quiet forever. The reporter had said that Bug showed in court with no lawyer and the judge had told him to get one. The lawyer would be working Bug too, advising him to strike a deal. A matter of time.

Chino boiled two hot dogs for lunch and ate them between slices of white bread. As he was finishing he heard tires on the gravel outside. He jumped to his feet, his pulse racing, thinking it had to be the cops. Instead it was Vanhizen, rolling to a stop behind the wheel of his new GMC three quarter ton pickup. As Chino watched he climbed out, hitching his pants as he looked in the direction of the yard, where the burning coils still trailed smoke into the air. Chino lit a cigarette and walked out on to the sagging back porch.

'You burning tires?' Vanhizen demanded.

'Nope.'

'You're burning something.' The farmer was a big man, wearing navy blue overalls and a John Deere cap.

Chino gestured to the rising smoke. 'No shit.'

'It's against the law,' Vanhizen said. 'I doubt very much you have a permit. And even if you do, it's against the law to be burning rubber.'

'I was cutting up an old escalator and the belt caught fire,' Chino said by way of apology. He needed to back off a little. Vanhizen was the type to call the cops and the timing was bad on that account.

'Must have been a big belt.'

'It was,' Chino said.

Vanhizen shook his head, turning to give the place the once over. 'All this mess, I wonder you don't have more problems like that. Just asking for trouble.'

It came to Chino in that instant. 'What will you give me for it?'

'What?'

'You heard me,' Chino said. 'Make an offer on the place.'

Vanhizen squinted at Chino. 'You're serious?'

Chino nodded. 'I put it on real estate, you're going to pay them too.'

The big farmer suddenly went from arrogant prick to friendly buyer albeit one looking for a bargain. He began to walk around the yard, evaluating the place. What was there to evaluate? Three acres, a knockdown bungalow, a rusted steel shed full of old tools and torches and a scrap yard in behind, scattered with corroded farm equipment and truck parts. None of it even mattered to Vanhizen, Chino knew. All that he cared about was the three acres. That, and wiping the rest of it from his line of sight. One day with a bulldozer would take care of that.

'What were you thinking?' Vanhizen asked.

'What were you thinking?'

The farmer balked. He wanted Chino to name a price. He was loath to make an offer that might be too high.

'I have to talk to the bank.'

That was bullshit, Chino knew. From what he'd heard,

Vanhizen either owned or leased over four thousand acres. He didn't need the bank's permission to buy Chino's patch of ground. Still, he nodded. 'Talk to the bank. I was going to call a real estate agent this afternoon.'

'Don't do that until I get back to you,' Vanhizen urged. 'What's the hurry anyway?'

'I'm thinking about taking a trip,' Chino said.

Now his mind was working. He knew that nothing could happen as quick as he needed it to happen. There would be lawyers and title searches and possibly even a survey of the property required. He had to move soon.

'Tell you what,' he said. 'Get your shit together and come up with a price. If I like it, I'll make the deal without even talking to an agent. But I'll want twenty-five grand on the spot and I'm talking cash.'

Vanhizen was nodding his head as Chino talked. He could see a bargain in it, keeping it away from the agents and their percentages.

'I'll get back to you later today,' he said.

'How fast can you get the money?'

'We agree on a price, you'll have the down payment tomorrow.'

'Get to it,' Chino told him.

TWENTY-THREE

Pulford called Dunbar on the landline, after failing to get him on his cell. Martha answered.

'He's just in the shower,' she said. 'Should I get him?'

'Let him dry off first,' Pulford said.

'So it's not urgent?'

'Maybe not urgent,' Pulford replied. 'But definitely interesting.'

Dunbar called her back fifteen minutes later. He came downstairs, dressed for work, carrying his Browning and shield, which he placed on the island counter. He'd eaten earlier and Martha had his second cup of coffee waiting. Pulford answered on the first ring.

'The money's moving,' she said.

She didn't say much more, other than that Dunbar should come to the station. He thought about the possibilities as he drove downtown. They'd been waiting for something to break. Larry Murdock didn't have a lot of friends but the ones they had talked to were all disclaiming any knowledge of the home invasion. Dunbar did learn that Murdock used to pull break and enters with a guy named Snider. They hadn't been very good at it, particularly at fencing the stolen goods, and had been busted a few times. Dunbar had checked Snider out, thinking he might have been involved at the farm, but it turned out he was doing time down east for breaking and entering. Obviously he'd changed his location but not his ways.

'Murdock's buddies would know if he was spreading money around,' Pulford had said at one point.

Dunbar was in agreement. But maybe that just meant that Murdock *wasn't* spending the money. But why the hell not? A smart crook might sit on it for a few months, or even longer, but Dunbar wouldn't put Larry Murdock anywhere close to that category.

At the station he and Pulford walked to the desk of Burt Fisher, who was working the Ken Hubert case.

'I've never been so popular,' he smiled. 'Everybody wants to talk about crooked Kenny.'

'So how did this come about?' Dunbar asked.

'You know the background obviously,' Fisher said. 'The councilor got busted for taking bribes and peddling influence and all that. Well, in the ongoing investigation we served warrants on his house out by the lake. Lo and behold, we found some hundred dollar bills from your home invasion.'

'The marked bills from the bank,' Pulford said.

'That's right.'

'How the hell did they end up in Hubert's pocket?' Dunbar asked. 'You're not going to suggest *he* was involved in that business at the farm?'

Fisher laughed. 'That was about the only thing the slippery bastard wasn't involved in.'

'Then how did he come by the money?' Pulford asked.

'I can tell you,' Fisher said. 'But wouldn't you rather hear it from the source?'

'Is he singing?' Dunbar asked.

'Like Pavarotti. Did you ever meet a politician who could keep his mouth shut?'

A half hour later they were sitting in an interrogation room with Councilor Ken Hubert, the same room where Dunbar and Pulford had met with Larry Murdock two days earlier. Hubert was awaiting his bail hearing and he wasn't wearing the jail-house jumpsuit. He was dressed in khakis and a polo shirt, what he'd been wearing when he was arrested. His hair was neatly combed and he had shaved. He had a fleshy, round face and a big gut, straining at the shirt. He was loose and relaxed.

'We've met,' he said to Dunbar.

'Yes,' Dunbar said. 'A thing at the community center.'

'That center has been a huge success,' Hubert said in his hearty politician's voice. 'A boon for the city.' The councilor turned to Pulford. 'You I have not met. I would have remembered.'

'Detective Pulford,' Fisher said.

Hubert showed his best smile. 'About time the city got around to hiring some good-looking cops.'

Pulford ignored the compliment. 'Would you be willing to talk about the money they found in your house? Specifically the new hundred dollar bills?'

'Sure, I'll talk about it. I'm yours, detective.'

Pulford stopped shy of rolling her eyes. 'The money is of interest to us as part of a separate investigation. Nothing to do with . . . your situation.'

Hubert leaned forward and dropped his voice to a whisper. 'Somebody rob a bank?'

Pulford glanced to Dunbar for aid.

'Where'd you get the money, Ken?' Dunbar asked.

Hubert leaned back, smiling. 'It came to me as partial payment for services rendered.'

'What kind of services?'

Hubert kept his eyes on Pulford as he spoke. 'If you have been reading the papers, you know that I am being investigated for taking money in connection with certain projects in the city. Some of those claims happen to be true. I have in the past periodically accepted payment in return for influencing bids. Keep in mind that the projects in question have helped our city a great deal. The community center you mentioned is just one example.'

Dunbar nodded. 'Who gave you the money?'

'Indulge me a moment longer,' Hubert said, holding up his hand. 'I just want you to know that I am not the mercenary evil-doer you might have heard. I may be a sinner, but I have been looking out for our city in the process. My political hero is Huey Long.' He paused. 'The money came from an organization called Wild Lucifer.'

'The bike gang?' Dunbar asked.

'Oh, they are much more than that,' Hubert said.

Dunbar glanced at Fisher, who cocked an eyebrow and then nodded toward Hubert as if to say, *Let him talk.*

'Why is a bike gang paying you money?' Pulford asked.

'Do you think they just run drugs and strippers these days?' Hubert asked. 'That's old school. The Wild is involved in a lot of things. For instance, they have majority ownership in Lake City Construction. Silent ownership, I might add. LCC won the contract for the downtown sewage project last year. They've done a lot of other work in the city over the past ten years. They built the new administration building on Main, for instance.'

'And you've been involved with them getting the contracts?' Dunbar suggested.

Hubert showed his palms. 'Come on. This is just standard procedure. How do you think the world operates? Keep in mind these people do good work. So why wouldn't I steer things in their direction? And if I happen to make a few bucks along the way, well, that's the way the world operates too.'

'Except it's illegal,' Pulford reminded him.

'Don't be judgmental, detective. That's not your job. I was this close to asking you out for a drink.' Hubert paused. 'You know, as soon as I make bail.'

'Right,' Pulford said.

'When did you receive the money in question?' Dunbar asked.

'That money,' Hubert said, thinking about it. 'That was last Sunday, I believe.'

'For what project in particular?'

'Nothing in particular,' Hubert replied. 'That was just . . . maintenance.'

'So you're on a retainer?' Pulford suggested.

'Something like that.'

'Who gave you the money?' Dunbar asked.

'Wild Lucifer.'

'Who specifically?'

'A man named Bones.' Hubert smiled. 'I have a feeling that's not his Christian name.' He looked at Pulford again. It seemed she was his main point of interest. 'So when are you going to tell me what this is about? What's the mystery with the hundred dollar bills? Are they counterfeit by any chance?'

'No,' Pulford said.

'That's all you have to say?' he persisted.

'Yes.'

'Whatever happened to quid pro quo?' Hubert joked. 'Here I am playing ball and I'm getting nothing in return.'

'Sorry,' Pulford told him, her tone clearly indicating that it wasn't going to work like that.

Dunbar knew there was no point in asking the councilor where the bike gang had happened upon the marked bills. The councilor wouldn't know. Dunbar was convinced that Hubert had nothing to do with the home invasion at the Rourke farm. After a few more questions, he decided to send him back to his cell. They called for an officer and as they waited Dunbar thought of one more question.

'You're being awfully cooperative, councilor. Why is that?'

'Because I want one thing,' Hubert said. 'Redemption. I fucked up and I have to pay for that. But I have been one of the best civil servants Rose City has ever seen. I love this city. So I will admit to my transgressions and pay the price for same. But then I will return. Mark my words – I will be re-elected as councilor. And maybe even mayor, down the road.' He paused. 'People love tales of redemption, don't you think?'

When he was gone Pulford looked at Fisher. 'What the hell was that?'

Fisher smiled. 'What did I tell you?'

'But are we buying this?' Pulford asked.

'I think we are,' Dunbar said. 'He's not going to make up a story like that. Plus, you heard him – he's baring his soul. If he knew what the connection was, if he knew about the murder and the robbery, he might not be so free and easy with his mouth. But he doesn't know. The guy thinks he's in a movie or something.'

'So you're thinking the bikers for the home invasion?' Fisher asked.

Dunbar shrugged. 'Sure looks that way. It doesn't seem to fit their business model these days but who knows who they have in their membership and what they're into? They had the money in their possession and that's what we've been waiting for.'

'If it looks like a duck and quacks like a duck,' Fisher said.

Pulford regarded him for a moment before nodding.

'There's something that doesn't fit, though,' Dunbar realized. 'What's the connection between Larry Murdock and the bikers? We never came across anything like that in his background.'

'Maybe he's a hanger-on?' Pulford suggested. 'A wannabe?'

'Or maybe your witness – the Burns character – fingered the wrong guy,' Fisher suggested.

'He didn't finger the wrong guy,' Dunbar said. 'Besides, we have Murdock's truck at the scene. Could be that Murdock's tied up with the Wild on some other level. They've been known to use these bottom feeders to do their dirty work. We'll see what the Wild has to say about him.'

'We're going to need warrants,' Pulford said.

Dunbar turned to Fisher. 'Where are they keeping Hubert?'

'The cells down below,' Fisher said. 'We were going to ship him out to county but he's a cinch to make bail so we didn't bother.'

'Can you stick him in seg for a couple of days?' Dunbar asked. 'In case he gets antsy and decides he needs to give the bikers a heads-up.'

Fisher nodded. 'I'm a little surprised he rolled over on them like he did. Why would he think that's a good idea?'

'Redemption,' Dunbar told him.

Tommy Jakes paid Billy a visit that afternoon. First he talked to Montreal. The coke was coming in that night. Tommy got into his Escalade and drove to Tareytown.

Billy was in the driveway alongside his house, lying underneath a twenty-year-old Mustang, just his legs sticking out from the vehicle, which was raised up on jacks. There was a large red toolbox on the ground, drawers open to the various compartments. It was a cold day. Too damn cold to be working on a car outside, Tommy thought.

'Hey,' he said, getting out of the Cadillac.

Billy shifted his body beneath the Mustang, trying to get a look at the visitor. Tommy crouched down in the gravel to show his face.

'You're Billy?'

'Who are you?'

'Tommy Jakes.'

The Indian didn't say anything to that. Tommy saw now that he was removing the car's rusted brake lines. There were lengths of new lines on the driveway, along with a quart container of brake fluid.

'You need a garage with some heat in it, son,' Tommy said.

The Indian grunted a reply, and continued in his work. Tommy straightened up and had a look at the house and the yard behind. There was a Pontiac parked in the driveway, ahead of the Mustang. Neither vehicle was in particularly good condition.

'What year's your Mustang?'

'Not mine,' Billy said. 'I'm fixing it for a guy.'

'Paying job?'

'Yeah.'

Tommy knelt down again. 'Hell of a way to make a living. I know Bones has made you a better offer.'

'Fixing brakes ain't against the law.'

'I guess it's not,' Tommy said. 'But I'm thinking it's not all that lucrative either. What are you going to make on a job like this?'

'Flat rate, twenty bucks an hour.'

'Shit. So you're going to lie on the cold ground all day and you won't make two hundred dollars. My grandmother always warned me against lying on the cold ground. She said I'd get cold in my kidneys. You ever worry about that?'

'No.'

'Well, she was about half-baked anyway,' Tommy said. 'Started drinking rye every morning about nine o'clock, just to put up with my grandfather's bullshit.'

Billy came out from under the car now, with a pair of twisted and rusted brake lines in his hand. His face was flecked with dirt from the undercarriage and there was a smear of grease across one cheek. Like the war paint of his ancestors, Tommy thought. 'Point is, why not come work for me?' he asked. 'You made the run once. It'll be easier this time. Not only that, but this time you'll get paid.'

Billy didn't look at him. 'I don't like the risks.'

'There's risk in everything. This car could fall off those jack stands and crush you like a cockroach. Where's your twenty bucks an hour then?'

Billy took one of the rusty brake lines and placed it alongside a new one, checking it for length. Tommy reached into his pocket and took out a wad of fifty dollar bills, wrapped with an elastic band. 'Here's a thousand, good faith money,' he said. 'Make the run tomorrow and there'll be another four grand in it for you when you get back. That's five grand for a day's work. And you don't have to deal with Chino.'

He held the money toward Billy but the Indian, still measuring the lines, ignored the gesture. Tommy waited a moment before placing the cash on top of the toolbox. Billy glanced at it and away.

Tommy laughed. 'Bones told me you don't have a fuck of a lot to say. He wasn't joking. You realize this could be a steady gig for you. Once every couple weeks. You got other prospects, other than fixing clunkers in your driveway for peanuts?'

'Like I said, it ain't against the law, fixing cars,' Billy said.

'No, it's not. But you want to know what is? Murder, for one. Home invasion is two. And then there's arson and robbery and assault.'

Now the Indian looked at him.

'Oh, that got your attention,' Tommy said. 'I'm a smart man, Billy. I can put two and two together. Now, I couldn't care less about Chino or that dipshit Murdock. But I'd hate to see you go down on this, Billy.'

The Indian looked at the shiny new brake line in his hand. After a moment he glanced at Tommy and then walked over to pick up the wad of cash from the toolbox. He held it in his hand for a long moment, as if weighing it, before shoving it into the pocket of his jean jacket.

Tommy smiled. 'See you tomorrow morning.'

TWENTY-FOUR

While Pulford dealt with the search warrants Dunbar drove downtown to have a talk with Pearce Walker. He'd heard from sources around the courthouse that Walker had taken Larry Murdock on as a client. If it was true, he was obviously doing it on the taxpayer's dime. Murdock couldn't afford a haircut, let alone a lawyer in Walker's price range.

Walker was in his outer office talking to his secretary when Dunbar walked in. The two had been joking about something and Walker held the smile as he looked at the newcomer.

'Tara, check the day book,' he said. 'Does the detective here have an appointment?'

The woman named Tara was apparently used to Walker's humor and she did not bother to check any book.

'I was in the neighborhood,' Dunbar said.

'I'm pretty busy,' Walker told him.

'No, you're not.'

'All right, what's this about?' Walker asked. 'As if I didn't know.'

'I thought we should have a talk about Larry Murdock.'

Walker smiled. 'Yes, let's do that.'

Winking at the woman, he led the way into his office and

closed the door behind them. Dunbar took a seat on a leather chair and Walker sat on a matching couch against the wall. He was in his shirtsleeves, his tie loosened.

'You realize,' he said, 'that there isn't much to discuss until I get a look at discovery.'

'Maybe there is,' Dunbar said. 'We need those other two names, Pearce. And Murdock can provide them.'

'You seem convinced that my client is guilty, detective. Have you guys done away with due process over there?'

Dunbar ignored the shot. 'There were three people involved that night. I get the impression that Murdock is a sheep. We're pretty sure somebody else was the leader. A big guy with a teardrop tattoo. Murdock can do himself a big favor if he gives us the names.'

'My client assures me he is innocent,' Walker said. 'Wouldn't he be admitting guilt if he started rattling off names?'

'I suppose you need to play it that way,' Dunbar said.

'The presumption of innocence, detective. It's common knowledge that your department has struck out big time on this one. How do I know that this isn't a giant witch hunt, that you didn't collar my client in the hopes that he heard something in a bar somewhere?'

'We have an eyewitness.'

'That eyewitness is Carl Burns. I have learned a little about him in the past forty-eight hours. He has a criminal record for starters. Not only that, but he was found on the lawn the night of the fire, unconscious, bleeding profusely from wounds on both wrists. There are rumors of a murder/suicide attempt. A doctor tells me that the man nearly died from a lack of blood, which means that his mental capacities would have been impaired on the night in question. A couple of weeks later he goes Rambo on my client, an innocent man, involves him in a high speed chase and then viciously assaults and kidnaps him.' Walker smiled. 'And this is the guy who's going to put my client at the scene of the crime? He's all you got, detective?'

'Murdock's truck was at the scene and he lied about it. Why would he do that?'

'No idea,' Walker shrugged. 'Maybe a knee-jerk reaction

from a guy who's been in lots of trouble and is basically a dimwit. That doesn't put him in the house.'

'He was in the house.'

'You saying it doesn't make it true. And it certainly doesn't mean squat in a court of law.'

'He was in the house, and he would be smart to give us those names,' Dunbar persisted. 'It could mean the difference between a murder conviction and one for accessory. Besides, doesn't it bother you that these people are out there on the loose?'

'Not really,' Walker said. 'They are your problem. But since you took the trouble to drive down here, I will tell you this. I've now had two lengthy interviews with Mr Murdock. He's an innocent man. If you want the names of the *three* people who were in the house that night, you're going to have to find them on your own.'

Pulford was still waiting for the paperwork when Dunbar got back to the station and told her about his conversation with Pearce Walker. Listening, she doodled on a pad on her desk, making circles inside of circles.

'So he's telling Murdock he's going to walk,' she said. 'And as long as Murdock believes that, he's never going to give us anything. Because that would be the same as a confession.'

'That's right.'

'Fucking Walker,' Pulford said. 'All he thinks about is his cred, what this means to his profile. He couldn't care less about what happened out there that night. Why couldn't Murdock have hired a public defender with a heart?'

'Walker has a heart,' Dunbar said. 'It happens to be made of stone.'

Pulford sighed. 'You know he's never going to let Murdock testify. Not a chance he'll put that guy on the stand.'

'Not a chance.'

Pulford gave up on her doodling. 'That leaves us with the bike gang. And just because they've been caught leading a crooked councilor around by his nose doesn't mean they're going to tell us anything about this situation.'

'I wouldn't think so.'

'So we're back to Murdock as our best lead.'

'And that's a problem,' Dunbar said. 'Murdock is never going to roll over on anybody from the Wild. He would be signing his own death warrant.'

'Does Walker know about the bike gang's involvement?'

'I don't think so,' Dunbar said. 'Unless his client told him. I sure as hell didn't.'

Pulford began absently tapping the pen on the desk, like a drummer hitting a snare. 'I still don't get that part.'

'What part?'

'The bike gang's involvement,' Pulford said. 'Especially after talking to Hubert earlier. It sounds as if they're getting rich through white collar crime these days. All of a sudden they pull this home invasion shit?' She paused, thinking. 'With his past, you don't think there's a chance that Burns is connected to the bikers, do you? And maybe this could be some sort of revenge scenario?'

Dunbar considered the idea. 'That would mean that he knows what's behind this. If he does, he's a hell of an actor. And why would he be tracking Murdock's plate number and chasing him around the countryside if he knew who it was all along?'

'Maybe he made up the story about the turkey receipt and the plate number.'

'If so, he took his own sweet time doing it,' Dunbar said. 'And keep in mind he could just have given us the plate number.'

'I suppose,' Pulford admitted. 'But it's something to think about. Maybe he crossed them somewhere along the way and doesn't want to tell us about it.'

'The bike gang is the key,' Dunbar said. 'We need to know who was in on this and why. Maybe tonight we'll get some answers.'

Carl opened two bottles of beer and handed one to Rufus Canfield, who was sitting on a pine plank laid across two sawhorses, his legs dangling above the floor of the sugar shack.

'So you know him?' Carl asked.

'Pearce Walker?' Rufus said. 'Only by reputation.'

'And what is that?' Carl pulled a bundle of shingles over and sat down.

'He's a bit of a dandy,' Rufus said. 'Wears fedoras and fur coats, that sort of thing. Loves the limelight, craves high profile cases. Seems not to be bothered by the more venal natures of some of his clients.'

Carl had a swig of beer. 'I would assume he is expensive?'

'No question about that.'

'How would Murdock afford him?'

'Oh, I'd say he's doing this on the court's stipend,' Rufus said. 'He knows this will be a big case, with lots of opportunities to preen for the gallery and smile for the cameras afterward.'

Rufus took a long drink. He had shown up unexpectedly, carrying a six pack of beer, after stopping at the warehouse looking for Carl. Norah had told him how to find his way to the bush lot. It had rained again in the night and Rufus had arrived at the cabin with his loafers encased in mud and his pant legs dirty to the knees. He had used a broken cedar shingle to clean most of the muck from his shoes before entering the shack.

'Speaking of Mr Walker,' Rufus continued, 'you might like to know that he petitioned the Rose City police to have you arrested.'

'For what?' Carl asked.

'Felony assault and kidnapping. With regards to Mr Murdock.'

'Shit.'

Rufus smiled. 'I was told that it was considered briefly but in the end nobody wanted to prosecute a kidnapping case where the alleged victim was hog-tied and dropped off in front of the police station. Particularly when the victim was a man the cops hadn't been able to identify, let alone apprehend.'

Carl drank from his bottle. He was hoping to finish shingling the roof today. The temperature was going to drop overnight and they were calling for snow by the weekend. He thought briefly about putting Rufus to work, then dismissed the idea. Putting the lawyer on the roof would probably mean having the lawyer fall off the roof. As it was, Carl was going to have to transport him back to his car on the wagon. Those loafers wouldn't survive another trip through the muck.

'What's next for Murdock?' he asked.

'He'll have a bail hearing sometime within the next few days,' Rufus said. 'Given the charges, I doubt he'll be offered bail. On the off chance that he is, it will be a couple of million dollars. I don't think he has it.'

'No,' Carl said.

'Next up would be the preliminary,' Rufus went on. 'You would be part of that, as I suspect you are the key witness. However, I'm assuming that the police would very much like to round up the other two suspects before that comes about, and present them before the court together. I have no idea if they are any closer to doing that. Have they told you anything?'

Carl shook his head. 'Just that they're hoping Murdock will talk. They said he might, after he talks to a lawyer.'

Rufus finished his beer and reached for a fresh one. 'He may very well have the wrong lawyer for that.'

'Why is that?'

'Pearce Walker isn't interested in taking on a case where his client makes a deal and pleads guilty on a lesser charge.' Rufus opened the beer and, seeing that Carl was in need, handed it over before reaching for another. 'There's no spotlight in that scenario. Walker wants an acquittal, or at the very least a long-drawn-out trial where he can showcase his talents for verbosity.'

'Maybe Murdock will want to talk,' Carl said.

'Maybe,' Rufus said. 'But if his lawyer is telling him he could go scot-free, I think it's unlikely. He's a different cat, Walker. I think he fancies himself one of those bigger-than-life lawyers that exist only in fiction. Some people seem inclined to believe that being on television affirms their importance somehow.'

'Pretty much the opposite of what Frances believes,' Carl said.

'True.' Rufus sipped at the beer, watching Carl over the bottle. 'Has there been any change?'

'Not really,' Carl said. 'She apparently has fluid on her brain. They mentioned surgery as an option.'

'No signs at all of waking?'

'No.' Carl finished the first bottle of beer and picked up the second.

'You know Frances,' Rufus said. 'She'll bloody well wake up when she wants to.'

Carl nodded. 'That's how I have it figured.'

They hit three locations at once. The Wild Lucifer clubhouse out on route 10, the bar called Hard Ten a few hundred yards away and the home of Tommy Jakes in the north end of Rose City. The raids were timed for precisely one in the morning, as the bar was closing. Dunbar and Pulford were with the team that battered in the door of the clubhouse – not an easy task since the entrance was fortified with steel rebar set in concrete jambs.

It was chaos from the start and there were some anxious moments where Dunbar feared the whole thing might end up in a shoot-out. The cops knew there would be weapons in the clubhouse and gang members willing to use them. The first six officers through the door were in complete SWAT gear. They entered shouting at the top of their lungs, demanding that everybody hit the floor. The bikers, most of whom had been lounging in front of a big screen TV, were on their feet as one. They were confused. And pissed off.

Dunbar and Pulford, wearing flak jackets, their sidearms cocked and ready, entered behind the SWAT team. There were four more officers behind the building, covering a second entrance. For a long thirty seconds the bikers stood in defiance, as if ready and even eager to make a fight of it. At least one that Dunbar could see had his hand inside his jacket. Dunbar put the front sight of his semi-automatic on the man's chest and waited, his heart pounding. The SWAT guys continued to shout and finally the bikers stepped down, one and then another, grudgingly dropping to their knees before stretching out on the floor.

As that was happening Dunbar saw Tommy Jakes moving toward the rear of the building. Dunbar shouted at one of the team and the man caught up with Tommy before he made it to a door there. Tommy gave the guy a resigned half smile before putting his hands behind his neck.

The raid was worth the effort. Not only was Tommy Jakes in the house, but Robert 'Bones' Sirocco was there as well, along with eight other members of the gang. Found on the premises were a few ounces of grass, four sawed-off shotguns, a half dozen handguns and roughly three hundred assorted pills. There was close to forty thousand dollars in an unlocked safe. Some of the money was in new hundreds.

Attached to the rear of the clubhouse, where Tommy Jakes had been headed, was a garage of sorts in which several Harleys were parked, some in various states of disrepair. Tommy's Cadillac Escalade was also there. In the back of the SUV was a spare tire, obviously not made for the vehicle. When Dunbar cut open the tire he found inside what later proved to be a quantity of cocaine with a street value of roughly a hundred thousand dollars. The assumption was that it had either just arrived at the clubhouse or was in the process of being shipped out.

Dunbar cuffed Tommy Jakes and put him in the back of a squad car before going back inside to help in the search for anything that might tie the bike gang to the home invasion. He kept in touch with the other searches in progress. In the end, nothing much of consequence resulted from the bar, while in the city the wife of Tommy Jakes went ballistic and threatened to sue everyone from the chief of police to the mayor. A small quantity of drugs and a couple of handguns were found in the house.

They arrested everybody on the clubhouse property as well as the manager of the bar, a woman named Joni Stensen, after finding four ecstasy pills in her pocket. Dunbar knew that she would not be charged with anything in the end; the arrest was primarily a way of getting her into custody and under interrogation in the hope that she might know something about the home invasion on River Road.

The bikers, for the most part, took the raid in stride. Two or three, probably under the influence, got a little mouthy with the cops loading them into the vans, offering idle threats and suggesting that there would be retribution down the road. The cops ignored them and pretty soon they all fell quiet, knowing they were heading to the lockup for a few days at least.

Dunbar and Pulford took Tommy downtown themselves, processed him at around four in the morning and went home to their respective beds. They would deal with the more specific charges in the days to follow. At that point, everybody – including Tommy Jakes – was interested in getting some sleep. In fact, Dunbar thought as he drove home, Tommy didn't seem all that concerned about the arrest, other than to comment on the fact that the cops had just cost him a lot of money.

TWENTY-FIVE

I t would be several days before the charges against the bikers would be sorted out. Dunbar didn't get to bed until nearly dawn and he slept until half past noon. When he got to the station he met with the chief briefly to go over what had gone down the night before. There were still phone records and hard drives to dissect but to this point nothing had turned up that would tie the bikers to the home invasion at River Valley Farm. The next step would be to bring Carl Burns in to have a look at the men in custody, on the chance that one of them was involved that night. Dunbar had checked before going home early that morning: none of the ten had a teardrop tattoo. But he would have Burns look them over anyway.

Until then, the main beef against Wild Lucifer was the large amount of cocaine that Dunbar had discovered in the tire. It was obvious to Dunbar now why Tommy Jakes had been trying to make it to the garage during the raid. He wanted that tire out of his vehicle. Then the drugs would have been considered simply to be on the premises. The deed for the clubhouse was under a numbered company which meant the police would have had a tough time assigning ownership of the cocaine to any one individual. It was just Tommy's bad luck that the tire happened to be in the back of his Cadillac. It meant that he – and not one of his subordinates – would be charged with possession for the purpose of trafficking. Tommy had a record going back to when he was sixteen, everything from assault to impaired driving to gun charges. He'd been clean in recent years but that didn't matter. Unless the suspected coke turned

out to be baby powder, he'd be going to prison on the trafficking charge.

Not only that, but the gang was now also part of a bigger
investigation regarding bribery and racketeering, based on
what Ken Hubert had been telling the department. It seemed
unlikely that Tommy Jakes even knew about that wrinkle at
this point. Detective Fisher was seeking warrants against Lake
City Construction's books to back up the charges. Nothing
of those accusations would be mentioned to Tommy or any
of the other bikers until after those warrants were served and
the hard drives seized.

After being processed early that morning, the bikers had
been sent to Clark County Detention outside the city since the
downtown cells couldn't accommodate them all. The bar
manager remained in a holding unit at the station. It was soon
pretty evident that she wouldn't be talking and, since there
was little to be gained in charging her with possession of a
few pills, she would probably be released before the day was
out. She could be back at work for happy hour.

Dunbar had decided to let Tommy stew in a cell for another
day or two before questioning him about the incident at the
farm. He wanted the biker president to have time to think
about what was in store for him. He had to know that his
chances of wriggling free on the trafficking charge were pretty
much nil. If he was willing to finger whoever in his gang had
been involved in the home invasion there might be a chance
Dunbar could convince a prosecutor to go easy on him – to
drop the trafficking to mere possession, or something along
those lines. Tommy Jakes would still be going to jail but for
a much shorter stretch. Dunbar thought it was a good idea to
let Tommy ruminate on all of that for a time. The idle mind
could be an active thing.

And so he was surprised to get a call from Tommy's lawyer
that afternoon around five o'clock. Tommy was ready to talk
to Dunbar now. According to the lawyer, he was being quite
insistent about it.

Dunbar drove out to the detention center, where the three
of them met in the visitation area. Visiting hours were over
and they had the room to themselves. The lawyer's name was

Beth Sawchuck. Dunbar had seen her around the courthouse but had never spoken to her before. He knew her father; he was also a criminal lawyer, now pretty much retired, and she had taken over the practice. She was small and intense, with toned forearms and short cropped dark hair. She looked like an athlete.

'What's going on, Tommy?' Dunbar said after introductions were made.

'You shit in my cornflakes, detective. That's what's going on. Why the hell would you pick last night of all nights to come calling?'

Dunbar leaned back in his chair and regarded the gang leader. Tommy didn't look much like a biker these days. His hair was styled and had blonde highlights. He favored suits over leather jackets, Escalades over Harleys. Dunbar knew all of that. What was puzzling him was Tommy's attitude at this moment. He was acting as if he'd been pulled over for running a red light.

'Next time I'll call ahead,' Dunbar said.

Tommy laughed at that. Dunbar glanced at the lawyer Sawchuck, who was sitting quietly, her legs crossed, showing taut calf muscles. She didn't laugh.

'What did you want to talk to me about?' Dunbar asked.

'About me getting out of here,' Tommy said. 'I can't handle the food.'

'You're going to have to put up with it for a while. We're still figuring out what all we're going to charge you with. But I'd advise you to get comfortable.'

'Maybe not, detective. Maybe I can lighten your load a little. You know – so you don't have to do all that paperwork.'

'How can you lighten my load?' Dunbar asked. 'Are you thinking you'll just plead guilty to everything and expedite the proceedings?'

'I'm thinking I'd like to avoid the courtroom altogether.'

'How would you do that?'

'Like this,' Tommy said, leaning forward. 'I read something in the newspaper a week or so ago. About a home invasion out near Talbotville. There was a fire and a robbery and a woman was killed. Your name was mentioned in the article. Said you were looking for three people. Now I see a couple of days ago you busted some guy named Murdock. I kept watching the news, thinking you were about to nail the other two. But I don't think you have nailed the other two. Have you?'

'I can't discuss that with you, Tommy.'

Tommy smiled. 'Well, either you have them or you don't. From what I've heard, that was a real shit show out there. A much bigger deal than a couple of ounces of cocaine in a spare tire.'

'A couple of ounces?' Dunbar repeated. He fell quiet for a time. He glanced at the lawyer Sawchuck, who was watching her client intently. He looked back at Tommy.

'Are you telling me you have the names, Tommy?'

'I do.'

'And these guys are patched?' Dunbar asked.

For the first time, Tommy was taken aback. 'What?' he asked. 'No. They've got nothing to do with the Wild. Why would you think that?'

'What about Murdock? He's not connected to the Wild?'

'I've seen him around,' Tommy said. 'But he's got fucking zilch to do with the organization. You think we'd let a mutt like that in?'

In truth, Dunbar didn't think that. 'What are you looking for?'

'Come on, you know what I'm looking for.'

'All right,' Sawchuck interrupted. 'This is where I need to get involved. We need to set some ground rules before we go any further. My client is willing to give you the names. But there are conditions here.'

'I figured that much,' Dunbar said.

'First of all,' Sawchuck said, 'there will be no drug-related charges filed against my client as a result of the raid last night.'

Dunbar showed no reaction. 'What else?'

'This remains quiet. My client doesn't want it known that he's the one who identified these men.'

'He should be proud of it,' Dunbar said.

'It doesn't work that way in his world,' the lawyer said.

'It doesn't work that way in my world,' Tommy repeated. He was smiling at Dunbar, obviously enjoying the exchange. He was like a poker player with a pat hand.

'I hope you're not thinking of just pulling a couple of names out of a hat, Tommy,' Dunbar said. 'That's not going to fly.'

'Now why would I do that?' Tommy asked.

'You know why,' Dunbar said. 'But I have an eyewitness who can positively identify at least one of these men.'

'We make the deal and I'll give you the guys who were there,' Tommy said. 'Absolutely. Hell, I'm doing your work for you. You should put me on the payroll. You guys got good benefits, right?'

Dunbar glanced at the lawyer again. She was still watching her client. In fact, she hadn't looked at Dunbar once since being introduced at the start.

'How do you happen to know this, Tommy?' Dunbar asked.

'I can tell you that once you tell me we have a deal,' Tommy said. 'If I tell you now, you might figure things out for yourself. Where would that leave old Tommy?'

Dunbar got to his feet. 'I'll get back to you on this.'

'Hold on,' Tommy said. 'You going to leave me dangling here? I want an answer. You think this offer's going to be good tomorrow or the next day?'

'Yeah, I do,' Dunbar said.

Later that afternoon Dunbar and Pulford met at the courthouse with the chief and the prosecutor Diane Mathews. They gathered in Mathews' office on the second floor.

'So you're waiting to grill this Jakes about whether or not he knows anything about the home invasion and all of a sudden he just hands it to you on a platter?' Mathews said when she'd heard the proposition.

'That's about it,' Dunbar said.

'I don't understand,' Mathews said. 'How does he happen to know this?'

'It's beginning to make sense now,' Pulford said. 'The night of the robbery, one of the thieves said that maybe the forty-seven grand was enough. We kept asking ourselves – enough for what? We know now the money ended up with the Wild, which means these guys were buying something from the bikers, probably drugs. And in large quantities.'

'Or maybe they already owed the money,' Dunbar suggested.

'Either way, Tommy Jakes got to reading the newspaper and figured things out. Ordinarily Tommy wouldn't be offering this information but we got lucky. We just happened to hit the clubhouse when there was a shitload of coke in the trunk of Tommy's Cadillac. Otherwise, I have a feeling this wouldn't be happening. But Tommy Jakes is in high cotton these days. He has no interest in a prison stretch.'

'How close are you to finding these individuals on your own?' Mathews asked.

'Not close,' Dunbar admitted. 'After the cash showed up in Ken Hubert's closet, we thought we had something. The money came from the Wild so we assumed that somebody from the club was involved at the farm. But it doesn't appear that way, not after what Tommy Jakes told me today.'

'Maybe they were involved and he's planning on handing you a couple of ringers,' Mathews said.

'I already told him that wouldn't work,' Dunbar said. 'Tommy's been around the block. He knows he couldn't get away with that.'

Mathews turned to the chief, her eyebrows raised to ask the question.

'We need those names,' he said. 'If we let him skate on the drug charges, at least we got the coke off the streets. Question is – do we want to see Tommy Jakes walk?'

'I hate to see that,' Mathews said.

'Keep in mind, this has nothing to do with his other problems,' Pulford interjected. 'We're assuming he doesn't know that Ken Hubert's been singing about the Wild's involvement with the bribery case. We can let him walk on the drug charges but he's still got bigger problems down the road. This deal doesn't give him immunity on that.'

Mathews nodded. 'Something ironic about this. Everybody's ratting everybody out.'

'That's what happens when you get a bunch of rats together,' Pulford said.

Mathews looked at Dunbar. 'I think I know what you want to do here.'

Dunbar merely nodded.

'Do it,' she said.

TWENTY-SIX

Chino sat on the back step drinking a beer and looking at Vanhizen, who was standing a few feet away. It was the farmer's third visit to Chino's place that day. He knew he had a chance at the property and he would be a dog with a bone until he got it. There were a couple of sticking points, though. One, it was Vanhizen's nature that he didn't want to pay what the place was worth. Two, Chino wanted the deal done immediately. That meant the title search and survey and anything else involved would have to come after the fact.

'Farmland's going for six grand an acre right now,' Vanhizen had said that morning, the first time he'd stopped by.

'It's more like ten grand,' Chino said. 'I can read the fucking real estate section. Doesn't matter anyway cuz this isn't farmland. It's a commercial business.'

'You saying you have a license to deal scrap?' the farmer had asked.

Chino ignored the question. 'If you think you're going to get this place for farm prices you better be on your way, you fucking hick.'

Vanhizen chafed at the profanity but he didn't complain about it. He was focused on the transaction. Chino could tell he was anxious, probably worried that Chino might change his mind. They went back and forth over the course of three conversations and eventually settled on a price of one hundred and ten thousand. Chino knew he was selling on the cheap but time was a factor. The closing was in thirty days. Chino would have until then to remove all he wanted from the property. What he wanted wasn't much.

'My lawyer's concerned about how we're doing this,' Vanhizen said now.

Chino tilted his bottle up and drank. He hadn't offered Vanhizen a bottle. Why would he? 'What's his problem?'

'The title search, for one thing.'

'I own the fucking place,' Chino said. 'Tell him to quit pissing his pants.'

'And he wants to know why you have to have cash for the down payment.'

'That's the way I roll,' Chino said. 'You can like it or lump it. I been dealing strictly in cash my whole life and I'm not going to change now because you and your lawyer are a couple of pussies. You'll get a receipt.'

Vanhizen hesitated. He was like a man trying to decide whether or not to buy a new convertible he really didn't need. Chino's three acres didn't mean a thing to him as far as his farm operation was concerned. But Chino could see he wanted it anyway, and wanted it badly. He wanted it because it was adjacent to his farm, but more than that he wanted it so he could at long last get rid of the buildings and all the surrounding junk. And in the process, be rid of Chino too.

'I get it,' Chino said then. 'You're one of those guys, always got to play by the rules. Then let's do it your way. I'll call a real estate agent in the morning and put it on the market. Then you can put in an offer, along with anybody else who wants it, and if I like your offer, then you're good to go. The asking price is going to be closer to a hundred and fifty, but hey – at least your lawyer will be a happy little girl.'

Vanhizen looked away, a stubborn set to his eyes. That scenario would solve all of his concerns and yet he wasn't remotely interested in it. He glanced across the fields to his home farm. The two story house, the painted barns and the landscaped grounds. He had married into the place but the upkeep had always been a source of pride to him.

'Make up the receipt,' he said without looking at Chino. 'I'll have your money here within an hour. But I'll be bringing my lawyer with me. I want this whole transaction witnessed.'

'You can bring your mommy with you if you want,' Chino said. 'So long as you have my twenty-five grand.'

Vanhizen wasn't gone ten minutes when Digger Bagley pulled into the yard. He stopped by the shop and got out, unsteady on his feet as usual. When he saw Chino up by the house he got back in his truck and drove over, even though the distance was no more than a couple hundred feet. Digger wasn't much on walking.

'Got a couple more rolls of that copper,' he said as he got out. He had a full can of beer in his hand and he opened it as he approached.

'Can't help you with that,' Chino said.

'Why not?'

Chino looked at the fat man a moment. Digger's shirt front was covered with bits of pretty much whatever he'd eaten in the past three days or so and his jeans were torn open at the crotch.

'Taking some down time,' Chino said.

Digger sat heavily in the grass, wheezing, as if he couldn't go any further. 'Well, shit,' he said.

Chino watched as he slurped from the beer. He considered for a moment lighting a fire out back and burning the coils, then dropping them off at the depot on his way out of town in the morning. It would mean a few extra bucks in his pocket. But then he decided, fuck it, he'd have the twenty-five grand from Vanhizen. He needed to get the hell out. Who knew what Bug was telling the cops at this point?

'What will you give me on it?' Digger asked. 'You can burn it later.'

'You hit that same place, Digger? You're gonna piss in that pot once too often. You think they don't know they're losing copper?'

'Aw, fuck 'em.' Digger drank more beer and it ran down his chin. 'How about I burn it here? I'll give you a cut.'

Chino started to refuse, but stopped. He thought about it a moment.

'I got a better idea, Digger. I'm taking off for a bit. Why don't you stay here for a month or so? You can use the yard for whatever you want. Clean up what you can and I'll split the money with you down the middle.'

He could see that Digger was all in favor of the idea. Chino didn't know where the man lived these days, but it was usually with one of his relatives and they were always giving him the boot after a few weeks. Chino's place probably looked like a mansion to Digger.

'I can look after the place if you want,' Digger said. 'Where you going anyway?'

'Just heading out.' Chino was warming to the idea himself. If the cops came looking for Chino, at least this way he would know about it. 'Yeah, you can look after the place. Collect my disability check and hang on to it. And you know – let me know if anybody comes snooping around.'

'Who's gonna come snooping?'

'You never know,' Chino said. 'Bill collectors, Jehovah Witness. Cops.'

'I'll run 'em off.'

Chino drained his beer. 'I'm heading out in the morning. Come back then and you can burn that copper off. I'll tell you where to take it and call ahead so they know you're cool. OK?'

When Digger was gone Chino went inside and opened another beer. He turned on the TV and lay out on the couch, flipping through the channels. He settled on a show where two guys in cowboy hats drove through the countryside in a Volkswagen van, looking for antiques.

Chino looked at his watch. Vanhizen had said within the hour and it was nearly that now. Chino didn't think the farmer could drive to the city and go through whatever paperwork a bank would make him go through to withdraw twenty-five grand and be back in an hour. Which meant he had the money at home. He'd probably withdrawn it earlier that day, before his lawyer had started harping on at him about title searches and all that shit. Chino wished there was a way that he actually could rip the snotty fucker off for the twenty-five. It would be pretty hard to do though, unless he could pack up the three acres and take it with him.

Thinking about it, he needed to decide if there was going to be any way to get the rest of the money from Vanhizen if the cops happened to issue a warrant for Chino. He would have to leave the country if that happened, which meant he'd probably never see the other eighty-five thousand. Maybe he could use Digger to collect it. He doubted it. Digger wouldn't be capable of it and even if he was, he couldn't be trusted.

Maybe Bug would keep his mouth shut and he wouldn't have to worry about it. Chino didn't have a lot of faith in that

either. Bug might be keeping mum for now, but Chino didn't
see that happening long term. Sooner or later, he'd spill. Even
if he managed to get acquitted, he'd get stoned and tell
somebody, somewhere down the road.

The show was ending when he heard Vanhizen pull into the
yard, the truck tires crunching on the gravel drive. As Chino
started to rise, though, he heard another vehicle, and then what
seemed like another. Maybe half a dozen in all.

He didn't need to go to the window to see who it was.

Carl picked up Rufus Canfield at his office at seven o'clock
and the two of them drove into the Rose City police station
together. Both Dunbar and Pulford were waiting by the front
desk. Rufus and Dunbar were acquainted; Carl introduced the
lawyer to Pulford and they all went downstairs.

The two men were in separate rooms, behind one way glass.
The young Indian was sitting at a table, staring straight ahead,
not moving. He wore a jean jacket and brown work pants. His
hands on the table were clean but there was grease beneath
the fingernails. A mechanic's hands. Carl looked at him and
shook his head. After all, he had never seen the man's face
that night. If this was the man.

'Nothing?' Dunbar asked. 'Height or build?'

'Ballpark,' Carl said, shrugging.

They walked along the corridor to the next room. Inside
Chino was pacing.

'That's him,' Carl said, his voice tight, his pulse rising.

'Are you certain?' Pulford asked.

'That's him.'

They went into a different room after that where Dunbar
showed Carl a revolver they had seized at Chino's house. It
was a thirty-eight caliber Smith & Wesson that had seen better
days. Carl couldn't say for certain that it was the gun Chino
had been waving around that night.

'I suspect it is,' Dunbar said.

The four of them went for coffee at a diner down the block.
There was coffee at the station but it wasn't good, Dunbar said.

'How did you get the names?' Carl asked. 'Murdock?'

'Murdock isn't saying anything,' Pulford said.

'Then how?'

'Somebody talked,' Dunbar said.

'Who? Somebody who was involved?'

'No. Somebody who wasn't.'

'Are you sure about that?' Carl asked.

'Yeah,' Dunbar said. 'But I can't tell you who it was.'

'If they weren't involved, then I don't care who it was,' Carl said. 'What are these two saying?'

'Nothing so far,' Pulford said. 'But we just pulled them in a couple of hours ago. Stanley Carter – known as Chino – is a habitual. The Native kid doesn't have a record but he's known to police. Carjacker who's never been convicted.'

'The young man goes from stealing cars to home invasion?' Rufus asked.

'Apparently,' Pulford said.

'Do we have any idea what was behind this?' Rufus asked.

'We know a little bit,' Dunbar said. He looked at Carl. 'These guys had incurred a debt to some people and it looks as if they were desperate for money. Why they decided they could get it at your farm is something we don't know.'

'You're saying it was random?' Rufus persisted.

'We don't know that,' Pulford interjected.

'What's that mean?' Carl asked. He'd been mostly quiet since leaving the station. He kept seeing Chino's face before him. He could see the man's hands on Frances's throat. Over the past weeks his image had begun to fade in Carl's mind, but now it was back in spades.

'We're just trying to figure out who these guys are,' Pulford said. 'At this point we don't know what was behind them choosing the farm.' She looked at Carl. 'You've never seen any of the three before that night?'

Carl shook his head, watching her carefully. He always felt that Pulford was suggesting something without ever getting to it.

'Is there any chance one of them could have worked on the farm in the past?' Pulford asked.

'Not since I've been there,' Carl said.

'But you've only been there a few years, right?' Pulford persisted. 'What about before you got there?'

'How would I know the answer to that? That's a question for Frances.'

'Unfortunately we can't ask Frances.'

'You can when she wakes up,' Carl said sharply.

At that Pulford glanced toward Dunbar. Nobody spoke for a few moments.

'What does it matter why they picked the farm?' Carl asked. 'These are the guys. I can ID two of them. Why does the rest matter?'

'We would like to establish motive,' Pulford said. 'For the trial.'

'The money is the motive,' Rufus reminded her.

'You're right,' Dunbar said.

Pulford tapped her finger on the table. 'But if we can show *why* they chose the farm, we can use that as proof that they were there.'

'I can prove they were there,' Carl told her.

'I realize that,' she said. 'But in a case like this we can't have too much evidence.'

'You're assuming that none of these individuals will talk?' Rufus asked.

'It's too early to say,' Dunbar said. 'Those two you just had a look at haven't even been indicted yet. With the murder charge hanging over them, there's a good chance one of the three will want to talk before we get anywhere close to going to trial.' He paused. 'Taylor might be the key. You said he seemed reluctant to be there?'

'Yeah,' Carl said.

'Let's see how it plays out,' Dunbar said. 'He's got a wife and kid. It could be he'll want to deal, once this all sinks in.'

'I can see what you mean about detective Pulford,' Rufus said. They were sitting at the bar in Archer's, eating chicken wings and splitting a pitcher of beer.

'What's your take on it?' Carl asked.

Rufus skinned the meat from a wing with his teeth and dropped the bone into a wooden bowl to the side. 'She wants a motive to show to a jury. Something other than just money. She's trying to make sense of a senseless crime, at least to the twelve people in that box. Keep in mind they have no physical evidence. Fingerprints, DNA, none of that. They want to be able to tell a jury not just who did it, but why.'

'What if there is no why?' Carl asked. 'What if it was completely random?'

'Then they have your testimony.'

'Isn't that all they need?'

Rufus wiped his mouth with a paper napkin and reached for his beer. 'One would think so. An eyewitness is a powerful thing.'

'Two eyewitnesses,' Carl said.

'Two?'

'This thing won't go to trial for months,' Carl said. 'By that time, Frances will be awake.'

TWENTY-SEVEN

'Do you have any money?' Walker asked.

Chino looked across the table at the lawyer. He said he'd just come from court, and he looked it. Pinstripe suit, hair combed perfectly with some sort of gel to hold it, the smell of cologne on him. He'd been joking with the guards when they brought Chino up from the common area on the first floor where he'd been pacing for hours, waiting for the man to show.

'No,' Chino said.

'Then what do you want with me?'

'I hear you do legal aid cases,' Chino said.

'Rarely,' Walker told him.

'I know you're representing Bug Murdock on the cuff,' Chino said.

'Which is why I'm not looking for anything else that pays ten cents on the dollar. You sure you have no money?'

'Nope,' Chino said. 'I got a small disability pension.'

'No equity?'

Chino shook his head.

'Is that true?' Walker asked. 'Because I've heard you own some property.'

'Bug's got a big mouth.'

'If Bug had a big mouth they would have arrested you a week ago. I saw the indictments that are coming down. I'm not taking you on for nothing, sport.'

He got to his feet and started to walk away.

'Hold on,' Chino said.

'What?'

'You figure on getting Bug off?' Chino asked. 'Well, if he walks I walk. And the other way around.'

'The other way around? What does that mean?'

Chino shrugged.

Walker came back. 'Are you saying that you'll roll over on Murdock if I don't play ball? That can be a two way street. You know what I mean?'

Chino still said nothing. Walker regarded him for a moment, his petulant attitude.

'Now you're going to pout?' Walker said. 'OK, I'll make it simple for you. If you want for you and Mr Murdock to be a package deal, you'd better show me some money. You heard what I said – I have one fucking charity case on my hands and I'm not taking on another. So if you're interested in this, say so now. I'm not driving out here again at your request.'

Chino looked at the guards behind the glass. One of them was showing the others something on his cell phone, a picture or a message or something. Like a bunch of fucking teenagers. They were knocking down eighty grand a year to play with their phones. And Chino was stuck there, a few feet away, with no choices.

'What do you want up front?' he asked.

'Ten thousand to start.'

Chino had actually been thinking it would be more than that. 'All right,' he said after a minute. 'My place is two-three-five Featherstone Road, outside Buckley. You need to talk to my neighbor, a guy named Leonard Vanhizen. He's holding twenty-five grand for me as a down payment for my property. There's a receipt made out in his name on my kitchen table, unless the cops took it when they ransacked the fucking place, which I assume they did. There might be a fat guy named Digger Bagley hanging around. He's nobody. Talk to Vanhizen, he owns the farm to the east. He'll probably want to get his lawyer in on it, he's afraid to take a shit without his lawyer being there.'

Walker took a small notebook from his pocket and wrote down the address. 'This Vanhizen is buying your place?'

'Yeah,' Chino said. 'So you take that twenty-five and do whatever legal shit you need to do to hold it for me. Take your ten grand out of it. I guess I might as well hire you to collect the rest in thirty days too. There's another eighty-five coming and I'm hoping to use that for bail.'

Walker smiled. 'Let's take it one step at a time. The ten thousand might get you through the discovery and preliminary. We don't know exactly what you're being charged with yet. If the charges are the same as Murdock's you can forget about bail, unless you plan to add a zero to that eighty-five number.'

'I want a bail hearing,' Chino said.

'You'll get a hearing,' Walker told him. 'Might be all you get. This is premature. We need to find out what the prosecution has.'

'They got fuck all.'

'They've got something or you wouldn't be sitting here. Story is there's an eyewitness.'

'Bullshit,' Chino said.

'You're telling me they don't?'

'I'm telling you they got fuck all.'

Walker looked at his watch before glancing toward the guards. 'You never heard this from me,' he said, lowering his voice. 'But I suggest that you and Mr Murdock tell the same story from here on in. Precisely the same story. If you guys weren't there, then you guys weren't there.'

Chino nodded.

'All right,' Walker said. 'I'm going to track down this Vanhizen character and see if you're telling me the truth about the money. If you are, then I'll see you at the indictment. If you're not, I'll see you at the trial. You and whatever lawyer you manage to hire.'

'Why would I lie?' Chino said.

'Look where you are,' Walker told him, and left.

Billy sat on the floor of the common room, his back to the wall, and watched as Chino returned. He'd been led out half an hour earlier. Billy had seen him that morning, talking to a guard about something before writing out a request on a sheet of paper. From then until the time they had come for him he had paced constantly, never stopping.

Now he came into the common area and headed straight for Bug, who was playing cards with three other inmates at a table in the middle of the room. Chino gave Bug a look and Bug finished the hand and quit the game. The two of them began to walk and talk.

The cops had grabbed Billy the day before. It was late afternoon and he'd taken Seth for a walk through the woods and down to the park by the river. It had been cold but he'd bundled the boy up in jeans and a hoodie, Superman mittens on his hands. They had sat by the broken bridge, watching for frogs in the shallow water. They saw none. It was late in the season and snow could come any day. Presumably the frogs were settling in for winter.

Billy had reluctantly shown up at the Wild Lucifer clubhouse at nine that morning ready for the border run, as he'd been instructed by Tommy Jakes. There had been a few bikers standing outside the building, smoking and talking. They seemed pretty wound up over something and when Billy asked where Tommy Jakes was he'd been told to fuck off. He was more than happy with the option and left without asking any questions. Watching the noon news, he found out about the raid the night before. Relief washed over Billy. He hoped that the raid meant that Tommy Jakes wouldn't bother him again about making the run. On top of that, after lunch he got a call from Chum's Service Center offering a job doing oil changes and lubes, maybe some brake work. Billy had given up on hearing from the garage. He told Cheryl the news when she came home from work and then took the boy for the hike.

When they came out of the woods and walked up to the street Billy saw the cars from half a block away. There were three cruisers and two unmarked SUVs. He would have made a run for it but he couldn't, not with Seth there. He stopped and stood on the slope, thinking what to do, and pretty soon the cops saw him and started for him. The uniforms had their guns drawn and when they got closer they began to shout at him, telling him to get down on the ground. Seth began to cry as Billy did what he was told.

Cheryl was following the cops and she was crying too. When she tried to run to Seth, one of the plainclothes cops, a woman, grabbed her and held her back. After they searched Billy for a weapon and cuffed him and pulled him to his feet, the woman allowed Cheryl to pick up the boy, who was sobbing, scared and confused.

'What's going on?' Cheryl kept asking as the cops led Billy down the street to the cruisers.

Most of the neighbors were outside now, on their front steps or their lawns, watching the situation unfold. Billy kept his head down as he walked.

'Tell me what's going on!' Cheryl shouted.

She tried to get close to Billy but the cops held her back. When they put him in the back seat of the car, he finally looked at her. He didn't know what to say so he said nothing. Cheryl had Seth on her hip, holding him tight with both arms.

'You'd better call someone,' Billy heard the woman cop say as they drove off.

They had taken him into Rose City, to the station there downtown. After processing he'd been loaded into a van and driven out to Clark County Detention. By that time it was after ten o'clock and they put him in a cell with a guy about his age. It wasn't until this morning, when he was released into the common area, that he saw that both Bug and Chino were there. Billy had heard about Bug's arrest and in the days afterward he'd been expecting the cops to show up at his place. After a week went by and they didn't, he began to think that maybe Bug wasn't talking. Obviously something had changed.

He noticed the two men watching him from time to time but neither spoke to him all day. Billy was fine with that. It was speaking to them in the first place that had led to him being here. He'd been told that he would be making an appearance in the Rose City courthouse the next morning to be formally charged. He was also informed that he could make a phone call. The only lawyer Billy knew was Darren Crowder from out at the rez, and he didn't feel like calling him at this point. Billy hadn't had much to do with the rez lately and he knew that certain people there were going to be pissed when they heard the new allegations. Billy making the Indians look bad.

He could call Cheryl, but what was he going to tell her? This was the day he'd been dreading since the night at the farmhouse and now that it had arrived it was every bit as bad as he had imagined it would be.

He was pretty sure it would only get worse.

Carl was at the courthouse for the indictments on Billy Taylor and Stanley Carter, the one they called Chino. The charges were carbon copies of those laid against Murdock. It was the same judge and the same prosecutor, the woman named Mathews. Taylor had duty counsel for the day, and Chino was represented by the man named Walker. As Rufus had suggested, he was a bit of dandy, with a carnation in his lapel and the tendency to strut.

Dunbar was there but Pulford wasn't. Dunbar had called Carl the night before to see if he would be attending. He said he wanted to talk to him afterward. After the prisoners were led away, he and Carl walked the four blocks back to the station, where they sat in an empty room. Dunbar had stopped at his desk and picked up a file.

'I want to go over your statement once more to make sure I have everything,' Dunbar said. 'Unfortunately, this is the part of the process where everything slows to a crawl. But I want to nail down everything you saw and everything you heard before we hand your statement over to the defense.'

'When's the preliminary?' Carl asked.

'A couple of months, maybe three,' Dunbar said. 'We have to deliver our case to the defense and give them time to go over it.'

'What about bail?'

'These guys aren't making bail,' Dunbar said. 'I doubt they'll even ask.'

'And how long between the preliminary and the trial?' Carl asked.

Dunbar shook his head. 'That's the tough part. It will be a year at the very least. And it could be as long as two years.'

'I expected that.' Carl indicated the paperwork. 'So what do you need?'

Dunbar opened the file. 'We need you to be rock solid on the stand during the preliminary. The memory can be a tricky thing, especially involving something as traumatic as what you went through. After a few months things can get foggy. So we're going to go over everything again. I'll print it out and give you a copy of the statement, the same copy we'll be giving the defense. That way, whatever they throw at you on the stand, you'll be ready.'

'OK,' Carl said.

Dunbar led him through the night in question again, going slowly. Carl found that he recalled a couple of things he hadn't before. The third man – Billy Taylor, they were calling him now – wore black sneakers that night. He also remembered that Murdock wore a ring; Carl had seen it when the man had been coming on to Stacy, running his hand up her leg. He remembered no details about it though, just that it was silver.

He and Dunbar talked for over an hour. When they were finished Carl drove to the hospital. He told Frances about the new arrests and he also told her that she would have to be patient. There was a long road ahead of them.

'At least they're not out there anymore,' he said.

He drove home with that thought in his head. He needed something to hang on to in the coming months. He was feeling let down for some reason. Up until now all he had been able to think about was finding the three men. And while those men were now sitting in jail, they were getting three squares a day. Joking and laughing, playing cards, working out. While Frances remained unconscious and Stacy was just ashes.

Carl was right when he told Frances to be patient but he needed to take his own advice. There was a difference, however, between patience and complacency. He couldn't allow the passage of time to dull how he felt about the three men in custody. That was not about to change in twelve months or twenty-four, or however long it took.

For now, all he could do was work. He wished that Frances would wake up. He wished she would come home, where she belonged. Carl could cook for her, help her to get her strength back. It wouldn't take long. Once she came out of the coma, it would be a matter of a week or maybe two for her to recover. Then she would be back at work, precisely where she needed to be. Where the two of them needed to be.

Maybe she'd be back in time for maple syrup season. The sugar shack was nearly finished. He'd found an evaporator for sale near Windsor and he called the man and told him he would take it, sight unseen. He planned to head there later in the week to pick it up. He needed to prod the insurance company again about the house. He wanted construction to begin. When Frances woke up she would need a place to live and Carl didn't think she'd be overly thrilled about moving into the motorhome. Then again, she might be fine with it, as least temporarily. She was never all that interested in material things.

When Carl got to the farm it was growing dark, too late to head back to the bush lot. Norah was gone for the day. He went into the motorhome and opened a beer. He needed to call Kate and give her an update but it was nearly midnight in Scotland. He'd call her in the morning. There was no reason for her to come home at this point, not with the trial being so far away. She could fly home then. Carl would like that, and so would Frances.

He drank the beer and opened another. The worst times were when he had nothing to do. When his mind was otherwise occupied he could keep his thoughts at bay. On occasion his subconscious would suggest to him that in due time everything would be back to the way it was. But his waking mind knew better. He needed to leave behind the way it had been and look forward to the way it could be in the future.

'The way it will be,' he said, sitting in the dimly lit trailer, beer in hand and dark thoughts in his head.

*   *   *

Dunbar was wrong when he predicted to Carl that there would be no request for a bail hearing. Pearce Walker insisted on a joint hearing for his two clients. There was no such request from Billy Taylor, who was being represented by a lawyer Dunbar had never heard of, a woman called Lafleur.

At the time of the hearing, Walker had received partial discovery from the police. The hearing was set for a Wednesday morning at nine o'clock. Dunbar had promised Carl that he would keep him in the loop with whatever happened and he'd called a few days earlier to let him know. Carl was at the courthouse. Both Dunbar and Pulford were there, sitting in the front row, a few feet behind the prosecutor Mathews. The judge was the same man Carl had seen earlier, the older guy named O'Brien. Chino and Bug were shuffled in from the back room, both wearing blue jumpsuits from the detention center.

There was a considerable media presence and it was obvious that Walker was aware of it. He made a long speech about the questionable nature of the charges and the sketchy evidence, as he described it. As he spoke he constantly turned away from the judge to address the reporters at the back of the courtroom.

When he was finished the judge set bail at five million dollars apiece and left the room.

Walker had no illusions about the hearing going in. He merely wanted to test the air around the case. When he came to trial he would do everything he could to get another judge in the chair. He didn't want O'Brien anywhere near it. Before they took the prisoners back out to Clark County jail, he met with them in a duty counsel office on the second floor of the courtroom.

'Five million, for fucksakes,' Bug said when they came in.

'Sit down,' Walker told them.

Bug, always compliant, did so. Chino remained on his feet. He wasn't about to let the lawyer order him about. Walker was working for him, not the other way around. Apparently there had been considerable back and forth between Walker and Vanhizen and the farmer's lawyer over the twenty-five grand. It had finally been paid, after a bunch of paperwork, and Walker had charged Chino an additional two grand for his role in it.

Walker looked at the two men for a moment. 'So – either one of you boys sitting on five million, or do we just let that slide?'

'Funny man,' Chino said.

Walker smiled. 'All right then. Looking forward to the preliminary. From what I'm seeing so far they have two things. One, Mr Murdock's truck was parked a quarter mile from the farmhouse that night. That means nothing. Two, they have the eyewitness Burns. This guy's got red flags all over him. I'm pretty sure I can take his story apart on the witness stand. Now there's supposedly a second eyewitness, the woman who owned the house, one Frances Rourke. She was injured in the fire and apparently she's still in the hospital. I heard a rumor that she's unconscious. Whatever's going on, there's no statement from her in the discovery.' He paused. 'Keep in mind that I don't have everything yet. But at this point, to put you two in the house that night, they have Burns and nothing else. Is that how it seems to you, gentlemen?'

Bug looked at once to Chino. Walker could see how it was between the two.

'That's right,' Chino said.

'I'm not going to receive any surprises down the road?' Walker asked.

'We weren't there,' Chino said.

'We was never there,' Bug repeated.

Walker stood up. 'Have a nice trip back, gentlemen.'

TWENTY-EIGHT

A month passed. Winter arrived and with it a good deal of the work at the farm came to a halt. Carl kept himself busy with the chickens and the brood hens. It had been apparent for some time that the farm couldn't keep up with the demand for eggs. Once Carl no longer needed the sling on his arm, he expanded the brood house by half again and brought in another four dozen laying hens. He took over the delivery of the eggs himself, enlarging the route to supply markets and wholesale outlets as far as fifty miles away. Anything to keep busy.

He drove to Windsor for the evaporator and installed it in the sugar shack. On a whim, he decided to rewire the old machine shed, getting rid of the tangle of extension cords and forty watt light fixtures installed by Frances's father fifty years earlier. As he worked, he waited for an answer from the insurance company on when construction could begin on a new farmhouse.

And he visited Frances daily. There were other doctors on the case now, other surgeons. Without actually telling Carl, they seemed to have come to the conclusion that something needed to be done at this point. Frances was showing no signs of waking up. One doctor, a woman named Aluz, appeared to be at odds with Harkness as to exactly what type of surgery was required. Harkness was hedging his bets, saying now that the fluid was not the source of the problem. It seemed, though, that everybody was of the opinion that surgery was needed.

'We have to relieve the pressure on the brain,' Aluz told Carl. 'Whether we do it now or later doesn't change anything. It has to be done.'

Frances was growing smaller in the bed. Her eyes were sunken. It seemed to Carl that she was a different person lying there. For the first time he wondered if she was actually gone. He began to ask the various doctors and staff when the surgery would happen. He received vague replies. Apparently nobody wanted to be the one to make the call.

Carl was walking along the corridor one afternoon, heading for Frances's room, when he looked up to see the lawyer Pearce Walker at the nurses' station talking to one of the staff. Carl waited until he was gone and then approached a nurse sitting behind the desk. He knew her by sight if not by name.

'That guy that was just here,' he said. 'He's a lawyer named Walker. What did he want?'

The nurse hesitated, as if weighing the ethical concerns of

a reply. Apparently she decided there were none. 'He was asking about Frances Rourke.'

'Why?' Carl demanded.

The nurse shrugged. 'I don't know. He's been here a couple of times. He seems concerned about her condition.'

When Carl got back to the motorhome he called Dunbar and told him.

'You sure it was Walker?'

'I'm sure,' Carl said.

Dunbar didn't say anything for a moment.

'What does he want from her?' Carl asked.

'Nothing would be my guess,' Dunbar said. 'Precisely that.'

It was a couple of days later that Dunbar got the call from Mathews saying that Pearce Walker was asking for a meeting. She set it up for a Friday afternoon in her office, after court was done for the day. Dunbar and Pulford walked over to the courthouse from the station together. After a balmy morning the day had grown cold, with flurries in the air, tiny pellets driven sideways by an east wind. Both cops were poorly dressed for the weather and they were chilled to the bone on the walk. When they arrived at the office Walker was already there sitting in an armchair, legs crossed, a black folder balanced on his knee. He was dressed down for Pearce Walker, a brown suit and white shirt. No lapel blossom.

Mathews had coffee for them and she poured for everybody except the lawyer, who declined.

'You have the floor,' she told him once everyone had settled.

Walker tapped the folder. 'I've been going over this discovery. I have to say it's pretty thin.'

'How is it thin?' Mathews asked.

'In every way.' Walker smiled at Mathews. 'You want to go down the list? Let's start with these charges of arson. You have a fire, cause unknown. The fire marshal suggests that there was a gasoline can found near the hot spot. However, the hot spot just happened to be beside the fireplace, where they have determined a fire was lit at the time. The fire could very well have started accidentally, sparks from the burning logs, whatever. Which means that the arson charges are very iffy. Now, the young woman died as a result of the fire. *If* the fire was accidental, then so was her death. Is that not accurate?'

He paused, as if expecting someone in the room to agree with him. He'd be waiting a long time for that. He shrugged contentedly and continued on.

'OK, so let's forget about the murder indictments for the moment. What else do we have? Well, robbery and extortion. No money was ever found in my clients' possession. Where's the proof that they were involved?' Walker tapped the folder again. 'Show me where you've connected my clients to the money. You don't have them in possession of it, you don't have them spending it, you found nothing incriminating in either of their houses. You have nothing there.'

Again he paused for effect. Dunbar drank his coffee, watching the lawyer quietly. Pulford looked at Mathews, who was sitting back in her chair, fingertips pressed together in front of her face.

'Still no comment, eh?' Walker said. 'Well, you know what they say – the truth hurts. Let's see – we also have allegations of a home invasion. Based on one piece of evidence, and that's the supposed eyewitness statement of this guy Carl Burns. Now isn't he an interesting character? Three years ago we wouldn't even be talking about him because at that particular point in time he was in prison for shooting a former mayor of this city down in cold blood.'

'You're referring to the rapist who was at the time attacking Burns' daughter?' Dunbar asked.

Walker waved away that detail with a flick of his hand. 'What else do we know about the man's past? Well, it turns out that he was also in prison a previous time. I'm trying to recall what that was for. Oh, I just remembered—it was *arson*. Now isn't that a coincidence?'

Dunbar glanced at Pulford. He knew that Carl's arson charge would surface at some point. Walker was rolling now.

'And then there's this strange story about the man's behavior the night of the fire. Something about an attempted murder/ suicide. The woman was beaten and then Burns tries to off himself by slitting his wrists? I've been told by the fire marshal that you guys knew about it but didn't bother to follow up.'

'We did follow up,' Pulford said. 'In the end we decided to prosecute the people responsible. Two of whom are your clients.'

Walker smiled again. 'I don't know if the story has merit or not. But I would certainly allow a jury to consider it. You know, in the interest of fairness and transparency. Just as I suppose that the prosecution will paint a picture of Mr Murdock and Mr Carter as being a couple of lowlifes, in and out of jail, known to the police. The problem with that is – I can paint a pretty similar picture of Carl Burns.'

Walker had been leaning forward, elbows on his knees, and now he sat back and crossed his legs again, perhaps to indicate that he had finished his discourse. He deliberately looked at the three of them, one at a time, as if conducting a census of sorts. Mathews reached for her coffee cup.

'So – did you call this meeting so you could share your defense strategy with us, counsellor?' she asked after she drank.

'Hardly.' Walker held the file up. He had not opened it since arriving. 'I called this meeting to see if we can't whittle this list down somewhat. As I think I have shown, you have no chance for a conviction on the arson or murder charges. And the rest are, quite frankly, contingent on the testimony of this Burns character. You have yourself a one-trick pony here, Diane. So what do you say – can we pare this thing down and save the taxpayers some money in the process?'

'Worried about the taxpayers now, are you?' Mathews asked.

'Oh, my concerns are many.'

Mathews snorted through her nose before glancing quickly at Dunbar and then Pulford. Both were sitting quietly, watching Walker, their body language such that she didn't need to ask the question.

'The charges will remain,' she told Walker. 'Was there anything else?'

'Yes,' Walker said after taking a moment to feign disappointment. 'There is something else. My clients are anxious to move on this. Any chance this preliminary could be fast forwarded?'

The request took Mathews by surprise. 'This office was under the impression that you weren't ready.'

'Wrong again,' Walker said, getting to his feet. 'I was born ready. So why don't you check your dance card and send me the date, Diane? As quick as quick can.'

'I will do that, counsellor.'

Walker let himself out. When he was gone, Mathews stood and poured more coffee for herself. She offered the carafe to the two cops but they refused. It was five o'clock. Dunbar, after listening to Walker, was thinking a couple of ounces of Scotch might better clear the taste in his mouth.

'So what was that?' Mathews asked.

'Good question,' Pulford said. 'Did he think he was going to walk in here and convince you to drop some of the charges? Is this guy stupid?'

'He's a lot of things,' Mathews said. 'Stupid isn't one of them. I can't figure it. Unless he was just fishing, trying to get an idea of how strong we think we are on the evidence. It's interesting that he brought up the murder/suicide rumor. I think he was hoping that we might tip our hand as to how we're going to handle it.' She paused to take a drink. 'By the way, how are we going to handle it?'

'There's nothing to it,' Dunbar said. 'Keep in mind that Frances Rourke drove into Talbotville that night and withdrew nearly fifty thousand dollars in cash from the bank. How does that fit into this scatterbrained theory of a domestic dispute? The money was for the home invasion.'

Mathews nodded. 'What about Walker pushing for the preliminary? I didn't see that coming.'

'I did actually,' Dunbar said. 'As far as I'm concerned, that was the only reason he called this meeting. The rest was just a smoke screen. It seems that Walker has visited Frances Rourke in the hospital. Or at least he has visited the medical staff treating her, asking questions. If she wakes up, she's going to be a key witness for us. Even more so than Burns, because she was there for it all. And Walker does not want that. So he's going to roll the dice with Burns.'

'Well, it's always nice to get the preliminary out of the way,' Mathews said. 'What about Carl Burns? Are you confident putting him on the stand?'

'Did you hear how he ran Murdock to ground?' Dunbar asked.

'I did,' Mathews said.

'This guy is not going to cave.'

Mathews sat in silence for a moment. 'What about the money? Walker said we can't tie these guys to the cash. Why not? We know they paid the bikers off with the bills from the bank.'

'We made a deal with Tommy Jakes. We had to guarantee him that his name isn't connected to this. He doesn't want to be the rat.'

'He is a rat.'

'But we made the deal,' Dunbar said. 'Without him we wouldn't have Chino or Taylor in custody at this point and we wouldn't even be having this conversation. The price you pay.'

'Things could change down the road,' Pulford said.

'How?' Mathews asked.

'The corruption charges against Ken Hubert,' Pulford replied. 'Once that shakes out, he's going to testify that he was taking bribes from the Wild. Presumably he'll also testify that that's where he got the marked hundreds. So we put Tommy Jakes on the stand and ask him where *he* got the money. He says he got it from Chino and Bug, payment for an unnamed debt. He's not ratting out anybody about any home invasion, he's just answering a question. Like the good citizen he is.'

'Right,' Mathews said.

'The thing is, that's still in the investigation stage,' Dunbar said. 'We won't have that testimony for the preliminary. But we should have it for the trial. Tommy's not going to like it, but he'll do it because he doesn't want to go to jail for perjury.'

'What about Walker's nonsense about the fire?' Pulford asked. 'Is there something there we should worry about? How do we prove it was arson? Like he says – if it's not arson, it's not murder.'

'We need Carl Burns to put these guys in the house,' Mathews said. 'If he can do that, nobody's going to believe the fire was accidental.'

'He can do it,' Dunbar said.

'All right,' Mathews said, opening her laptop. 'Let's find a date.'

TWENTY-NINE

By the middle of a cold February Carl was becoming desperate for something to do. That fall, he'd noticed that the Ferguson was blowing blue smoke and using oil on the trips back and forth to the sugar shack and so, when the cabin was finished and ready for use, he had pulled the tractor into the machine shed and set about rebuilding the engine. There was an oil heater in the shop that would, on a good day, raise the temperature to about fifty degrees, which was fine for working. For all the use the tractor got, Carl could have let it go. A quart or two of oil a month was no expense. But it was winter and work on the farm had slowed. Frances was still in the coma. Carl would rebuild the engine.

He was honing the cylinders late in the morning when he heard a car pull up outside. He looked out the window to see Dunbar climbing out of a sedan, pulling his collar up against the wind. When he headed for the motorhome, Carl rapped sharply on the glass. The cop saw him in the window and started over.

'You're a jack-of-all-trades,' he said when he saw what Carl was up to. The pistons from the engine were in a row on the work bench, the cylinder head clamped in a large vise. Carl had removed the valves earlier that morning and washed everything thoroughly with diesel oil. He had new rings and rod bearings on order from a dealer in Talbotville.

'What's going on?' Carl asked.

'We have a date for the preliminary,' Dunbar told him. 'It starts a week from today.'

'That was quick.'

'The defense is pushing for it.'

Carl nodded, absently running his fingertips inside a cylinder, feeling for ridges from the old rings. 'How will it work?'

'Should be pretty cut and dried,' Dunbar said. 'I've been on the force thirty-one years and I can only remember one case that never made it past the preliminary stage. And that was because the primary witness skipped the country. It's basically a formality. All we need is for you to testify that they were in the farmhouse that night. Demanding the money. Committing the assaults.'

'What if they have somebody lie for them?' Carl asked. 'Maybe one of their buddies, saying they were someplace else that night? What happens then?'

Dunbar shook his head to dismiss the notion. 'I suppose if the Pope were to show up and testify that Murdock and Carter were with him at the Vatican the night in question, we would have a problem. As it is, your testimony is all we'll need to hold this over for trial. And even if someone did testify that they were elsewhere that night, Murdock would still have to explain why his truck was parked a quarter mile away.'

'What about Taylor?' Carl asked. 'I can't ID him.'

'He'll have a separate preliminary. This is just for Murdock and Carter. They have joint representation so we'll do the two of them together.'

'You say it's Walker who's pushing it?'

'Yes.'

'Because he doesn't want to wait for Frances to wake up,' Carl said.

'That's my take on it,' Dunbar said. 'He doesn't want her on that stand. He doesn't want you on the stand either but there's nothing he can do about that. You can have a mountain of forensic evidence and circumstantial evidence and all kinds of other things, but there is nothing as powerful as an eyewitness.'

'So Walker will try to discredit me?'

'He'll try. He'll bring up your past and make allusions about this and that. But your job is easy, Carl. All you have to do is tell the truth.'

Carl nodded.

'I'm going to let you get back to work,' Dunbar said. As he opened the door to go, he stopped. 'What is the latest on Frances anyway?'

'They've decided to do surgery,' Carl said. 'I'm waiting to hear when.'

He heard that afternoon. He worked on the tractor until one o'clock and cleaned up and drove to Rose City to the hospital. The two doctors, Harkness and Amuz, met him in the corridor outside Frances's room.

'We were about to call you,' Amuz said.

They took Carl into a consultation room and told him they had decided on a course of treatment. They would do surgery on the coming Monday, to remove the remaining fluid from the brain. They would then do a CAT scan to try to determine if there was damage there they hadn't been able to see with the previous scans. They were making no promises but they felt that something needed to be done. The patient was making no progress.

'Big week coming up,' Carl had told Frances later, sitting by her bed.

He stayed longer than usual, holding her hand and not saying much. Her fingers and wrists were small and fragile in his rough palm. He thought about how strong she had been, how capable in nearly everything she did. In the fields, in the kitchen, in bed. She had been Carl's equal in every way, other than those in which she was more than that. And they were many. She had more compassion than he did, more sympathy. She was much more patient. Maybe that patience was helping her now. Like Rufus had said, Frances would wake up when she was bloody well ready to wake up. On top of everything else, she was smarter than Carl. The only time he had ever questioned her intelligence was when she had told him she loved him.

Maybe next week she would tell him that again.

When he got into his truck in the hospital parking lot, the cell phone he'd left on the seat was ringing. It was Rufus.

'I've finally heard back from the insurance company,' he said. 'Looks as if they're going to give you the green light.'

Things happen in threes.

'I'm in the city,' Carl said. 'I'll stop at your office on my way home.'

'Well, let me know if anyone's there,' Rufus said. 'I'm heading to Archer's.'

Which was where Carl found him, perched on a bar stool, already into his second pint of ale. Carl ordered a beer and a sandwich. With all that had been going on, he hadn't bothered to eat lunch.

'So I called the rep again,' Rufus said. 'And after the usual runaround I got off the phone and called his boss, a man named Strome. I explained to him that you were, by proxy, in charge of the situation until Frances returns. When he began his double-talk I pulled a number out of the air, the amount I told him it would cost him down the road for temporary accommodations for you and Frances due to his company dragging their feet. I admired his petulant silence so much that I threw another number at him for good measure, this one a punitive amount for deliberately dragging this out.'

'What did he say?'

'Goodbye, basically,' Rufus said. 'But he called back an hour later and said everything had been cleared. He blamed it all on a vague clerical error somewhere in head office. Standard procedure, I should think. The blaming, that is, not the error itself, which probably never occurred.'

Carl's roast beef sandwich arrived and he had a bite. 'How quick will they start?'

'He said for you to go ahead and hire someone to come in and clean up the debris on site. When that is done, they'll dig the new basement and begin construction. You will have to decide on plans, you realize.'

'We'll build the same house,' Carl said. 'I've drawn it all out myself, the rooms and dimensions as best I can remember. I just need to take them someplace and have blueprints made.'

'There's a place in town,' Rufus said.

Carl had another bite and talked around the sandwich. 'Frances is going to have surgery on Monday.'

'She is?'

Carl nodded. 'And the preliminary starts on Wednesday.'

'Well now,' Rufus said. 'I assumed that would be a couple of months away at least.'

'Walker is pushing it.'

'How do you feel about that?' Rufus asked.

'I feel good, Rufus,' Carl said after thinking a moment. 'I feel good about all of it.'

*   *   *

Walker met with Chino and Bug at the jail on Thursday afternoon and told them about the upcoming preliminary. Bug
spoke first.

'We don't got to testify, do we?'

'No,' Walker said. 'You won't be testifying. Not ever.'

Chino looked at Bug disdainfully, then pointed his chin
toward Walker's briefcase. 'So what have they got?'

'So far, an eyewitness and not much else,' Walker said. 'I
need to ask you again. Do either of you guys have anybody
who can put you someplace else that night? Have you been
thinking about it?'

'I already told the cops I was home watching the football
alone,' Bug said. He looked at Chino. 'Like we said.'

'We didn't say fuck all, dummy,' Chino told him. He looked
at Walker. 'I don't have nobody. Nobody the judge is gonna
like, anyway. Why are they pushing it up?'

'I'm pushing it,' Walker said.

'Why?'

'Because at this point their case is thin,' Walker said. 'The
woman's still unconscious and as far as I know the Indian
isn't talking. If he'd given evidence, they would have to share
it with me.'

'We see him every day,' Chino said. 'He don't talk to anybody.'

Walker nodded. 'So I want to do this now. If I can get Carl
Burns to recant on anything he's said so far – and I mean
anything – then we have a chance of walking out of there next
week. I have seen it happen on occasion. The right judge and
a shaky witness can produce wonders. If nothing else, I'm
going to find out what kind of witness he is. Maybe he's the
weak link.'

Chino laughed. 'Bug didn't think so, the day Burns caught
up to him.'

'In the alley and on the stand are two different things.'
Walker hesitated. 'How should I put this? If by chance Burns
comes face to face with the people who were in the house
that night, he's going to be nervous. Maybe even scared
shitless. I want to see what he's made of.'

'Go for it,' Chino said.

'I intend to,' Walker said, rising. 'I'll see you boys next week in court.'

The guard let him out and Chino and Bug were left sitting there for a time, Chino staring across the room at the door Walker had used to exit. Bug watched Chino. After five minutes another guard came in to take them back to the cells.

'I need to make a phone call,' Chino told him.

Digger came around that night during visiting hours. He didn't exactly dress for the occasion, wearing dirty baggy jeans and a T-shirt that was torn and soiled. When he sat across from Chino, he smelled. Chino wondered if the man ever used the bathtub at the house. It was a wonder the guards even let him in.

They sat off in the corner, Chino leaning forward, his voice low, eyes on the guards behind the glass. It took a fair amount of convincing to get Digger on board. It was a risky move, with Digger's record and reputation. At first Chino wanted Digger to do the job as a favor, in return for living in Chino's house. But Digger wasn't going for that, not with the stakes involved, so Chino had no choice but to offer money. He started at a thousand dollars and kept upping the number. Digger finally nodded when they got to five grand.

'How do I get paid?' He gestured at their surroundings. 'You in here.'

'That dipshit Walker is holding money for me,' Chino said. 'I'll get him to pay you. After, not before.'

'Who is he?'

'Walker, my lawyer,' Chino said.

Digger pouted like a child. 'How the fuck you gonna tell your lawyer about this?'

'I'm not telling him anything. Just to give you the money.'

'Like he ain't gonna ask?'

Chino took a moment. 'My hog sitting in the yard. I'll say I bought it from you and there's been five owing on it for a while. None of his fucking business anyway.'

'I guess,' Digger said. He was still having doubts, more

about the job at hand than whatever the lawyer was going to think. 'But he better pay.'

'He will,' Chino said. 'You can't drag your heels on this, Digger. This has got to be done this weekend. That going to be a problem?'

'No,' Digger said reluctantly. 'I already got what I need stashed.'

'OK.' Chino stood up.

Digger remained seated, looking at the table top. 'I don't like this, Chino.'

'You don't have to like it,' Chino said. 'You just have to do it.'

THIRTY

D unbar and Pulford found Carl in the machine shed, putting the carburetor on the Ferguson. It was just past eleven on Sunday morning. Carl had waited until ten o'clock to phone Dunbar, not wanting to bother him too early on his day off. Dunbar had called the station and arranged for a team before picking Pulford up on his way out of the city. When they got to the farm, they had walked around what was left of Carl's truck before heading over to the shed. Carl had already told Dunbar the story but told it again for Pulford's benefit.

'And what time was it?' she asked.

'Just after three.'

'And you didn't hear anything beforehand?'

Carl shook his head. 'I don't sleep all that well but I never heard anything. The wind was up, making a racket.'

'The first thing you heard was the explosion,' Pulford suggested.

'I did hear that,' Carl said.

He pulled a jacket on and the three of them went outside for another look. The truck was parked in the drive, a hundred feet or so from the motorhome. The doors were blown open and the paint blackened. The interior was scorched. The glass was melted in place and one of the side mirrors was propped against the front tire of the motorhome where it had landed, still intact. The hood was partially raised, the hinges bent. The smell of burned fabric and cordite hung in the cold morning air.

Pulford indicated the charred seats, flecked with foam. 'Did you call the fire department?'

'No,' Carl said. 'I had a fire extinguisher in the RV.'

Dunbar knelt down and looked under the truck. 'There's your bomb.'

Carl crouched as well. He saw the ruptured remains of a length of steel pipe, maybe two feet long. It was blown completely apart.

'We'll leave it for the team,' Dunbar said, straightening up. 'They're on the way. They'll want to check for prints but they won't find any.'

Pulford stood huddled in her leather jacket, looking at the destroyed truck. After a moment, she turned to Carl.

'Any idea who might have done this?'

'Yeah, I have an idea,' Carl replied. 'Don't you?'

'I meant other than the obvious.' She elaborated. 'Anybody else who might want to send you a message?'

'No,' Carl said. 'You keep beating that drum, though.'

'I'm not beating any drum. It's called doing my job.'

Dunbar interceded. 'I don't think we're looking at much of a mystery here. We might not know who did it but we know who's behind it. The preliminary is three days away.'

Pulford glanced from Dunbar to Carl. 'This doesn't change anything in that regard, does it? I mean, as far as you testifying.'

'No,' Carl said. 'It doesn't.'

'Good.' Pulford watched him a moment. 'Do you want to go over your statement again?'

'No.' Carl looked at the gray sky. 'Cold out here. I'd just as soon get back to my tractor.'

'Go ahead,' Dunbar said. 'The bomb guys might have some questions for you when they get here.'

Carl headed back to the machine shed. Dunbar and Pulford

waited until the team arrived in the van and hung around for a while after that, watching as they crawled in and around and under the ruined truck. The leader told them it was a standard pipe bomb, one that any high school kid with access to a computer could learn how to build.

Back in the city Dunbar dropped Pulford off at home, pulling up to the curb in front of her condo building.

'Do you think Walker is behind this?' Pulford asked.

'No,' Dunbar said. 'But that doesn't mean he's going to be unhappy about it.'

'So how did it go down, with the principals all in lockup?'

'Somebody called in a favor is my guess,' Dunbar said.

Pulford nodded as she removed her seat belt and opened the car door. 'Do you think Burns is rattled?'

'I don't know,' Dunbar said. 'I know I would be.'

She got out and Dunbar drove out of the city again, heading for the jail. He asked for a list of the names of people who had visited the three defendants since they'd been there. Billy Taylor had just one – his girlfriend, almost daily. Bug Murdock had none.

Chino Carter had one.

Dunbar drove back downtown to the station. He downloaded the file and did some printouts. By the time he got back to the farm the team had finished going over the scene of the bombing. They didn't have much for Dunbar that he didn't already know. No prints, and any DNA was very unlikely. After he talked to them they packed up and left.

In the motorhome Carl was cleaned up and preparing to do the same. He had the keys to Frances's car in his hand when Dunbar entered and showed him Digger Bagley's mug shot.

'Ever see this guy before?'

'No,' Carl said. 'Who is he?'

'Probably the guy who blew up your truck.'

Carl nodded. 'You talk to him?'

'Not yet.' Dunbar indicated the car keys in Carl's hand. 'Where you headed?'

'The hospital. Frances has her surgery in the morning.'

'That's good.' Dunbar paused. 'Listen, the reason I'm here – we can put you up in a hotel until this preliminary is over.'

'I'll stay here,' Carl said. 'Thanks.'

Dunbar thought to argue the point but decided against it. 'Then I'm going to put a uniform out here. This guy won't be back, but I'm going to anyway. You can refuse but I'm still going to do it.'

Carl nearly smiled at that.

'I hope the surgery goes OK,' Dunbar said before he left.

The surgery the next day did go as planned, according to the doctors. Carl spent the afternoon at the hospital, and into the evening. There was no immediate change in Frances's condition. The surgeon had said not to expect anything for a few days as there would be renewed swelling due to the procedure. They also said that Frances would be in an intensive care unit for a couple of days.

Carl put on a gown and a mask and sat with her there for a couple of hours. He told her about the upcoming preliminary. He said that when the actual trial came about the two of them would walk into the courtroom together. He didn't say much else, just sat there, holding her hand and watching her breathing.

He left the city at half past nine that evening. Driving through Talbotville he thought to stop at Archer's for a beer but in the end he kept going. When he got to the farm, an officer was sitting in a cruiser in the driveway. Carl gave him a wave and went to bed.

THIRTY-ONE

D unbar spent two days looking for Digger Bagley. At the time of his last arrest, for possession of stolen goods, he was listed as "no fixed address". There was a twenty-year-old GMC pickup registered in his name, though, and that was the focus of Dunbar's search.

He was driving past a south side liquor store late Tuesday afternoon when he spotted the truck parked in the lot there.

Dunbar pulled alongside, had a look inside the truck and was leaning against the fender when Digger walked out a few minutes later, carrying a brown bag with a bottle inside. Dunbar indicated the cruiser.

'Get in.'

'What for?' Digger complained. 'I ain't done shit.'

'Get in the car.'

Digger sat in the passenger seat, cradling the bottle like it was a new born baby. His bottom lip bounced as he listened.

'You were out to see Chino Carter last Thursday,' Dunbar said.

'I was not,' Digger said. He sat silent under Dunbar's gaze for a moment. 'Well, what if I was?'

'What did you talk about?'

'Nothing.'

'You drove out there to talk about nothing?'

'Nothing that concerns you.'

'That's where you're wrong,' Dunbar said. 'When you blow up a vehicle with a pipe bomb, it does concern the police. Don't you remember the last time, when you went to jail for it?'

'I got no idea what you're talking about.'

'I'm talking about the pickup truck you blew up in the early hours of Sunday morning out near Talbotville. What did Chino promise you for the job?'

'I never blew up nothing.'

'Yeah, you did,' Dunbar told him. 'Where you living these days, Digger?'

'Out to—' Digger began, then stopped. 'Sometimes I stay at my sister's.'

'If I go to your sister's, am I going to find the makings of a pipe bomb?' Dunbar asked.

'No.'

'Give me the address.'

Digger hesitated, then gave it up. 'I ain't been staying there lately,' he said as Dunbar jotted it down.

'Where have you been staying?'

Digger looked out the window at his truck and was struck by inspiration. 'I been sleeping in my truck mostly.'

'It's February,' Dunbar reminded him. He reached over and

took the brown bag from Digger. There was a mickey of whisky inside. 'That's a small bottle, Digger. I'm guessing you haven't been paid for the job yet.'

'I never did nothing.'

'Tell you what, Digger,' Dunbar said. 'We'll just wait a while. When Chino stiffs you, like we both know he's going to do, then you and I can have another discussion about this. You'd better toe the line until then. I don't like a guy who thinks he can blow things up just because he feels like it. A guy like that belongs in jail, and that's where I'm going to see you. Now get out.'

Digger took his bottle and did as he was told. He couldn't resist smirking, though, as he got into his truck. Dunbar, backing up, saw the look. He glanced at the license plate on the rusty GMC and saw that the sticker was expired. He put the car in park and got out.

He cited Digger for no valid plates and no insurance. He called for a tow truck and had the GMC towed into the police compound to be searched for evidence of the bombing. He left Digger standing in the parking lot, with his mickey of whisky. He was no longer smirking.

Dunbar felt no satisfaction as he drove away. In fact, he felt impotent in the face of what was happening. He could have charged Digger Bagley with blowing up Carl Burns's truck but the case would have been thrown out. There was no forensic evidence against the man and the fact that Dunbar knew exactly what had happened didn't matter. What had he expected – that Digger would confess? It was discouraging to think that he'd been outmaneuvered by Chino Carter and Digger Bagley.

He drove home. Martha was gone; a note on the table said she was shopping with her sister. Dunbar poured two fingers of scotch for himself and sat down in the study, where he could look out over the back yard. The ground was covered with snow and there were a dozen or more birds in the yard, pursuing the seed Martha had thrown for them earlier. Grackles and chickadees and a lone cardinal, standing bright red against the snow.

The Digger encounter bothered him and he was aware that the bother was bigger than just Digger Bagley. It had to do with the home invasion at the farmhouse in general. It was the worst case Dunbar had worked on in all his years on the force and he wondered if that meant that he'd been lucky or simply that the world was spiralling downward. More and more he came up against things that made no sense. Men who would kill for a few thousand dollars. Men who would blow up a vehicle as a favor. Men who seemed to have no regard for mankind in general.

Maybe it was just that he was getting older, that he was growing nostalgic for a world that he remembered being kinder, even if perhaps it hadn't been. But it sure seemed that way in Dunbar's mind. Either way, he was happy to be through with the job. He would, of course, be obliged to testify at the trial for the home invasion, and he would be glad to do so. If his last act as a police officer was to help put those three men in prison, he would walk away with some degree of satisfaction.

But the world was getter harder and he had no desire to get harder with it. Today he had overreacted to a smirk from a punk in a liquor store parking lot. And he had charged the man with insignificant things because he knew he could not nail him on that which was significant. And in the end, he had succeeded only in frustrating himself.

He was ready to be done with it.

On Wednesday morning Pulford stood in the atrium outside the courtroom, checking her watch occasionally. The hearing was to start at ten o'clock and it was now ten minutes to the hour. Walker had come through a half hour ago wearing a black pinstripe, a white carnation and his self-assured smile.

'You sure you don't want to plead this down, detective?' he'd said to Pulford before he went into the courtroom. Pulford, refusing to look at him, made no reply.

Dunbar came up from the lower level, carrying coffee for the two of them.

'Nothing yet?' he asked.

Pulford shook her head as she took the coffee from him and blew on it. 'He's pushing it.'

'He'll be here.'

Carl came through the front doors five minutes later, wearing jeans and a leather jacket. He hadn't shaved.

'I thought he might have worn a tie,' Pulford said to Dunbar. 'He looks like shit.'

They all went inside. Carl sat in the front row of the gallery waiting to be called while the two cops sat in chairs along the wall, not far from where Bug and Chino were seated in the prisoners' dock. The prosecutor Mathews was standing behind a wide oak table, shuffling papers. Walker was also on his feet by the defense table, joking with the bailiff.

At ten past the hour the judge was announced. Her name was Whiteside. She was around sixty, with a helmet of stiff hair and dark-rimmed glasses hanging on a chain around her neck. She went up the step to the bench and sat down. She had a long look around the courtroom, at the spectators and the usual phalanx of reporters, before nodding to Mathews.

As the charges against Chino and Bug were being read Dunbar saw movement and looked over to see Rufus Canfield entering the courtroom. Something about the little lawyer held Dunbar's eye. He stopped just inside the rear doors, looking over the full gallery until he found Carl Burns in the front row. He came forward but stopped again. After hesitating he slid into a bench a couple rows behind Carl. There was something off about him, Dunbar thought.

Mathews stood. 'Your honor, I would just like to note in starting that this is the first of two preliminaries in this matter. A third accused, William Brian Taylor, will come before this court at a later date. The defense for Mr Murdock and Mr Carter has requested that this hearing be expedited. The prosecution asks that these charges be held over for trial based on the evidence you will hear today. Said evidence will show that the two accused did, on the night in question, force entry into the home at two hundred twenty-three River Road, outside of Talbotville. It will show that the two accused assaulted a young woman, Stacy Fulton, as well as Carl Burns. It will show that they laid in wait for Frances Rourke, assaulted her and then demanded money from her in return for the safety of all three of the victims. It will show that Frances Rourke drove to the First Equity Bank in Talbotville and withdrew forty-five thousand dollars in cash, as well as an additional two thousand from two separate ATM machines. She returned to the house and gave the money to the accused, who proceeded to further assault her and Mr Burns and Ms Fulton. They then set the house on fire and left the three victims there to perish. Ms Fulton died in the blaze while Mr Burns and Ms Rourke managed to escape. The court will hear today from two employees from the First Equity Bank, who will verify the claims of withdrawal. The court will also hear eyewitness evidence from Carl Burns, one of the victims that night.'

Mathews paused as she finished her remarks. As she reached for another file, ready to proceed, Walker was on his feet.

'Your honor,' he said. 'A moment of the court's time?'

The judge gave him a look. 'Go ahead.'

Walker took a couple of steps forward. 'With all due respect to my friend here,' he said, indicating Mathews, 'I feel I need to question her version of events. I realize that she is obliged to take on whatever the police might deliver to her, regardless of evidence or lack thereof, but she has in this case elevated a tragic house fire to a fanciful tale of malicious malfeasance and murder, none of which occurred. Not only that, but she has implicated my clients in these events when she has no real evidence connecting them to it, aside from a suspect witness who is, quite frankly, surrounded by questions about his own behavior that night. Given the lack of evidence in this matter, I ask that these charges be stayed, your honor. Surely the court has more credible cases to pursue.'

'Request denied,' the judge said.

'Your honor—' Walker began.

'Sit down, Mr Walker.'

Walker sat, and as he did he glanced over at Dunbar and winked. In a preliminary hearing he was not permitted any opening remarks, but he'd managed to make them anyway. More to the point, he had put on a show for the reporters in the room.

Mathews watched him before turning to the judge. 'Given Mr Walker's concerns, we will begin with the testimony of Carl Burns.'

The bailiff called Carl and he rose and walked slowly through the wooden gate and up to the stand. Dunbar watched closely as he was sworn in. Carl kept his eyes straight ahead, as if there was something on the far wall of the courtroom that held his interest. His movements, even in placing his hand on the Bible, were deliberate in the extreme. Dunbar wondered if he had taken something to calm his nerves.

'Mr Burns,' Mathews said. 'You have heard my description of the events in question, including my statement that you were present that night. Is that true?'

Carl turned his head slowly in her direction. 'Yes.'

'Do you agree with my version of events?'

'Yes.'

'Mr Burns, I want you to look at the two men in the prisoners' dock, Mr Carter and Mr Murdock. Are these the men who forced their way into the house that night?'

Carl did not do as she asked. Instead he kept his eyes on Mathews. His breathing was shallow, his eyes blank. Ten seconds went by.

'Mr Burns? Are these the men who assaulted you that night?'

Now Carl looked out at the crowded gallery, to the spectators and reporters and courthouse workers. There had been murmuring earlier but now the place was quiet and every eye was on him.

'Mr Burns, are these the men?' Mathews insisted.

'No.'

There was stunned silence in the courtroom. Walker, who had been lounging in his chair, legs crossed, came forward, his elbows hitting the table.

'Mr Burns,' Mathews said sharply. 'Will you please look at the two men to your left? Are these the men who assaulted Stacy Fulton and Frances Rourke?'

Carl glanced briefly at Bug and Chino and then away. 'No.'

Mathews was in panic mode. She looked to the judge and then over to where Dunbar and Pulford sat. Dunbar was staring at Carl, while Pulford's eyes were cast downward, as if she couldn't watch.

'Mr Burns,' Mathews said, her voice rising. 'You identified

both of these individuals earlier. *These two men.* Are these
the men responsible for the home invasion at two hundred
twenty-three River Road?'

'I made a mistake,' Carl said. 'I've never seen those men
before.'

'Mr Burns—'

Walker jumped to his feet. 'Your honor, how many times does
the prosecution intend to ask the question? It's been answered
three times. Even Judas Iscariot only got three chances.'

The judge turned to Carl. 'Mr Burns, are you certain you
do not recognize the defendants?'

'I'm certain.'

The judge looked in resignation at Mathews before turning
back to Carl. 'You may step down, sir.'

Carl walked away from the stand and returned to his seat
in the gallery. He kept his eyes down. Walker was moving
toward the bench now.

'At this point,' he said, 'the court has no option but to
dismiss, your honor. The prosecution has freely admitted they
have but one eyewitness. Now that number is *none.* The court
has no choice but to stay these charges.'

'You will not dictate to this court, Mr Walker,' the judge
said. She looked from Walker to Mathews. 'We'll recess until
two o'clock this afternoon. Ms Mathews and Mr Walker, I
will see you in chambers at one o'clock. I need time to think
about this.'

Dunbar and Pulford watched Carl leave the courtroom
through the rear doors that led to the street. They walked out
the side entrance, hoping to intercept him out front. They
were waiting there as he came down the steps. He slowed
but didn't stop.

'I'm sorry,' he said, not looking at either of them.

Dunbar called to him but he kept walking, toward a parking
lot a block away. After a moment Dunbar felt a presence
beside him and turned to see Rufus Canfield standing
there. His eyes were narrow and he too was watching Carl
as he walked away.

'Did you know he was going to do that?' Pulford demanded.

'No,' Rufus said quietly.

'A heads-up would have been nice,' Pulford said. 'This is a disaster.'

'It is that,' Rufus said. 'Do you have enough to hold them for trial?'

'I doubt it,' Dunbar said. 'They'll be back on the street by the weekend.'

Rufus shook his head, still watching in the direction Carl had gone.

'I *asked* him,' Pulford said bitterly. 'I asked him on Sunday if he was good to testify after the pipe bomb. He claimed he was. He told me to my face he was good to go. Goddamn it.'

Rufus turned to the two cops. 'What are you talking about?' He stared at them as he realized. 'Christ, you don't know, do you?'

'Know what?' Pulford snapped.

'Frances Rourke died during the night.'

'Oh lord,' Dunbar said softly. 'What happened?'

'Her heart stopped,' Rufus said. 'As, I suspect, has Carl's.'

THIRTY-TWO

The sap ran early that spring. The last week of February was warm and by the first of March the maples were flowing freely. The days were sunny and in the forties while the nights remained cold and crisp, the temperatures slightly below freezing, perfect weather for gathering sap.

Carl tapped fifty-seven maples and ran a total of roughly four hundred feet of plastic tubing from one to the other, using a transit to determine the gravity flow, moving everything toward the sugar shack. On the third day of tapping he began to boil the sap. He had stacked four cords of seasoned hardwood against the back wall of the building and he kept the fire box going day and night.

He had Norah order five hundred jugs – pints and quarts and gallons – for the finished product. Carl was constantly on

the move between the bush and the warehouse at the
farm, driving the Ferguson tractor with the rebuilt engine and
pulling the wagon behind. He built a plywood box atop the
wagon to transport the jugs.

The insurance company sent a trailer to haul Carl's truck
away and a few days later he bought a used Ford – a red
pickup – from a lot outside of Talbotville. He could use the
truck to deliver the syrup to the farmers' markets and other
stores in the area. When he was ready to start selling he had
Norah design a label for the maple syrup. She came up with
a retro image of a horse drawing a cutter through the woods.

'I think we should put Frances's name on it,' she said to
Carl.

They were standing in the warehouse, just the two of them,
and she had just shown Carl the image on her computer screen.
He looked at it for a time before replying.

'What were you thinking?'

'I don't know. Maybe something like this?' She leaned
forward and typed *Rourke's Old Tyme Maple Syrup* on to the
screen beneath the image.

'That's exactly the type of thing she hated,' Carl pointed
out.

'Shit – I'm sorry.'

'Don't be.'

'What would she want, then?'

'River Valley Farm,' Carl said. 'That's what she would want.'

After the first week of boiling sap, Carl built a plank bed
against the end wall of the sugar shack and put a piece of
foam on it for a mattress. After that, he slept most nights
there in a sleeping bag, cooking his meals on the wood fire
and tending to the boiler and evaporator. At nights he read
by an oil lamp he'd found in the garage at the farm. His books
had been lost in the fire so he bought more in a used book
store in Talbotville. He re-read early Steinbeck and Faulkner,
a couple of Zane Greys. He read modern spy novels that
didn't hold him. Books on raising poultry, on farming, on
syrup production. Various magazines he picked up in town.
He read until he was tired and the next morning he got up
and carried on again.

During the day, when the sap was slowly evaporating, he had time on his hands. He cut more dead trees for firewood and split the logs by maul and wedges, even though there was a hydraulic splitter in the machine shed up at the farm.

Rufus came to visit a couple of times, again making his way down the muddy lane in his street shoes. Carl suggested he invest in a pair of rubber boots but Rufus told him that he'd lived over fifty years without such footwear and wasn't about to change now. The two men drank beer and talked about things of little consequence, mostly the weather.

Carl was surprised at the sheer volume of syrup he was producing. Halfway through the month of March Norah had to order more jugs. The temperatures rose late in the month and the sap slowed, but then a cold snap came and it began again. Carl kept the boiler going.

He knew that Frances would have enjoyed the process. She loved being in the bush in general, away from the computers and telephones. She would have been in her element spending the month in the woods, even if they only produced a single pint of syrup. It was something she had talked about constantly, something she and Carl would do together.

They had been so close to doing it.

The sap finally slowed and then stopped during the first week in April. Carl boiled the last of it off, filtered it and siphoned it into quart containers. He passed the next two days shutting down the operation. He hauled a hundred gallons of water to the bush and spent a day in the shack, cleaning the boiler and the evaporator and the rest of the equipment. He swept the pine floor clean and treated it with boiled linseed oil. He brought back a generator and air compressor on the wagon and blew out the plastic tubing running to the trees. He removed the spikes and stored them in the cabin.

He finished in the bush at the end of the second day and drove the tractor and wagon up to the farm and into the machine shed. He stacked the equipment on shelves there. It would be ready for the next year, should anybody decide to use it.

Maple syrup season was over.

The next morning Carl got up and made oatmeal. He drank a cup of coffee after he ate, then went into the bathroom and shaved and took a long shower. As he got dressed he could hear Norah's car coming down the drive, heading for the warehouse. He looked out the window and watched as she unlocked the door and went inside. It was a bright spring morning. The grass in the yard was beginning to show green.

Carl retrieved the canvas bag from beneath the mattress and left.

THIRTY-THREE

Friday would be Dunbar's last day on the job. He knew that they were planning something for him, a little celebration of sorts in the squad room, probably something low key with cake and coffee and gag gifts. The veterans on the force knew that he wouldn't be thrilled with anyone making a big deal and most of the younger cops barely knew who he was. Dunbar had decided he would go along with whatever they came up with. It would only happen once.

On the Wednesday that week he got a call from a detective out in Markham County, a cop named Linklater whom Dunbar had known casually for years. He said he was at a homicide scene that he thought might be of interest to Dunbar, and to Pulford as well.

'Why's he calling you?' Pulford asked. "Markham isn't our bailiwick."

'I can't say,' Dunbar replied. He was driving and they were on the parkway, heading out of the city. It was shortly past noon and they had stopped at a burger place on Main for take-out. They were eating on the run.

Dunbar hadn't seen much of Pulford the past couple of months. With his time short Dunbar hadn't been given any new cases, and so Pulford had been working on other investigations with other cops. Other than passing hellos at the station, they hadn't talked much. Now she finished her burger and balled the wrapping up and placed it on the seat.

'He didn't give you any details?'

'Nothing,' Dunbar said. 'He was being kind of coy, actually. I can tell you this – if he wants me to be involved, it had better be something we can clean up in two and a half days.'

Pulford smiled. 'You know where we're going?'

'Oh, he sent the address to my phone.' Dunbar took his phone from his pocket and handed it over. 'Put it in the GPS.'

Pulford looked at the info. 'Did you see the address?'

'No,' Dunbar said.

'Sonofabitch.'

Chino was sitting on the ground, his back against a broken chain link fence. He wore greasy coveralls and work boots with the steel toes worn through the leather. He had welding goggles propped on top of his head and two holes in his chest. There was a set of acetylene torches a few feet away, the hoses and cutting torch lying in the dirt. A length of rusted angle iron, stretched over two oil drums, was cut partway through. It seemed as if the gunshots had interrupted Chino's work day.

The body was behind the metal shed located across the yard from the bungalow where Dunbar and Pulford had arrested Chino a few months earlier. All around was scrap iron, along with a couple of coils of copper, the insulation burned away, the odor of the melted plastic in the air.

The local police were on the scene – a forensics team sniffing about, a few constables talking in the driveway, drinking take-out coffees. Linklater had met Dunbar and Pulford when they pulled up in the sedan and led them through the shed to have a look at Chino out behind.

'Who found him?' Dunbar asked.

Linklater pointed to a farmhouse, a quarter mile to the east. 'Next door neighbor heard the shots and came over to investigate.'

'Curious sort, is he?' Pulford asked. 'I would have thought gunshots would be pretty common out here in the boonies. Hunters and whatnot.'

'Oh, he's got a story to go with it,' Linklater said. 'I heard all about it. It seems he and the deceased have been fighting over a real estate deal that went sour. Farmer claims that he's owed twenty-five grand he put down on the place.'

Dunbar knelt down for a closer look at the body.

'This *is* Chino Carter, right?' Linklater asked.

'It's him.'

'Well, I remember you guys busting him so I thought I'd give you a call,' Linklater said.

'I guess we have a time of death,' Dunbar said. 'If the farmer heard the shots.'

'He says around twenty past ten this morning.' Linklater waited until Dunbar stood up. 'Any idea who might have done it?'

'The farmer who claims he's owed money?' Pulford suggested.

'You think so?' Linklater asked.

Pulford shrugged. 'I'd be having a conversation with him. He's got motive and maybe he thinks he's got a built-in alibi, saying he found the body. He put himself at the scene before you or anybody else could.'

'He did that,' Linklater said. 'Come to think of it, he was in a big hurry to tell me his story too.'

'What else is he saying?' Dunbar asked. 'Did he see a vehicle?'

'No, but he says he can't see the driveway out front from his place. Says the house here blocks it.'

'He just might be your man,' Pulford said. 'People have been killed for a lot less than twenty-five grand.'

Dunbar walked around the body, looking at the ground. 'If it's not him, I can tell you there's probably only about a hundred people in the world who had it in for Chino. You might want to talk to a lawyer named Pearce Walker from the city. He and Chino had dealings.'

As Linklater wrote the name down Dunbar knelt again, this time along the chain link fence. Pushing the dead grass aside, he took a pen from his pocket and used it to retrieve a shell casing. He smelled it before showing it to the other two cops.

'Forty-five ACP. Smells recent. Should be another one around here somewhere, unless the shooter retrieved one but couldn't find the other.'

He handed the pen and casing to Linklater, who called to one of the forensics guys and had him put the casing in a baggie. They looked around for a while for the second casing but never came up with it. Dunbar and Pulford walked out to their car shortly after that, with Linklater tailing.

'Any other ideas where we might look?' he asked.

'Chino had dealings with Wild Lucifer,' Dunbar said. 'I'm not sure the Wild would be involved in this but he did rip them off in the past. They've got their hands full these days with the Hubert bribery thing, but you never know. Seems as if people like that can always find time for revenge.'

Neither Dunbar nor Pulford said much on the drive back to the city. Dunbar knew that Linklater was merely exercising common courtesy in calling him, but in truth he could just have told Dunbar over the phone what had happened. It had nothing to do with him or Pulford at this point. Still, Chino had been their concern at one time, right up until the charges against him and the other two had been dismissed.

Pulford must have been thinking along the same lines. As they got close to the city she looked over at Dunbar.

'What goes around comes around, eh?'

THIRTY-FOUR

On his last day of employment by the Rose City Police Department, Dunbar was awakened by his cell phone at half past six in the morning. After hanging up he told Martha to stay in bed and he got up and dressed in the half dark. He bought a coffee for himself at the Tim Hortons drive-thru. He was about to call Pulford when he remembered she was away for a long weekend, visiting her sister in Winnipeg. She would miss Dunbar's retirement party later that day.

Coffee in hand, he drove out to the city's north side. It was the first he had been to the bar called Hard Ten since the night they'd raided it a few months ago. The parking lot was full of cops when he pulled in.

Bug Murdock's body was behind a dumpster in the back

corner of the lot. He was lying on his side, his eyes closed, and he looked to be sleeping. His fly was open. Whoever had shot him had caught him about to take a leak, or just finishing the task. There was a bullet hole in his temple. Without turning him over Dunbar knew that the other side of his head would be mostly missing.

As Dunbar knelt beside the body an unmarked cruiser pulled into the parking lot and Detective Fisher got out and went around and opened the rear passenger door. The bartender from Hard Ten got out. Her name was Joni, Dunbar recalled. She didn't look particularly happy about being summoned at that hour. Fisher led her over to where Dunbar stood.

'Yeah, I know him,' she said when asked. 'Calls himself Bug. I got no idea what his real name is.'

'Was he in the bar last night?' Fisher asked.

'Yeah. He's been hanging around.'

'Is he involved with the Wild?'

'Fuck you, man. You think I'm gonna answer questions about the Wild?'

Dunbar glanced at Fisher before turning to the bartender. 'You happen to remember when he left?'

'Maybe midnight. He was drunk. Usually is.'

'You remember him arguing with anybody?' Fisher asked. 'Any sort of altercation at all?'

'No,' she said. 'He sits in the fucking corner all night, eyeballing me.'

So that was how it was, Dunbar thought. He wondered why Bug would be patronizing the Hard Ten after what had gone down between him and Chino and Tommy Jakes. But then Bug wouldn't have known it was Tommy who put the finger on Chino and the Indian.

'And he left alone?' Dunbar asked.

'He always does.'

After a few more questions they let her go, with Fisher asking a uniform to drive her home. She didn't bother to say goodbye.

'Chino Carter yesterday and now this,' Fisher said. 'Looks like the Wild is settling some hash.'

Dunbar regarded what was left of Bug Murdock for a moment.

'I don't think so,' he said. 'They're not going to shoot Murdock and leave his body five hundred yards from their clubhouse.'

'So you're thinking they're not connected?' Fisher asked. 'Kind of a bizarre coincidence, isn't it?'

'I didn't say coincidence.' Dunbar knelt by Bug's body. The stench from the dumpster was strong. 'You didn't find a shell casing?'

'Nothing. Good-sized hole, though.'

'A forty-five would be my guess,' Dunbar said.

Dunbar ended up being late to his own party. While the office staff was mixing non-alcoholic punch (not like the old days) and putting up banners, he was driving around Tareytown looking for a red Ford pickup.

At four thirty he had given up on the search for the truck and was parked in the lot by the city park, down the block from Billy Taylor's house. It was a warm day and there were a number of people in the park, a few adults and quite a few kids, playing on the playground equipment. There was a wide wooded area that separated the park from the street where Taylor lived.

Dunbar recognized the white Pontiac as it came down the street and pulled into the driveway. Billy got out, wearing work clothes and carrying a lunch pail. He went inside the house as Dunbar watched the surrounding area.

A few minutes later Billy came out again and crossed the street to a path that led through the woods. As he disappeared into the trees Dunbar saw a man approaching along the river to his right. It was Carl Burns, and he was heading in the direction of the park and the woods where Billy had gone. He wore jeans and a leather jacket. A baseball cap, pulled low.

Dunbar got out of the car and began to move. As he did he saw Billy emerge from the trees and walk to the playground. He went directly toward a group of kids surrounding a young woman wearing a bright yellow hoodie. One of the kids, a boy of about two, saw Billy and started for him on a run. Billy scooped the boy up. Dunbar saw Carl stop now, watching the scene in the playground.

The woman, obviously a daycare worker, came over and spoke to Billy. After a few moments Billy lifted the boy up on to his shoulders and started back through the trees.

Carl was a hundred yards away. He'd been moving at an angle that would have him intercepting Billy in the woods. He began to walk again now, sliding his right hand into his jacket pocket as he did. Billy and the boy approached the woodlot, the boy laughing atop his father's shoulders. Dunbar picked up his pace, coming at Carl from behind. He pulled his Glock from the holster.

He was about to shout out when he saw Carl slow, his eyes fixed on both Billy and the boy, and then stop. Dunbar was directly behind Carl now, fifty yards back. He kept his eyes on Carl's right hand in the jacket pocket. Billy and the boy went into the woods, the boy still bouncing on his father's shoulders.

Carl let them go.

Dunbar stood still in the parking lot and watched. After a long while, Carl turned away and began to walk aimlessly toward the river, his motions slow and robotic. He stopped at a wooden bench along the bank and sat down. Raising his chin, he looked out over the water.

Dunbar put his gun away and followed. Carl didn't see him until the very last. He was staring straight ahead at the river and seemed weary to the point of collapse. Dunbar sat down beside him. He waited a couple of minutes before he spoke.

'Give me the gun, Carl.'

Carl did it, pulling the forty-five from his jacket and handing it over without a word. Both men watched the river flow past. Dunbar waited, thinking that Carl might say something. He was hoping he would, because he himself was having trouble coming up with any words that might fit.

'You know this is my last day on the job?' he finally asked. 'I'm retiring.'

Carl glanced over at him, as if confused by the news.

'I'd rather my last act as a cop was something different.'

Carl nodded.

'But I've had a pretty good career,' Dunbar said after a moment. 'I've had a good life, I guess. I'm married, you know. I guess you wouldn't know that. But I am, and it's a pretty fair marriage. Not perfect, but I can't imagine there is such a thing. My wife and I – her name's Martha – have plans now. She retired a year ago, and we figure to travel and whatever. Typical things, I suppose.'

Dunbar shifted on the hard bench. He realized he was still holding the forty-five in his hand and now he put it in his coat pocket. He sat quietly for a while, thinking of all that had happened since he'd first met Carl Burns lying in a hospital bed, half dead from loss of blood, six months earlier. All the things that had led them to this spot on this day. It seemed like six years.

'Thing is, I don't know what I'd do if somebody took her away from me,' he said. He looked at Carl and got to his feet. 'I have to read you your rights now, Carl.'

Afterward they walked up the slope to the parking lot. Dunbar put Carl in the back seat without handcuffing him. Then he slid behind the wheel. He put the keys in the ignition and he stopped. He sat there for a time, watching the activity in the park along the way. The kids running and playing, taking turns on the slide, the parents watching, talking among themselves. The way life should be but not the way it always was.

Dunbar opened the door and got out of the car and started for the river. When he got to the bank, he took the gun from his pocket and threw it as high and as far as he could. It splashed down fifty yards out and sank like a stone.

He left Carl standing in the parking lot. Before driving away he rolled the window down.

'I'm late to a retirement party,' he said. 'Go home, Carl.'

Carl watched as the cruiser pulled out of the lot and headed back to the city. The wind came up then, whipping across the river, creating tiny whitecaps out in the current. Carl put his collar up and began to walk.